Unhallowed Ground

The fourth chronicle of

Hugh de Singleton, surgeon

MEL STARR

MONARCH
BOOKS

Oxford, UK & Grand Rapids, Michigan, USA

First published in the UK in 2011 by Monarch Books
(a publishing imprint of Lion Hudson plc)
Wilkinson House, Jordan Hill Road, Oxford OX2 8DR, England
Tel: +44 (0)1865 302750 Fax: +44 (0)1865 302757
Email: monarch@lionhudson.com
www.lionhudson.com

Reprinted 2011.

ISBN 978 0 85721 058 6 (print)
ISBN 978 0 85721 237 5 (epub)
ISBN 978 0 85721 236 8 (Kindle)
ISBN 978 0 85721 238 2 (PDF)

Distributed by:
UK: Marston Book Services, PO Box 269, Abingdon, Oxon,
OX14 4YN
USA: Kregel Publications, PO Box 2607, Grand Rapids,
Michigan 49501

British Library Cataloguing Data
A catalogue record for this book is available from the British
Library.

Printed and bound in the USA.

By the same author:
(in sequence)

The Unquiet Bones
A Corpse at St Andrew's Chapel
A Trail of Ink

For Tony and Lis Page

Acknowledgments

In the summer of 1990 my wife Susan and I discovered a lovely B&B in the village of Mavesyn Ridware. The proprietors, Tony and Lis Page, became friends. We visited them again in 2001, after they had moved to Bampton. I saw that the village would be an ideal setting for the tales I wished to write. Tony and Lis have been a wonderful resource for the history of Bampton. I owe them much.

When Dan Runyon, Professor of English at Spring Arbor University, learned that I was writing *The Unquiet Bones*, Master Hugh's first chronicle, he invited me to speak to a fiction-writing class about the trials of a rookie writer. Dan sent some chapters to his friend, Tony Collins. Thanks, Dan.

And thanks to Tony Collins and the fine people at Monarch for their willingness to publish an untried author. Thanks also to my editor, Jan Greenough, who keeps the plot moving when I would digress.

Thanks also to Professor John Blair, of Queen's College, who has written several papers about the history of Bampton. Master Hugh's tales are fiction, but as far as possible the Bampton he lived in is accurate to the time and place.

Malgorzata Deron, a linguistics scholar from Poznan, Poland, has graciously volunteered to maintain my website. This is much appreciated from one who is digitally challenged. See her work at www.melstarr.net

Glossary

Alaunt: A large hunting dog.

Almoner: The monk responsible for a monastery's charity, he tended the deserving poor of the neighborhood.

Angelus Bell: Rung three times each day, dawn, noon, and dusk. Announced the time for the Angelus devotional.

Ascension Day: May 14 in 1366, forty days after Easter.

Bailiff: A lord's chief manorial representative. He oversaw all operations, collected rents and fines, and enforced labor service. Not a popular fellow.

Beadle: A manor officer in charge of fences, hedges, enclosures, and curfew. Also called a hayward.

Capon: A castrated male chicken.

Cataract couching: Excising the clouded lens from a patient's eye.

Chardedate: A confection made of dates, honey, and ginger.

Childwite: A fine for having a child out of wedlock.

Coney in cevy: A rabbit stew made with wine and a variety of spices.

Coppice: To cut a tree back to a stump to stimulate the growth of new shoots.

Corpus Christi: June 4, 1366. Celebrated on the first Thursday after Trinity Sunday, to give thanks for Holy Communion.

Cotter: A poor villager, usually holding five acres or less, he often had to labor for wealthy villagers to make ends meet.

Cow-ley: Pasture or meadow.

Cresset: A bowl of oil with a floating wick used for lighting.

Daub: A clay-and-plaster mix, reinforced with straw and/or horsehair.

Demesne: Land directly exploited by a lord, and worked by his villeins, as opposed to land a lord might rent to tenants.

Deodand: Any object which caused a death. The item was sold and the price awarded to the king.

Dexter: A war-horse, larger than pack-horses and palfreys. Also the right-hand direction.

Dorter: A monastery dormitory.

Dredge: Mixed grains planted together in a field, often barley and oats.

Farthing: A small coin worth one fourth of a penny.

Gentleman: A nobleman. The term had nothing to do with character or behavior.

Gersom: A fee paid to a noble to acquire or inherit land.

God's sib: Woman who attended another woman while she was in labor, from which comes the word "gossip."

Groat: A silver coin worth four pence.

Groom: A household servant to a lord, ranking above a page and below a valet.

Haberdasher: A merchant who sold household items such as pins, buckles, buttons, hats, and purses. ﹨

Hallmote: The manorial court. Royal courts judged free tenants accused of murder or felony; otherwise manor courts had jurisdiction over legal matters concerning villagers.

Hamsoken: Breaking and entering.

Heriot: An inheritance tax paid by an heir to a lord, usually the deceased's best animal.

Hocktide: The Sunday after Easter. A time for paying rents and taxes; therefore, getting "out of hock."

Host: Communion wafers.

Hue and cry: An alarm call raised by the person who discovered a crime. All who heard were expected to go to the scene of the crime and, if possible, pursue the criminal.

King's Eyre: A royal circuit court, presided over by a traveling judge.

Ladywell: A well dedicated to the Virgin Mary, located a short distance north of Bampton Castle, the water of which was reputed to cure ills, especially of the eye.

Lammas Day: August 1, when thanks was given for a successful wheat harvest. From Old English "loaf mass."

Laudable pus: Thick white pus from a wound, which was assumed to mean healing was progressing, as opposed to watery pus, which was assumed to be dangerous.

Lauds: The first canonical hour of the day, celebrated at dawn.

Leirwite: A fine for sexual relations out of wedlock.

Let lardes: A type of custard made with eggs, milk, bacon fat, and parsley.

Lombard stew: A pork stew with wine, onions, almonds, and spices.

Lombardy custard: A custard made with the addition of dried fruit.

Lych gate: A roofed gate over the entry to a churchyard under which the deceased rested during the initial part of a funeral.

Marshalsea: The stables and associated accoutrements.

Maslin: Bread made with a mixture of grains, commonly wheat and rye or barley.

Merlon: The solid upper portion of a wall between the open crenels of a battlement.

Mews: Stables, usually with living quarters, built around a courtyard.

Mortrews: A stew made with pork, ground or chopped fine, thickened with breadcrumbs, egg yolks, and spices.

New Year: By the fourteenth century, usually January 1, but the traditional earlier date of March 25 was also often used.

Noble: A gold coin worth six shillings and eight pence.

Nones: The fifth daytime canonical hour, sung at the ninth hour of the day, mid-afternoon.

Palfrey: A riding-horse with a comfortable gait.

Poitiers: A city in France which was the scene of the English victory over and capture of King John II of France (September 1356).

Pottage: Anything cooked in one pot, from the meanest oatmeal to a savory stew.

Refectory: A monastery dining-room.

Rogation Sunday: The Sunday before Ascension Day. Monday, Tuesday, and Wednesday were Rogation Days, also called "gang days." A time of beseeching God for a good growing season.

St Botolf's Day: June 17.

St George's Day: April 23. In 1366, a Thursday.

St Nicholas's Day: December 6.

Shilling: Twelve pence. Twenty shillings made a pound, but there was no one pound coin.

Solar: A small room in a castle, more easily heated than the great hall, where lords preferred to spend time, especially in winter. Usually on an upper floor.

Stone: Fourteen pounds.

Subtlety: An elaborate confection made more for show than for consumption.

Suffusio: The milky, opaque matter obscuring the vision of a cataract sufferer.

Terce: The third canonical hour, celebrated at the third hour of the day, mid-morning.

Toft: Land surrounding a house, often used for growing vegetables and keeping chickens.

Tor: A high, conical hill.

Trinity Sunday: One week after Whitsunday, May 31 in 1366.

Verderer: The forester in charge of a lord's forests.

Vigils: The night office, traditionally celebrated at midnight.

Villein: A non-free peasant. He could not leave his land or service to his lord, or sell animals without permission. But if he could escape his manor for a year and a day he would be free.

Wattle: Interlaced sticks used as a foundation and support for daub in building a wall.

Week-work: The two or three days of labor per week (more during harvest) which a villein owed to his lord.

Wether: A male sheep castrated before maturity.

Whitsunday: White Sunday; ten days after Ascension Day, seven weeks after Easter. In 1366, May 24.

Yardland: About thirty acres. Also called a virgate, and in northern England called an oxgang.

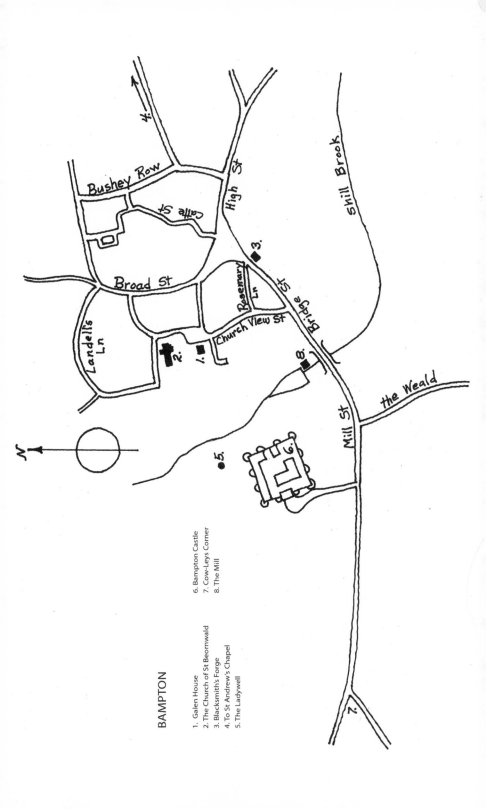

BAMPTON

1. Galen House
2. The Church of St Beornwald
3. Blacksmith's Forge
4. To St Andrew's Chapel
5. The Ladywell

6. Bampton Castle
7. Cow-Leys Corner
8. The Mill

Bushey Row

Catte St

High St

Broad St

Landell's Ln

Rosemary Ln

Church View St

Bridge St

Mill St

the Weald

Shill Brook

N

Chapter 1

A fortnight after Hocktide, in the new year 1366, shouting and pounding upon the door of Galen House drew me from the maslin loaf with which I was breaking my fast. The sun was just beginning to illuminate the spire of the Church of St Beornwald. It was Hubert Shillside who bruised his knuckles against my door. He was about to set out for the castle and desired I should accompany him. The hue and cry was raised and he, as town coroner, and I as bailiff of Bampton Manor, were called to our duties. Thomas atte Bridge had been found this morn hanging from the limb of an oak at Cow-Leys Corner.

Word of such a death passes through a village swiftly. A dozen men and a few women stood at Cow-Leys Corner when Shillside and I approached. Roads to Clanfield and Alvescot here diverge; the road to Clanfield passes through a meadow, where Lord Gilbert's cattle watched serenely as men gathered before them. To the north of the corner, and along the road to Alvescot and Black Bourton, is forest. From a tree of this wood the corpse of Thomas atte Bridge hung by the neck, his body but a few paces from the road. Shillside and I crossed ourselves as we approached.

Most who gazed upon the dead man did so silently, but not his wife. Maud knelt before her husband's body, her arms wrapped about his knees. She wailed incomprehensibly, as well she might.

Atte Bridge's corpse was suspended there by a coarse hempen cord twisted about the small oak's limb and his neck. After winding about the limb the cord was fastened about the trunk at waist height. The limb was not high above my head. If I stretched a hand above me I could nearly touch it. The man's feet dangled from his wife's embrace little more than two hand-breadths above the ground, and near the corpse lay an overturned stool.

"Who found him?" I asked the crowd. Ralph the herder stepped forward.

"Was on me way to see to the cattle. They been turned out to grass but a short time now, an' can swell up, like. Near walked into 'im, dark as it was, an' him hangin' so close to the road."

Hubert Shillside wandered about the place, then approached me and whispered, "Suicide, I think."

Spirits are known to frequent Cow-Leys Corner. Many folk will not walk the road there after dark, and those who do sometimes see apparitions. This is to be expected, for any who take their own life are buried there. They cannot be interred in the churchyard, in hallowed ground. Their ghosts rest uneasy, and are said to vex travelers who pass the place at night.

"Knew he'd be buried here," Shillside continued, "an' thought to spare poor Maud greater trouble."

That Thomas atte Bridge might wish to cause little trouble for his wife did not seem likely, given my experience of the man. He had twice attacked me in nocturnal churchyards, leaving lumps upon my skull. But I made no reply. It is not good to speak ill of the dead, even this dead man.

Kate had heard Shillside's announcement at Galen House and followed us to Cow-Leys Corner. She looked from the corpse to Maud to me, then spoke softly: "You are troubled, Hugh."

This was a statement, not a question. We had been wed but three months, but Kate is observant and knows me well.

"I will call a coroner's jury here," Shillside announced. "We can cut the fellow down and see him buried straight away."

"You must seek Father Thomas or one of the other

vicars," I reminded him. "Thomas was a tenant of the Bishop of Exeter, not of Lord Gilbert. They may wish otherwise."

Shillside set off for the town while two men lifted Maud from her knees and led her sobbing in the coroner's track.

"Wait," I said abruptly. All turned to see what caused my command. "The stool which lies at your husband's feet," I asked the grieving widow, "is it yours?"

Maud ceased her wailing long enough to whisper, "Aye."

Another onlooker righted the stool and prepared to climb to the limb with a knife, when I bid him halt. He had thought to cut the corpse down. Kate spoke true, the circumstances of this death troubled me, although I readily admit that when I first recognized the dead man I felt no sorrow.

I saw a man hanged once, in Paris, when I studied surgery there. He dangled, kicking the sheriff's dance and growing purple in the face until the constables relented and allowed his friends to approach and pull upon his legs until his torment ended. Thomas atte Bridge's face was swollen and purple, and he had soiled himself as death approached. His countenance in death duplicated the unfortunate cut-purse in Paris. It seemed as Hubert Shillside suggested: atte Bridge brought rope and stool to Cow-Leys Corner, threw the hemp about the limb and tied it to the tree and then to his neck, then kicked aside the stool he'd stood upon to fix cord to limb. All who stood peering at me and the corpse surely thought the same.

I circled the dangling corpse. The hands hung limp and were cold to the touch. A man about to die on the gallows will be securely bound, but not so a man who takes his own life. I inspected atte Bridge's hands and pushed up the frayed sleeves of his cotehardie to see his wrists.

Upon one wrist I saw a small red mark, much like a rash, or a place where a man has scratched a persistent itch. No such scraping appeared upon the other wrist, but when I pushed up the sleeve of the cotehardie another thing caught my eye. The sleeve was of coarse brown wool, and frayed with age. Caught in the wisps of fabric which marked the end of the sleeve I found a wrinkled thread of lighter hue. I looked up to the branch above atte Bridge's glassy stare. This filament was much the same shade as the hempen cord from which the dead man hung. Perhaps it found its way to his sleeve when atte Bridge adjusted the rope about his neck.

I stood back from the corpse to survey the place. I was near convinced that Hubert Shillside must be correct. My life would have been easier had he been so. But my duties as bailiff to Lord Gilbert Talbot have made me suspicious of others and skeptical of tales they tell – whether dead or alive. It was then I noticed the mud upon Thomas atte Bridge's heels.

I knelt to see better, and Kate peered over my shoulder. Mud upon one's shoes is common when walking roads in springtime, but this mud was not upon the soles of atte Bridge's shoes, where it should have been, but was drying upon the backs of his heels. Kate understood readily what we saw.

"Odd, that," she said softly, so others might not hear. She then turned to the righted stool and gazed down at it thoughtfully. I saw her brow furrow and knew the cause. I drew her from the corpse to the trunk of the tree where we might converse unheard by others.

"A man who walks to his death will have mud upon the soles of his shoes," I whispered, "not upon the backs of his heels."

"And he will leave muddy footprints where he stands," Kate replied. "I see none on yon stool."

"Walk with me," I said. "Let us see what the road may tell us."

It told us that many folk had walked this way. The previous week there had been much rain, and the road was deep in mud. Footprints were many, and one man who had walked there was unshod. Occasionally the track of a cart appeared. A hundred paces and more east of Cow-Leys Corner I found what I sought. Two parallel lines, a hand's breadth apart, were drawn in the mud of the road. These tracks were no more than one pace long. Kate watched me study the grooves.

"Did the mud upon his heels come from here?" she asked.

"Perhaps. It is as if two men carried another, and one lost his grip and allowed the fellow's feet to drop briefly to the road."

"How could this be? Was he dead already?"

"Nay. I think not. His face is that of a man who has died at the end of a rope. But if he did not perish at his own hand, someone bound him or rendered him helpless so to get him to Cow-Leys Corner."

While Kate and I stood in the road inspecting suspicious furrows, Hubert Shillside and eleven men of Bampton approached. The coroner saw us studying the mud at our feet and turned his gaze there also. He saw nothing to interest him.

"What is here, Hugh? Why stand you here studying the road?"

"See there," I pointed to the twin grooves in the mud. As Shillside had not seen Thomas atte Bridge's heels, he could not know my suspicion. He shrugged and walked on. The coroner's jury he had assembled followed and would have obliterated the marks in the way had not Kate and I stood before them so that they were obliged to flow about us like Shill Brook about a rock.

There was nothing more to be learned standing in the road. Kate and I followed the jury back to Cow-Leys Corner. Shillside and those with him studied the corpse, the rope, the stool, and muttered among themselves. The coroner had already voiced his opinion that atte Bridge died at his own hand. His companions, thus set toward a conclusion of the matter, found no reason to disagree. When a man has adopted an opinion it is difficult to dissuade him of it, but I tried.

I took Shillside to the corpse and bid him bend to inspect the stained and mud-crusted heels. "The tracks you saw me studying in the road... made by atte Bridge's heels, I think. Why else dirt upon the backs of a man's feet?"

"Hmmm... perhaps."

"And see the stool. If he stood upon it to fix the rope to the limb, he made no muddy footprints upon it."

Shillside glanced at the stool, then lifted his eyes to atte Bridge's lolling head.

"The fellow is dead of hanging and strangulation," he declared. "I've seen men die so, faces swollen an' purple, tongue hangin' from 'is mouth all puffy an' red."

"Aye," I agreed. "So it does seem. But if he stood upon that stool to fasten rope to tree, he left no mark. How could a man walk the road and arrive here with clean shoes... but for the backs of his heels?"

Shillside shrugged again. "Who can know? But this I'll say: not a man in Bampton or the Weald will be sorry Thomas atte Bridge is dead. He tried to kill you. Be satisfied the fellow can do no more harm to you or any other."

I saw then how it might be. Shillside drew his coroner's jury to the verge and they discussed the matter. Occasionally one or more of the group would look to the corpse, which now twisted slowly on the hemp. A breeze was rising.

Father Thomas, Father Simon, and Father Ralph, vicars of the Church of St Beornwald, arrived as the jury ended its deliberations. The vicars looked upon the corpse and crossed themselves. Those who yet milled about Cow-Leys Corner vied with each other to tell what the priests could see: a man was dead, hanging by a cord from the limb of a tree. More than this no man knew. If there was more to know, there were those who preferred ignorance.

Hubert Shillside approached me and the priests and

announced the decision of the coroner's jury. Thomas atte Bridge took his own life, choosing to do so at a place where it was well known that suicides of past years were buried. The stool was proof: Maud had identified it as belonging to their house.

The vicars looked on gravely while Shillside explained this conclusion. The stool and rope, he declared, would be deodand. What use King Edward might make of them he did not say.

Thomas atte Bridge was a tenant of the Bishop of Exeter, but was found dead on lands of Lord Gilbert Talbot. The priests and coroner's jury looked to me for direction. Lord Gilbert was in residence at Goodrich Castle. As bailiff of Bampton Manor, disposal of the corpse was now my bailiwick. My suspicions remained, but it seemed I was alone in my doubts. Other than Kate.

I saw Arthur standing at the fringe of onlookers and motioned him to approach. While he threaded his way through the crowd I spoke to Father Thomas.

"Will you allow burial in the churchyard?"

The vicar shook his head. Father Simon and Father Ralph pursed their lips and frowned in agreement. "A man who takes his own life cannot seek confession and absolution," Father Thomas explained. He had no need to do so. I knew the observances well. "He dies in his sins, unshriven. He cannot rest in hallowed ground."

Arthur had served me and Master John Wyclif well in the matter of Master John's stolen books. Now I found another duty for the sturdy fellow. I sent him to the castle to seek another groom and two spades.

There was no point in prolonging the matter. Shillside asked if the corpse might be cut down and I nodded assent. It was but the work of a moment for another of the bishop's tenants to mount the stool and slice through the rope. Thomas atte Bridge's remains crumpled to a heap at the fellow's feet. I told the man to unwind the cord from about the limb while he was on his perch. I knelt by the corpse and did the same to the cord which encircled atte Bridge's abraded neck. I then straightened the fellow out on the verge. He was beginning to stiffen in death and it would be best to put him in his grave unbent.

I knelt to straighten atte Bridge's head and while I did so I looked into his staring, bulging eyes and gaping mouth. I see them yet on nights when sleep eludes me. The face was purple and bloated, so I nearly missed the swelling on atte Bridge's upper lip. There was a red bulge there. And just beneath the mark I saw in his open mouth a tooth bent back.

I reached a finger past the dead man's lips and pressed upon the bent tooth. It yielded freely. I pulled gently upon the tooth and nearly drew it from the mouth. Thomas atte Bridge had recently been in a fight and had received a robust blow. I was not surprised to learn of this. I knew Thomas atte Bridge. I would congratulate the man who served him with a fattened lip and broken tooth.

But did this discovery have to do with Thomas atte Bridge's death, suicide or not? Who could know? Perhaps only the man who delivered the blow.

Arthur returned with an assistant and set to work digging a grave at the base of the wall which enclosed Lord Gilbert's pasture. Cows chewed thoughtfully on spring grass and watched the work while their calves gamboled about. An onlooker urged Arthur to make the grave deep so the dead man might not easily rise to afflict those whose business took them past Cow-Leys Corner. Arthur did not seem pleased with the admonition.

Kate left me while the grave was yet unfinished. She wished to set a capon roasting for our dinner and was already tardy at the task. Her business served to remind me how hungry I was. Some might lose appetite after staring a hanged man in the face. I am not such a one, especially if the face be that of Thomas atte Bridge.

Hubert Shillside approached as Arthur and his assistant shoveled the last of the earth upon the burial mound. "One less troublemaker to vex the town, eh?" he said.

"He'll not be missed," I agreed. "But for Maud."

"Hah. Them of the Weald say as how he beat her regular, like. She'll not be grieved to have that end."

"Aye, perhaps, but he provided for his family. Who will do so now?"

"There be widowers about who'll be pleased to add her lands to their holdings."

"A quarter-yardland? And four children to come with the bargain? I think Maud will find few suitors."

"Hmmm. Well, she will have to make do. Perhaps the oldest boy can do a man's work."

"Perhaps."

The throng of onlookers had begun to melt away when atte Bridge's corpse was lowered to the grave. These folks chattered noisily about the death and burial as they departed for the town. They did not seem afflicted with sorrow, but rather behaved as if a weight was lifted from their shoulders. Did Thomas atte Bridge guess this would be the response to his death, having lived as he did, at enmity with all men?

The coroner and I were among the last to leave Cow-Leys Corner. In my hand I carried the hempen rope, now sliced in two, which ended Thomas atte Bridge's life. We walked behind the vicars. I was silent while Shillside spoke of the weather, new-sown crops, and other topics of a pleasant spring day. When he found no ready response from me he grew silent, then as we reached the castle he turned and spoke again.

"The man is surely dead of his own hand, Hugh. You must not seek a felon where none is. And even was atte Bridge slain, there is no man in Bampton sorry for it. He was an evil fellow we are well rid of."

Chapter 2

𝔑ext day, near noon, I received a visitor. Maud atte Bridge appeared at my door, red-eyed from tears and a sleepless night. I opened the door for her entry and Kate, observing her condition, offered a bench by the fire. The woman sat and sighed, then looked up to me and spoke.

"They all say 'e hung hisself," she began, "but 'e din't."

"Why do you say so?"

"'E just wouldn't. I know my Thomas."

"What happened the night before he was found? Did he leave the house early in the morn, or was he away all night?"

"All night. We'd covered the fire an' was ready to go to our bed when we 'eard hens cacklin'. They ain't likely to do so after dark less they're vexed. Tom thought maybe a fox was at 'em, so took a staff an' went to the toft."

"Did he return?"

"Nay. Hens quieted an' I thought 'e'd run the beast off that troubled 'em. But 'e din't come to bed. After a time I went out to seek 'im, but 'e was not to be found. Never saw 'im again 'til folk took me to Cow-Leys Corner, an' there 'e was."

"The stool found there... you said it was yours."

"Aye. Went missin' two days past. Tom was workin' with the bishop's plow team an' I was plantin' onions in the toft. When we was done an' the day near gone we couldn't find the stool. 'Twas there in the morn."

"Your children saw no man enter the house and take it?"

"Nay. They was in an' out. Oldest was helpin' me in

toft. Babe was sleepin', an' couldn't know a man stole a stool anyway."

"Perhaps Thomas took the stool himself that day, having planned his death and the means?"

Maud looked to the flags at her feet. "Mayhap. 'E was right fierce about it bein' took, though. Said 'e was gonna watch others in the Weald to see did any have it, an' deal with 'em when 'e found it."

"Did Thomas fight with another the day before he died?"

"Fight? Nay… not that 'e spoke of."

"But he often quarreled with others, is this not so?"

"Aye, as you well know."

"But he'd been in no recent disputes?"

"Nay. He'd not spoke of any."

"And his face showed no sign of blows?"

Maud peered up at me suspiciously. "Nay. Why should 'e appear so?"

I decided to keep silent about Thomas atte Bridge's damaged lip and tooth. I was learning that knowledge can be a useful tool, and occasionally a weapon – a weapon most effective when an opponent knows nothing of its existence, like a dagger hidden in a boot.

"Vicars wouldn't bury 'im in churchyard," Maud continued. "'Ow'll 'e get to heaven?"

I did not reply. I saw no point in reminding the woman of her husband's many sins. The Lord Christ said the path to heaven is narrow, and few there be who find it. It seemed to me unlikely that Thomas atte Bridge would be among those few, no matter was he buried in hallowed ground or not. But Maud faced enough grief. She needed to consider no more.

"You bein' Lord Gilbert's bailiff, it'd be your part to find who slew Tom an' set things right, so he can be buried proper in the churchyard."

I looked from Maud to Kate, and saw in my bride's eyes a reflection of my own thoughts. Kate knew of Thomas atte Bridge's assaults upon me. I had told her how he left lumps upon my skull in Alvescot Churchyard and at St Andrew's Chapel when I discovered his part in the blackmail he, his brother Henry, and the wicked priest John Kellet had visited upon transgressors who had confessed to the scoundrel priest.

So although I had ample reason to leave Thomas atte Bridge in his grave at Cow-Leys Corner, I saw in Kate's eyes that I could not. Did some other murder him, it would be a great injustice to abandon him there, lost and unshriven. Atte Bridge was himself guilty of much injustice, but holy writ says the Lord Christ died for his sins as well as mine.

Who would murder Thomas atte Bridge? Surely it would be some man wronged at his hand. Atte Bridge had few friends in Bampton and the Weald. If I was convinced the fellow was murdered, and sought the man who took his life, I would likely seek one who did what others would have wished to do, had they the stomach for it. Who, then, would assist me? Who would wish to see a friend hang for slaying a reprobate?

I had faced a similar problem when I sought who might have struck down Thomas's brother, Henry. Henry was as despised as Thomas, perhaps more so. Townsmen were pleased these brothers would trouble them no more. They would not be happy was I able to lay Thomas's death at the feet of a friend. Again I caught Kate's eye. Did I seek approval more than justice? Even justice for the unjust?

I sighed and chewed upon my lip. Perhaps, I thought, I may discover that Thomas atte Bridge did indeed take his own life, and planned it so as to suggest some other had part in the business. This would be convenient. But justice can be often inconvenient.

I promised Maud that I would examine the circumstances of her husband's death. She departed Galen House with many expressions of gratitude, as if I had already resolved the matter.

I had discarded the rope taken from Thomas atte

Bridge's neck in a corner of the chamber. My eyes fell upon it as I sat at my table and pondered the obligation I had accepted. Two lengths of hempen cord lay tangled. Three of the ends were sliced through cleanly. I had seen a knife make one of these cuts when Thomas was cut down. The fourth end was frayed with age. When the rope was one piece it had one worn end and one newly cut.

Kate had prepared a coney pie for our dinner. My mind returned to the rope while I ate. Kate saw I was preoccupied, followed my gaze, and guessed the cause.

"You are silent, Hugh. Does Maud's complaint trouble you?"

"Aye. Lord Gilbert entrusts me with justice in Bampton. If a man is murdered here I must seek whoso has slain him. But if Maud speaks true and her husband was done to death by another, there are those who would agree the murderer has done a laudable deed."

"You think the same?" she asked.

"I am troubled. Murder is a grievous sin, but I am not sorry Thomas atte Bridge lies in his grave. What if I discover he was murdered and the felon is a friend? What then will I do?"

"You will do the right. I have faith in you," Kate replied softly.

"I might sleep more soundly did I have your confidence."

"I will do what I may to see you sleep well, your burdens forgot," she smiled.

I am sure my face reflected a lightened spirit after her words.

I could not drive the discarded rope from my mind that day. It seemed there might be significance to the odd number of cut and frayed ends to the two sections. Late in the day I took a length of the hempen cord with me and called at Maud's hut.

The door was open to the warm spring afternoon but only silence greeted me. A cottage with four children should be a noisy place. I rapped my knuckles against the door-post and heard the rustle of rushes on the floor in response. Maud appeared, her youngest child upon a hip, both of them blinking in the sunlight after the dim interior of the dwelling.

I showed her the rope. She recoiled as if I had swatted her with it, but regained composure when I told her I was about the work she begged of me. I asked if Thomas had owned rope like that in my hand. Such common stuff might be found about a cotter's house. Did a man have a field planted to hemp, it was easy enough to make. I thought Maud might produce a length of cord like it and I could compare the cut ends. She did not. Thomas, she contended, had no such rope nor had he possessed any or had need to for many years.

That Thomas atte Bridge might have owned things his wife knew not of I did not doubt. But it seemed unlikely he would keep possession of a hempen rope from her. He might, however, borrow such a cord from another and Maud know not.

If I displayed the rope, and asked if any owned the length it was cut from, word would soon find its way through Bampton and the Weald. Was Thomas murdered, as I believed, a guilty man would surely then hide any remnant. I decided to forego questioning neighbors in the Weald.

Kate was right. I fell readily to sleep that eve, and the next, but awoke two days later well before the Angelus Bell. In the pale light of early dawn, Kate's steady breathing beside me, I pondered the slashed ends of hempen rope. In my bed, before even Kate's rooster discharged his duty, it came to me where I might seek a fragment of rope like that which brought death to Thomas atte Bridge. Did I find nothing, I would know no less than I now did, but if I found a length of hempen cord it would go far to confirming my suspicions.

I rose from my bed, descended the stairs, and prodded

coals on the hearth to life. I sat on a bench and fed sticks to the growing blaze until the room was warmed. Kate appeared soon after. She produced from our cup board a maslin loaf and cup of ale for me, but declined to break her fast. She complained of an uneasy stomach.

I told her then of my plan to search for a short length of rope. Kate, for all her unease, would not consider remaining behind at Galen House. So when the sun was high enough to allow inspection of even a shadowy forest we set out for Cow-Leys Corner.

But six months past Kate had searched with me outside the wall of Canterbury Hall, in Oxford, for a broken thong. She had found the bit of leather, and now she prowled with me through the wood to the north of the road, seeking a length of hempen cord. She found it.

The rope segment was as long as my arm. It lay upon a compost of rotting leaves and broken twigs, its color blending with the forest floor. Kate knew what I sought, but not why. She held the length of hemp above her head and shouted success while I was kicking through fallen, rotting leaves twenty or so paces from where the cord lay.

"What means this?" she asked when I took the rope from her to inspect it.

"Stand here," I replied, "where you found it."

I walked to stand under the limb where Thomas atte Bridge hung in death. I wound the cord to a ball in my hand, then threw it toward Kate. The hemp uncoiled in flight and fell at her feet, or near so, perhaps one pace beyond where she stood watching, puzzled by this exercise.

"I found a small abrasion on Thomas atte Bridge's wrist," I explained, "as if perhaps his hands were tied before he died."

"Then Maud speaks true, and your suspicion is valid; her husband did not take his own life."

"I fear so."

"Fear?"

"Aye. Many will resent me seeking the murderer of

one like Thomas atte Bridge from among their friends."

"But you will do so?"

"Aye," I sighed. "Some man tied Thomas by the neck to that oak, then threw away the cord he used to bind his wrists. 'Twas two men, I think. The man who carried his feet dropped them, hence the mud upon atte Bridge's heels and the grooves in the road yonder."

"Did they bind his feet also?"

"Nay, I think not. The tracks in the road are a hand's breadth and more apart."

"Did he not struggle and cry out?"

"He could not, I think."

"Why so?"

"I found a great welt upon his lip when he was cut down. Beneath it a tooth was broken. Maud knew nothing of these injuries. He was knocked senseless, I think, then brought here and hanged so all would believe him a suicide."

"You told no one of his injury?"

"Nay, and I will not, I think."

"Not even Hubert Shillside?"

"The coroner is convinced that Thomas did away with himself... or is convinced that is what should be so and is what all men must think."

"He will be of no assistance to us, then."

"Us?"

"A wife's duty is to be always at her husband's side. And I found the rope," Kate laughed.

"It is your duty to feed me, which now interests me most."

"I have a leg of lamb ready to roast," Kate replied. "After dinner we must consider how to find a murderer."

"Such a discovery will require some effort. The man who did this planned well."

"But he did not consider the mud," Kate rejoined, "and he should not have cast aside that length of cord."

"Aye. No felon considers all the ways his crime might

go awry. We have found two misjudgments already. There may be more to discover."

We returned to Galen House past fields where men worked with dibble sticks, poking holes into the newly turned earth to plant peas and beans. Kate set to work upon our dinner, and shortly after Peter the Carpenter knocked upon our door. He had taken a gouge out of his wrist with a chisel and required my service. It was a serious wound and bled greatly. I stitched him, bathed the wound in wine from the castle buttery, and collected tuppence. I follow the practice of Henri de Mondeville, who taught that such injuries heal best when uncovered, left open to the air. I instructed Peter to keep the wound free of dirt but placed no salve or wrapping upon it. He seemed skeptical of this treatment, but I assured him good success was sure to follow, and that I would remove the stitches in a fortnight.

There was another matter I must soon raise with Peter. His daughter was heavy with child, and unwed. It was my duty to levy fines for leirwite and childwite. I resolved to await the birth. If the babe did not live I would levy leirwite only.

The leg of lamb sizzled on a spit over the coals, but Kate was not to be found. Odd, I thought, that she would not attend the spit to keep our dinner from singeing. Grease dripped to the coals and sputtered there. The smell of roasting meat caused my stomach to growl with anticipation.

Then I heard, through the open door, Kate retching in the toft behind Galen House. She had taken no loaf to break her fast, and now seemed unlikely to enjoy her dinner. I was much concerned, but when we sat to our meal Kate assured me that her belly was much improved and I was pleased to see her take a portion of lamb and wheaten loaf.

Four days later was May Day. Youth of the town were out of their beds before dawn, gathering hawthorn boughs and wildflowers from the forests of Lord Gilbert and the

Bishop of Exeter. Indeed, many, as is the custom, spent the night gamboling in forest and meadow, bringing in the May. Garlands of greenery decorated windows and doors before the third hour of the day. Hubert Shillside's son, Will, was chosen Lord of the May. His lady was a lass of the Weald whose father held a yardland of the bishop. Kate and I watched as the couple was paraded down Church View Street with singing and laughter. I would have joined the procession, but Kate was again unwell and I did not wish to celebrate the May and its carefree joy while she was afflicted so.

Hubert Shillside also observed the revelers. He watched with pride as Will, crowned with a circlet of bluebells, led marchers past his shop. The lad was becoming a man, no longer an assemblage of knees, elbows, and overgrown feet. His form was growing to fill the gaps between those adolescent enlargements.

Walking close behind the Lord and Lady of the May I saw Alice atte Bridge. She was subdued, and I knew why. No castle scullery maid would be chosen Lady of the May, no matter her comeliness. I had seen Will Shillside giving attention to Alice in the past, but this day the maid from the Weald supplanted her.

Hubert Shillside was Bampton town's haberdasher. He would want his son courting a lass who might bring a substantial dowry to the marriage. He had probably already had conversation with fathers of suitable maids in the town, and perhaps from Witney and Burford as well. The lass walking beside Will would have suited Shillside, but Alice, for all her beauty, would not.

Alice was half-sister to Thomas atte Bridge. Her father, a widower, had remarried late in life and Alice was the only offspring of that union. Near three years past the old man slipped on icy cobbles and broke his hip. I could do nothing for him but ease his pain as he made his way to the next world.

I could, however, help Alice. I found a place for the

child at the castle, free of the hatred and jealousy of her brothers. Henry and Thomas seized all of their father's few possessions after his death. Alice escaped to the castle with what she might carry, no more. Her father's hut now mouldered, derelict, in the Weald, beside the houses of Emma and Maud, the widows of Henry and Thomas.

I followed the merrymakers to the Broad Street and Cheapside, where they busied themselves raising a maypole at the marketplace. I found Hubert Shillside there, observing the youth of Bampton with a proud smile upon his face.

"Will is well chosen," I congratulated him. "And the lass also. Her father has a yardland of the bishop, does he not?"

"Aye. She has two brothers."

With four words the haberdasher had told me neither he, nor Will, I assumed, was interested in the maid. The lass might bring coin and some possessions to her marriage, but the land would stay with the older brother. And should he die, another heir was in place.

"Bampton has several comely maids."

"Hmmm. 'Tis so. But most will bring little to their husbands. You did well with Kate… a house in Oxford."

"Aye, but measured against her other virtues the house is of scant value."

"Hah. So you say now. When you are wed some years such a dowry will loom larger. Beauty does not last, houses and lands will."

"Perhaps."

Shillside must know of his son's attraction to Alice atte Bridge and be displeased. I thought to bait him on the matter. "Will seems more interested these days in pleasing his eye than his purse," I laughed.

Shillside peered at me and frowned.

"I have seen him in company with a comely maid who will bring nothing to her husband but herself."

"Ah," the haberdasher smiled. "You speak of Alice

atte Bridge. 'Tis true... Will is smitten with the lass. But she is not so poor as all think."

This was a surprise to me. When three years past I sent her to the castle I thought she owned nothing. Indeed, Alice believed so as well.

Shillside saw my astonishment and continued. "Alice's mother, Isabel, was second wife to the elder Henry atte Bridge, as you know. Isabel's dowry from her first husband was a half-yardland in the Weald. When she died, an' then Henry, the land came to Alice."

"Alice did not speak of this."

"She was but a child... perhaps she knew nothing of it."

"Isabel had no children of her first husband?"

"None," Shillside smiled.

"Henry and Thomas atte Bridge claimed their father's lands when he died."

"Aye, so they did. But not all of it was theirs to have."

"How did you learn this?"

"Isabel's sister is wed to William Walle. His brother Randall is haberdasher in Witney. We do business."

"Does Alice know?"

"Aye, she does."

"And the vicars of St Beornwald? Disputes in the Weald are their bailiwick. Do they know of this?"

"Aye. The matter is to be brought before hallmote."

"Thomas atte Bridge will not attend to defend his taking."

"Nay," Shillside smiled again. "Alice will gain her due, I've no doubt."

"And her husband, whoso that may be, will add a half-yardland and pasture rights to his holdings."

"Just so. Alice will not stand in the church porch so penniless as many would think of a scullery maid."

"Did Thomas atte Bridge know of Alice's suit to regain her mother's dowry lands?"

"Aye, he did. And was ready to dispute the matter, but I think Maud will not refuse Alice her due as Thomas would."

"'Tis convenient, then, for Alice and whoso she may wed, that Thomas hanged himself at Cow-Leys Corner."

"Aye, it is so."

Revelry continued that fine spring day but I felt no wish to join it. My Kate was unwell, and distasteful images flashed through my mind. As I retreated to Galen House I saw in my mind's eye Hubert Shillside prowling about in Thomas atte Bridge's toft, intentionally disturbing his hens. I saw atte Bridge stumble from his hut to investigate the uproar, and saw Shillside swing a cudgel to deliver a blow to the back of Thomas's head. I saw Thomas catch a glimpse of movement in the darkened toft, and turn so that Shillside's blow caught him in the face, upon his mouth.

I envisioned Shillside and his son binding Thomas by the wrists, leaving a strand of hempen cord upon atte Bridge's frayed sleeve, then taking him by shoulders and heels to carry him off to Cow-Leys Corner. I imagined the lad losing grip of Thomas's heels, allowing them to drag briefly in the mud. I saw the youth sneaking in to atte Bridge's hut some days earlier to make off with the stool, which would prove then to all that Thomas atte Bridge took his own life.

These images caused me much distress, for Hubert Shillside was my friend.

I entered Galen House in somber mood. What I found there did little, at first, to improve my dour outlook. Kate heard me enter and left our bed, where she had withdrawn. She was half-way down the stairs, coming to greet me, when she grew light-headed and fell. It was my good fortune that I heard her descending, so was at the foot of the steps when she stumbled. I caught her before she could do harm to herself, and carried her to a bench.

Kate came quickly to her senses, although I admit I did not. I took a cup of water from the ewer upon our cup board and splashed it into her face. She spluttered and protested and demanded I cease, which I did.

Kate dried her face with her apron, then began to giggle. I thought my wife had come unhinged. I found no humor in the scene. I sat beside her upon the bench to comfort her, and put an arm about her shoulder to support her should she again swoon. I did not wish to apply my surgical skills to repair her broken scalp should she fall back upon the flags.

"You are unwell," I said. "I will take you to bed, where you may rest."

"I have just come from there," she said. "I rose when I heard you enter, and did so too quickly. 'Tis why I became giddy on the stairs."

"You have not been well for many days."

"I am very well, or would be did you not dash cold water in my face. My illness is but what is common to women."

I am a surgeon, not a physician, and in surgical training I had learned nothing of swooning being customary female behavior. I said so.

"I will be quite well in a fortnight, or perhaps a little longer," she assured me. "This sickness which now afflicts me will pass, as it does with all womankind who are with child."

Chapter 3

Kate's announcement caused me to forget for a time what I had learned from Hubert Shillside. When thoughts of his conversation returned I attempted to excuse the knowledge. What had the fellow told me? Only that Alice atte Bridge might inherit a smallholding from her deceased mother.

I might wish ignorance of the matter but this was not given to me. I knew of Will's interest in Alice. I knew of the haberdasher's desires for his son. And now I knew of a reason Thomas atte Bridge might die at the hands of another. The thought brought bile to my throat.

Kate saw that my joy at her disclosure had faded, along with my appetite for dinner. She mistook my anxiety.

"I will soon be well, Hugh. I do not fear bearing a child... since Eve women have borne babes."

She did not say that her mother died in childbirth, and the babe with her, when Kate was but a wee lass, and so I did not speak of it either. But surely such apprehension must occasionally cloud her thoughts. Now that I knew of her condition such dark reflections would, I knew, come unbidden to me.

"Should our child be a boy," she continued, "shall we name him for his father?"

"Perhaps," I shrugged. "But when you summon him from the door of Galen House I would then think you called for me. And it would confuse the neighbors. Robert, for your father, would serve, I think."

"He would be well pleased. If the child is a lass I should like her named for my mother, have you no objection."

"Elizabeth? A fine name. I should enjoy my little Bessie playing about my ankles."

"You do not seem joyful."

"For your news I am much pleased. I have some worry... for you and the babe, but I know well the good in life is oft accompanied by sorrow. Woe is often the coin by which we pay for bliss."

"Then why have you left some custard in your bowl?" Kate had begun to serve me my dinner while we talked, and noted my lack of appetite, a thing highly unusual for me.

"I have learned a troubling thing."

"Do you wish to speak of it?"

"Aye. Perhaps you may discover some mitigating consideration. I have just come from speaking to Hubert Shillside. You will remember that I told you of Alice, the scullery maid? Shillside has told me she is not so penniless as I thought – or as she thought, I am sure."

"A cotter's daughter with two rapacious brothers?" Kate frowned. "How could such a maid be aught but a mendicant?"

"Her mother died when Alice was but a child. She brought to her marriage to Alice's father a dower of a half-yardland. The property fell into the hands of Henry and Thomas atte Bridge when their father died."

"Did they know it was dower land?"

"I am sure of it. But Alice was too young to understand such things, and all others who knew were dead, but for Henry and Thomas."

"How did Shillside learn of this?"

"The haberdasher in Witney is Shillside's friend and brother-in-law to Alice's aunt. He knew the terms of the dower."

"Why is Hubert Shillside concerned with the business?"

"Because Will is smitten with Alice."

Kate was silent, considering this. "Now Thomas is dead there is only Maud to protest Alice regaining her mother's dower."

"And Emma," I added. "Shillside is confident the bishop's hallmote will award the land to Alice."

Kate looked pensively past me, toward the fire, before she spoke again. "Would a man murder another for a half-yardland?" she said softly, to herself as much as to me. I had no answer, so spoke none.

"Would not the bishop's hallmote award Alice her due even was Thomas atte Bridge alive to protest?" Kate continued.

"Mayhap. But now that he is gone the issue may be in less doubt. And did he live and lose the suit, he might take vengeance upon those who bested him. Such a man was he."

"Will you pursue this?"

"I must. I would rather spend a month in Oxford Castle dungeon."

"Will you confront Shillside with your suspicion?"

"Nay. If he is guilty it will be easier to discover so does he not know of my suspicion. If he is innocent I would not have him aware that I thought him capable of such a felony."

"You believe he is... capable of such a felony?"

"Nay, but I have been wrong before."

"Surely there are others in Bampton and the Weald Thomas atte Bridge has wronged more grievously than Alice."

"No doubt, but men may respond differently to similar insults."

"And women also," Kate agreed.

The May Day revelers had gone to their dinners. Most were away from their beds before dawn, and now, with full stomachs, sought rest more than continued merrymaking. So Bampton was silent, and the scream, when it came, was audible although it came from Rosemary Lane, near two hundred paces away. Kate looked to me with a frown, and I returned the expression. Folk will not shriek so unless they are in great pain or anguish. I expected a summons, and work for either a surgeon or a bailiff.

Kate and I yet held each other's questioning gaze when there came a thumping upon the door of Galen House. But it was Kate's presence requested, not mine. Eleanor, the cobbler's wife, was come to fetch Kate. The carpenter's daughter, Jane, was about to deliver her child. Kate had agreed to act God's sib at the birth.

I heard another distant screech through the open door. The sound gave wings to Kate's feet. She ran off down Church View Street to her duty. Another scream echoed up the street as Kate disappeared 'round the corner of Rosemary Lane. Such distress in childbirth was not unknown to me, although, all praise to God, the birth of a babe is work for the midwife, not the surgeon.

I continued to hear Jane's shrieks, but soon after the evening Angelus Bell rang they faded and I supposed her travail over and the babe safely delivered. I was wrong.

Near midnight I gave up waiting for Kate's return and sought our bed. I expected to be disturbed in the night when she returned from her duty, but this was not so. When dawn glowed through the skin of our chamber window I was yet alone.

I had broken my fast and was finishing a cup of ale when Kate burst through the door of Galen House. "Midwife wishes you to attend her. You are to bring your instruments," Kate gasped.

"What has happened?"

"Nothing, and therein lies the trouble. Jane is near death. The babe is wrongly placed and Mistress Pecham cannot turn it."

Jane had struggled for many hours to deliver her child. She was surely exhausted, and no effort from her would produce the babe. It was likely she was doomed, but I would heed Katherine Pecham's summons and see was there aught I might do for the lass or the babe.

The midwife had done all she knew. Doors and

windows of the carpenter's house stood open, chests were open and all knots undone, this to open the womb. Galen, the great physician of many centuries past, did not write of these actions, and I distrust their potency. But such is commonly done, and if to no advantage, it can surely do no harm.

Katherine Pecham has been midwife to Bampton for many years. The crone has seen many babes brought to the world and knows well whether success or misfortune is likely. She had sent word to Father Thomas to be ready at St Beornwald's baptismal font, for if the babe did come forth it was sure to be feeble and must be baptized straight away. The godparents were notified also and awaited a summons. Mistress Pecham had done all needful things; all else was now in the hands of God. Or in my hands. I shuddered briefly at the thought. Kate, at my side, took note and grasped my arm.

Jane sat upon the birthing chair, near senseless from her vain exertions. The morning was cool, but sweat stood upon her brow and upper lip. As I watched a God's sib wiped her forehead with a cooling cloth. This caused the lass to raise her head and soon another ineffectual spasm racked her body. She cried out, but weakly. When the convulsion was done she lay back against the chair, more spent than before.

"The babe is placed wrong," Mistress Pecham whispered. "I have tried all I know to turn it, but have no success. I will make another attempt. If I fail the lass will likely perish. You must stand ready to take the babe does Jane die. I have felt the babe move. It lives, and may yet survive even if Jane does not."

My study of surgery in Paris did not include instruction in childbirth. Such things are best left to women. Students were, however, taught to open the womb with a blade so as to take the babe when the mother was dead or it was sure she soon would be so. A doctor of surgery at the University of Paris told me that he knew of such a surgery where both mother and babe survived. If so, this was the only such occurrence I have heard of. I have doubts.

Mistress Pecham attended to Jane, pressing her swollen belly to see could she not shift the babe. The midwife was soon sweating as heavily as Jane, but to no effect which I could see. I felt much regret that I would likely soon be called upon to release the babe with a scalpel. Kate saw my black mood and gripped my arm as if to steady me for the sorry work to come.

Mistress Pecham peered up at me, ceased her struggle, and shook her head in wordless despair. Kate looked to me with a plea in her eyes. I bid Kate follow and went to help the midwife to her feet. She was weary, and wobbled unsteadily as she stood.

"You must take the child," she whispered. "The lass is too young and small to allow the babe to pass, misplaced as it is."

"If I open her womb Jane will surely die. Is there no other hope?"

"Nay," the woman shook her head. "I have seen such misplaced babes before. If I cannot turn them, and the mother be so weakened as Jane, all is lost. I sent for Father Thomas at dawn. Jane has been shriven."

I looked to Kate. She and the other God's sibs stared back at me. I saw reproach in some eyes, as if I and my gender were responsible for the dread which infected the carpenter's house.

"I am hesitant to do this. I have no experience in such surgery."

"I know that if you open Jane's womb she will die," Mistress Pecham said softly, brushing a wisp of graying hair from her brow with the back of her wrist. "But if you will not, she and the babe will both perish."

Kate again took my arm. "Mistress Pecham speaks true. You must balance a certainty with the possible." She pressed my arm with both hands, as if to stiffen my courage.

I made no reply to these pleas for some minutes. Jane's pale face occupied my attention and thoughts. Her eyes were closed, her breathing shallow. I knew the midwife spoke true; Jane was likely soon to see the Lord Christ, yet I could not move from my place. It was as if my heels had taken root in the soil beneath the rushes.

"How long has she, think you?" I asked Mistress Pecham.

The woman shrugged, pursed her lips, then replied softly so Jane, was she sensible, might not hear. "She will be gone by the ninth hour, I think."

It was not yet the third hour of the day. "If, by the ninth hour," I replied, "she is yet unable to deliver the child, I will take it with the blade. Keep close watch on her. If she perish before then I must take the babe instantly. Are you certain it lives?"

"I felt it move when I last tried to shift it. I cannot say if it lives now."

A bed lay beside the birthing stool, and a small table stood near it. I laid upon this table the instruments I would need if called upon to open Jane's womb.

Peter Carpenter, with his wife and other children, awaited birth or death in the other of the two chambers of his house. As I placed my instruments I saw his haggard face at the door. He looked from me to Kate to Mistress Pecham and the God's sibs, saw despair writ on our faces, and disappeared.

Kate and the midwife sat upon a bench in a corner of the chamber to await the conclusion of the sad business. Once Jane cried out weakly as travail came again upon her. Both her agony and her cries soon ended.

When the lass lay still and silent again Mistress Pecham rose from the bench and approached the birthing stool. She stood silently, watching Jane. The midwife suddenly bent low over the lass. She studied her intently, then crossed herself, rose, and turned to me.

"Quickly, Master Hugh... Jane is gone."

I leaped to her side and saw it was so; Jane's shallow breathing had stopped. I picked up the lass from the birthing stool, set her upon the bed, drew the gown from her bloated belly, and with one hurried motion drew a blade from one side of her abdomen to the other. It was the work of but a few heartbeats to enlarge and deepen this opening until I saw beneath my scalpel the womb and the pattern of a tiny foot where it should not have been, pressed against the membrane. With less speed and more care I opened the womb. When I did so I saw the babe's foot twitch, as if pleased to be freed of its fleshly embrace.

A moment later I drew the babe from the womb and turned to Katherine Pecham. The midwife stood ready with a clean linen cloth to receive the child. It was a lad. I severed the cord and turned back to Jane, although there was nothing to be done for her. As I looked upon her still, bloodied form I heard a weak wail, then gasps from the God's sibs. The babe drew breath, and lived, at least for now.

I turned back to observe Mistress Pecham at her work. She first opened the babe's nostrils and purged them of bile, then bathed the infant in warm water. When this was done she anointed the babe with oil of acorns and wrapped it in bands of soft linen.

The cobbler's wife took the babe from her and with her husband, who had waited without all the while, hastened to the church. There Thomas de Bowlegh would unwrap the babe and immerse him in the font so that, should the infant perish, his soul would find its way to paradise. This is a shocking way to welcome a babe to the world, but perhaps, given the sorrows all men must endure, it is well to introduce the trials of life to the young, so to harden them for adversities sure to come.

Peter Carpenter and his wife sat together in the home's other chamber, drained of life and emotion. Two younger children, a lad of twelve years or thereabouts, and a lass a few years younger, peered up wide-eyed at me and Kate as we entered the chamber. A few embers glowed upon the hearth. Peter stood and spoke as we entered.

"Will the babe live?"

"The Lord Christ only knows," I replied. "Mistress Pecham believes him sound, if weak. She is practiced in such matters."

"But Jane is gone, for the babe to live?"

"Aye. When Mistress Pecham saw that Jane was dead she called for me to take the babe."

"Then for this, much thanks. Does he live, we may remember the mother by the son."

The carpenter's lips drew tightly together. He turned to his wife: "Sent her to an early grave, the wretch!"

I thought it was of the lad who had lain with his daughter that he spoke. "Who is that?" I asked.

"You'll get no leirwite for Lord Gilbert from the knave."

"Will you not name the lad?"

"Oh, I'll name the rogue. Won't do you nor me nor Jane any good."

"Who, then?"

"Thomas atte Bridge… him as hanged hisself. An' well he did, too."

"Jane named him as the father of her child?" I said, somewhat incredulously. I searched my mind for some memory of Thomas atte Bridge and could summon no feature of the man likely to appeal to a comely maid.

"'E come on her sudden, like, last summer. She were in the forest beyond the Weald, pickin' blackberries. She tried to cry out, but 'e beat her an' throttled her an' had 'is way with her. Knew somethin' was amiss when she come home… eyes goin' to black an' weepin' an' no berries."

"Jane told you what happened?"

"Aye."

"Why did you not seek me and charge the scoundrel?"

"Jane begged me not. Atte Bridge said to her if she

told, 'e'd do worse to her, an' take revenge upon her family, too."

I had experience enough of Thomas atte Bridge to know his words no idle threat.

"But when you saw Jane was with child, why then did you not seek justice?"

"Bah. What justice is there for a maid when such befalls her? An' even did hallmote find against Thomas, 'e'd soon seek us to take vengeance."

Peter spoke true. Atte Bridge nursed his grudges well. And the carpenter knew also of the prescript, which Galen wrote many centuries past, that a woman will not conceive except she be a willing partner. A lass who is with child cannot therefore accuse a man of rape, and if she does not bear a child any accusation is but the maid's word against the man's. Who would believe her but perhaps her father? I wonder if Galen might have been wrong about this. Surely Jane Carpenter did not willingly lie with Thomas atte Bridge.

The carpenter is a large man, his movements ever slow and measured. I had never seen the man hurried in walk or work. His temperament matched his manner. A frown seemed never to cross his face, until this day.

I am a peaceful man. How might I change, sixteen years hence, does Kate bear me a daughter and the lass be set upon by some miscreant like Thomas atte Bridge? Because Jane conceived no court would indict atte Bridge for rape. Galen had said it could not be so. The carpenter's shop would have many planks of proper size to deliver a blow across a man's skull. And Peter is strong enough that a stroke from him might render a man senseless. Senseless long enough to haul his body from the Weald to Cow-Leys Corner?

Did Peter's wife assist, or his lad? Perhaps she or he carried atte Bridge's feet, and briefly dropped them in the muddy road when the burden grew heavy.

Peter Carpenter, like Hubert Shillside, is a friend.

What if I were to discover that one of these indeed murdered Thomas atte Bridge? The mournful thought occupied my mind as Kate and I walked Church View Street to Galen House. On our way we met Martyn the cobbler and Eleanor hurrying from the church. Eleanor carried a pale bundle in her arms. The babe was properly baptized and the outcome now in God's hands.

Not entirely. How would the babe's life be altered did I discover that his grandfather had slain his father? I did not wish to think longer of the matter. But it is sure that when a man tries to dismiss a thought it will fix itself in his mind.

The day was far gone when Kate and I returned to Galen House. We ate a cold supper of capon and barley loaf and went silently to our bed. I found no rest, and heard Kate's steady breathing for much of the night before I fell to sleep some time shortly before Kate's rooster announced the new day.

Neither Kate nor I had appetite to break our fast. She set ale and a wheaten loaf before me. But I could manage only a small portion of the loaf. I am not usually so afflicted. Hunger can overwhelm my darkest moods, most of the time.

"Will you seek the carpenter's house this day," she asked, "to learn if the babe lives?"

"Aye."

"What fine must they pay?"

"Six pence for leirwite, another six for childwite is common."

"Common? You say so, but your manner says other."

I motioned Kate to our bench, placed more wood upon the fire, for it was a chill morn, then sat beside her and told her of Peter Carpenter's disclosure.

Kate's lips grew thin as I related the tale, and although the blaze upon our hearth grew warm I sensed a chill come over Kate.

"So a bailiff would make Peter Carpenter pay for the injury done his daughter?"

"Some would, to keep their position. Great lords are always in want. Most would have a shilling from even a pauper could they get it."

"Is Lord Gilbert Talbot such a man?"

"He will not turn profit away, but I think he would see unfairness in this matter."

"Think you so?" Kate replied with raised brows.

"He will not return from Pembroke 'til Lammastide. Perhaps he need not know."

"Or by Lammastide we may know the truth of Thomas atte Bridge's death."

She said "we" again. I wished no discord this day, so did not contest the word. I was not long practiced at being a husband, but I am a ready scholar.

Chapter 4

Next day I found Peter sitting upon the same bench where I had left him. I asked for news of the babe.

"He lives," he replied, "but cries weakly and does not take the breast of the wet nurse strongly."

As he spoke a curate and four others darkened the door of the carpenter's house. They had come to bear Jane to the churchyard.

Jane had been already wrapped in her burial shroud and placed in a coffin. Peter would not see his daughter await the return of the Lord Christ in only a black winding sheet. The curate's companions carried the coffin from house to street, and I joined the procession which made its way up Church View Street. Kate heard the wailing as we approached and followed as the mourners passed Galen House.

The bearers set Jane down in the lych gate, where Father Thomas awaited the procession. Before the sixth hour mass was said, the grave diggers had completed their work, and Jane Carpenter was awaiting the resurrection of the dead in St Beornwald's churchyard.

I had little stomach for business in what remained of the day, but busied myself at the castle so as to escape thoughts of recent black events. Next morn, after a loaf and ale, I bid Kate "Good day," and set out again for the castle. I came upon Peter Carpenter as I passed Rosemary Lane. He had a bag of tools slung over a shoulder and was evidently called to exercise his carpentry skills. Some lives must continue even when others cease.

"A fine day for labor," I remarked, finding any other subject of conversation uncomfortable.

"Aye. If I keep me hands busy I can keep me thoughts from Jane an' what befell her. Father Thomas says hate is an evil thing. We are to love others. How can a man love one who ravished his daughter, her but a maid, an' sent her to her death?"

Choosing a contrary subject for conversation with one who is single-minded is not readily done.

"The Lord Christ commands us to love our enemies," I replied. "Even those who use us badly."

"Aye, so the priests say. Don't say 'ow to do it, though, an' they don't have daughters to be despoiled... Well, there be some as do, I suppose."

"Where does your work take you this day? I will walk with you if it be toward the castle."

"In the Weald. Some man did hamsoken there while all were thought to be at mass. Broke down the door, an' I've got to place a new door-post an' set the hinges right."

"Who was attacked?"

"Philip Mannyng."

"He is an aged man, is he not?"

"Aye. Keeps to 'is bed most days. Amabil went off to church, an' come home to find 'im beaten. Senseless, he was."

"Who did such a thing?"

"Couldn't say. Amabil asked, of course. He couldn't remember. Whoso done it took a club to 'is head while 'e was sleepin'. Amabil said as 'e had great lumps on 'is skull an' 'is nose broke."

"Did they complain to the vicars?"

"Oh, aye. Father Simon come to see the damage an' what could be done. Philip could recall nothing."

"Do Philip and Amabil have enemies in the Weald? They are the bishop's tenants, so I know little of doings there."

"Don't know much of what 'appens in the Weald meself, but never heard anything against 'em. Arnulf is wrathful an' seeks whoso did it."

"Arnulf?"

"Arnulf Mannyng, Philip's son. Has a yardland of the bishop, an' works 'is father's lands."

I tried to fit a face to the name, but could not. Arnulf Mannyng had evidently done nothing to draw the attention of Lord Gilbert Talbot's bailiff. Probably, like most men, he is content to live a quiet life with wife and children. A man much like Peter Carpenter, perhaps. An attack upon an aged and infirm parent might cause even a placid man to do injury to the assailant. Who would be most angry, I wondered – a man whose daughter was violated to her death, or one whose parent was attacked? I resolved to learn more.

"I will walk with you to the Weald. Keeping the peace there is the vicars' business, but I would know more of the matter."

Peter said no more, but a man would not need to be clairvoyant to guess my interest. Together we crossed the bridge over Shill Brook and turned to the lane leading to the Weald. Philip Mannyng's house stood near the end of the narrow road. To reach it we passed the dwellings of Maud and Emma atte Bridge, two widows who now lived without beatings if also without a husband's labor at field and hearth. I wondered what they thought of the exchange.

A small, dirty face peered out of the open door of Emma's hut, but otherwise the houses were silent. That is, until Peter and I had walked twenty paces or so past. Then, of a sudden, we heard feminine voices. Father Thomas, deaf as he is, might have heard them. Indeed, he might have heard them from Mill Street.

The words were indistinct, but the shrieking came from behind the atte Bridge hovels. Peter peered at me from under questioning brows and we halted to better discover the source and meaning of the screeching. Across the lane I saw a woman look out from her open door, shake her head in disgust, then disappear about her work. Her reaction seemed token that such din was not uncommon in the Weald.

Emma and Maud appeared in the space between their tofts to the rear of their houses as we watched. Maud was in retreat, Emma shaking an angry fist in her face. Emma's oldest son, a strapping lad of fourteen years or so, advanced behind his mother to support her cause in the dispute. She appeared capable of defending her position unaided.

Tenants and villeins in the Weald are the Bishop of Exeter's concern. I had no wish to place myself between two angry women, especially as the dispute was not my bailiwick. Peter seemed to think likewise. He looked at me, shrugged, and we set off again for Philip Mannyng's house. We could yet hear Maud and Emma when we stood before Mannyng's broken door.

Amabil Mannyng opened the fractured door to Peter's call. The old woman was bent with age, an affliction of her sex common to those who have seen many years pass. She had expected Peter, but was surprised to see me.

"You've come to mend me door, then?" she asked, speaking to Peter, but examining me.

"Aye, an' do you know Master Hugh? 'E's bailiff to Lord Gilbert."

"Seen 'im about. Heard 'e patched Gerard's head."

Gerard is Lord Gilbert's verderer. Two years past he had the misfortune to stand where an oak his sons were felling might swat him with a plunging limb. His skull was badly cracked. I repaired the injury, but he walks now with a limp, which I suspect will always be so.

"Your man lies ill in his bed, I am told."

"Aye. Since Candlemas 'e's been low."

"And near a fortnight past someone beset him in his bed?" I added.

"They did."

"Perhaps I might see him. I have herbs which can comfort afflicted folk."

"Was going to call for you when I found 'im, but Philip wouldn't have it. Said he'd heal well enough, an' if not was ready to see God. 'No use payin' the surgeon,' he said. My Philip's always been tight with a penny."

I left Peter to inspect the splintered door and followed Amabil into the dim interior of the house. The woman's aged husband lay upon his bed, his form so shrunken with age and illness and abuse, he seemed but an assemblage of coppiced poles beneath the bed coverings. I found myself in agreement with the old man's prophecy: he was near to seeing the Lord Christ.

Philip heard our conversation and approach and turned in his bed to see who disturbed his slumber. A purple bruise, beginning to turn green and yellow, stretched from his forehead to cheek. A gash across his scalp, which I might have closed with needle and silk thread, bore a thick scab. Philip would, did he live, bear a wide scar where the blow caught him. His nose was swollen, purple, and bent.

A bench sat near the bed. I drew it to Philip's side and introduced myself.

"Know who you are," he wheezed. "Seen you about the town."

"I am told you lay abed a Sunday and were attacked while your wife was at mass."

"Aye. My time is short... know that well enough."

"Who was it tried to hasten your passing?"

"Dunno. Kicked in the door. That's what woke me. I don't see so well any more. All I remember is a fellow raisin' a club over me. Next I knew, 'twas Sunday eve an' Amabil and Arnulf was bendin' over me."

"Door was barred," Amabil added. "Arnulf thought it best. Philip can rise from 'is bed when needful, an' could unbar the door when I returned."

"Have you been in dispute with any man that you must bar the door?"

"Nay," Philip managed a chuckle. "I'm near seventy years old. Too old to quarrel with any man."

"Why, then, would a man wait 'til you were alone, then attack you?"

Philip shook his head weakly, and sighed. The effort seemed to pain him, for he closed his eyes and grimaced.

"Most folk in the Weald know Philip is afflicted," Amabil said. "It's no secret 'e's seldom from 'is bed."

"And none holds a grudge against him?"

"Nay. My Philip was always a peaceful man."

Then why, I wondered, bar the door while Philip was abed alone?

"I have preparations which will ease his pain. I will return at the sixth hour. 'Tis too late to mend the cut on his scalp, or do aught for his nose, but I can allay his hurt."

I left Peter Carpenter at work on the broken door and jamb and sought Kate and my dinner. When I returned to Philip Mannyng's house Peter was near finished repairing the splintered door. I had with me a pouch of herbs: pounded lettuce seeds to help the man sleep, and hemp seeds and leaves to reduce the pain of his broken nose. I brought also the crushed root and leaves of comfrey, to make a poultice for Philip's bruised face. Such a preparation should have been applied straight away after the injury was discovered, but perhaps the comfrey might do the man some good even yet.

I instructed Amabil to measure a portion of the herbs into a cup of ale three times each day for her husband to drink, and was ready to depart when Arnulf Mannyng entered the house. He did not notice my presence at first. The house was dim and the man was intent upon his injured father. He strode to Philip's bed and sat upon the bench I had recently vacated.

Arnulf Mannyng was as sturdy as his father was frail. In shadow against the window he appeared much like Arthur; not so tall as me but weighing thirteen stone or more. Arnulf is a prosperous tenant of the Bishop of Exeter. Since the plague much land lies waste for want of men to plow and seed and harvest. Mannyng had added a yardland to the property of his father which he had assumed a year past when the old man was no longer able to work. Rumor had it that Arnulf had paid but six shillings gersom for the vacant holding, which included a tumble-down hut the man now used as a barn for his three cows and two oxen.

I stood silent in a corner while Amabil tended the fire and Arnulf spoke to his father. It was not my intent to pry into family business, but I was there and could not avoid the conversation.

Arnulf began by asking his father how he did, which needed no reply, for any man could see he was likely to soon see the Lord Christ, unless there be a purgatory, which I am come to doubt. Perhaps I should not write so, but I think it unlikely a bishop will ever read these words of mine, or trouble himself with a heretical surgeon should he do so.

The son's next words brought me to quick attention. "I told you last week you'll need worry no more of bein' attacked again," he assured the old man. "Not as Thomas atte Bridge was found hangin' from a tree at Cow-Leys Corner."

"Amabil told me also," Philip whispered. "Little good his death'll do me now."

While his father spoke Arnulf shifted on his bench to observe his mother. She had placed a pot upon the coals. Arnulf had but to raise his eyes from the pot to see me standing between door and window.

"You have a guest," he said harshly.

"'Tis Master Hugh, him as is Lord Gilbert's bailiff. He has brought herbs to ease your father's suffering."

"Ah… well then," his voice softened, "we are in your debt."

"Mixed with ale, the herbs will bring some release from pain and aid your father's sleep. And comfrey made into a paste will speed healing of his bruised face."

"What is owed for this?"

"Tuppence."

Arnulf fished about in his pouch and brought forth the coins. He stood and delivered them to my hand without another word. It was I who spoke.

"Did Thomas atte Bridge deal the blows to your father?"

"Aye, so I believe."

"Why would he do so?"

"Because he was too much the coward to attack me."

"He had reason to dislike you?"

"So he thought."

"Was his thinking flawed?"

"Nay... I suppose not."

"You did harm to Thomas?"

"In a way. We both sought a yardland of the bishop. I offered a better price. 'Twas land vacant near two years since John Rugg died with all his family when plague returned."

"Thomas resented losing the property?"

"Aye. He offered but three shillings gersom to Father Thomas."

"I'm surprised he could afford even that."

"Said as how I'd enough land an' was takin' food from 'is table."

"But all this was near two years in the past, was it not?"

"Aye, 'bout that."

"Atte Bridge waited two years to vent his anger?"

"Nay, 'e's been at me since, but nothin' I could prove to the vicars. Lost two lambs last year. Seen 'em born an' two days later they was gone."

"Perhaps some beast carried them off?"

"Perhaps. But no fox will take a lamb, be there an angry ewe about. An' someone breaks into me barn at night. Things go missin': harness for the oxen, an iron spade, such like."

"Is it possible some other did these thefts?"

"It is, but I'm thinkin' there will be no more, now Thomas atte Bridge lies in a grave at Cow-Leys Corner."

I agreed that cessation of these misfortunes would point to Thomas atte Bridge as the source, bid farewell to Philip and Amabil, and set out for Galen House. I had found another man pleased that Thomas atte Bridge lay in his grave. But did he put him there?

Chapter 5

I found Kate munching contentedly upon a maslin loaf and was pleased to see her do so.

"Your appetite has returned?"

"Some. Not in the morn, nor do I pine for roasted meat. But a piece of fish or a custard is pleasing, and this loaf suits me very well."

It had been three months and a few days since I met Kate, her father, and the wedding party at the porch of the Church of St Beornwald. There Father Thomas made us husband and wife, and I gave to Kate a golden ring set with an emerald, which I had purchased from a goldsmith on Oxford High Street. All know emeralds may ward off illness. I would have been better pleased to wed Kate sooner, but Holy Church forbids marriage during Advent and the twelve days of Christmas. Why this must be so I do not understand. The birth of the Lord Christ is cause for much joy and celebration, as is a wedding. The bishops surely have an answer to this, but there are none in Bampton or Oxford to ask.

"The herbs you took to the sufferer in the Weald… will they ease him?"

"As much as can be. I can diminish a man's pain, but I cannot remove it wholly."

"And the man who attacked him, is he known?"

"The son believes so: Thomas atte Bridge."

Kate was silent, chewing thoughtfully upon the last crust of her loaf. She swallowed and spoke.

"There is no shortage of folk in Bampton and the Weald with cause to hate the man."

"True. Hubert Shillside would have faced him over

Alice atte Bridge's dower lands, did he yet live. Peter Carpenter's daughter was ravished, and Arnulf Mannyng has suffered theft and the beating of his father at Thomas atte Bridge's hands, so he believes."

"Three men with a grudge against atte Bridge," Kate mused. "You think there are more?"

"Likely so."

My apprehension was accurate, as I soon learned.

Two days later I determined to travel to Alvescot where I might learn from Gerard the verderer the condition of Lord Gilbert's forests now that winter was past. I did not expect to discover anything troubling. Gerard has served Lord Gilbert for many years and knows his business, although his sons and nephew do the work now under his guidance, crippled as he is since the blow to his skull.

At the marshalsea I ordered Bruce saddled and made ready. I might have walked, but I am grown fond of the old horse which carries me about the countryside and I believe the beast enjoys escaping the stable.

The way to Alvescot leads past Cow-Leys Corner. As I passed the tree where Thomas atte Bridge hung, my thoughts drifted from forest management to death. I had convinced myself that a journey to Alvescot was my duty, but was this so? Perhaps my travel was but an escape from confronting three men who had reason to murder Thomas atte Bridge. Indeed, if Hubert or Peter or Arnulf was guilty, I had no desire to know of it.

Gerard lives with his wife and grown sons across the street from the Church of St Peter. I remembered the place well, for on a dark night a year past Thomas atte Bridge had lain in wait for me behind the church wall and clubbed me upon my skull when I peered through the lych gate. I did not know at the time who delivered the blow, or who it was I had followed from Bampton. Indeed, at the time and for some hours after I knew nothing at all.

I found Gerard hobbling about in his toft, where were stored coppiced poles and a few beams cut from trees which had fallen in winter storms. There is little need, since the plague, for cutting timber for construction. Many houses lie empty; why build new? But should a tree fall, it is wise to hew it into beams and saw it into planks rather than allow it to rot upon the forest floor. I was pleased to see that Gerard, or his sons and nephew, had been active in this work. And coppiced poles will always find use: houses need new rafters when the old decay, fences must be maintained, and firewood and charcoal burning will consume what may remain.

Few trees, Gerard said, had fallen in the winter past, and those which did I saw now before me hewn and sawn in Lord Gilbert's wood-yard, drying under a crude shed. Deer were plentiful, Gerard reported, and when Lord Gilbert returned to Bampton at Lammastide he would find good hunting.

While we spoke Richard and a youth I did not know entered the toft with a bundle of new-cut coppiced poles carried between the two on slings. The poles were placed to dry upon a rack already near full with the product of their labor.

The day was grown warm. Richard wiped sweat from his brow with the sleeve of his cotehardie and eyed me with, I thought, some suspicion. I had caught out his brother poaching Lord Gilbert's deer a year past, which would have been reason enough to end the family's tenure as verderers to Lord Gilbert. This, as bailiff, I could have done, and there were some who aspired to the post who wondered that I did not. But Gerard had served Lord Gilbert well and, so far as I knew, so had Richard. Their worry would guarantee Walter's future good behavior, so I thought. Nevertheless, my appearance in Alvescot now always drew apprehensive furrows across the family brows. This is not a bad thing. A man unsure of his position will work more diligently.

I turned to leave Gerard, my duty complete, when the man spoke again.

"Heard about Thomas atte Bridge hangin' hisself," he said.

"So all believe," I replied. My response caused Gerard to peer at me with puzzled expression. He understood, I think, that I did not include myself in the words I spoke. I had tried to keep disbelief from my voice. To dissemble is a competence much desired among bailiffs, I think. Perhaps one day I may achieve it.

I stepped from behind Gerard's house and saw two figures approaching with another load of coppiced beech poles slung between them. It was Walter, Gerard's younger son, and another youth unknown to me, who turned with their burden into the yard. Walter saw me and averted his gaze, as well he might, poacher of Lord Gilbert's deer as he once was.

Here was another man with reason to dislike Thomas atte Bridge. With the aid of a scoundrel priest atte Bridge had learned of Walter's poaching and blackmailed the verderer's son for a portion of the venison he took. When Thomas was taken with the flesh he readily implicated Walter as his source, for which misdemeanor Walter was fined sixpence at hallmote. But for Thomas's admission Walter might never have been found out.

I watched as Walter and the youth dropped their poles beside the drying shed, and as I did Gerard and Richard stared at me, then Walter.

"Your father," I said to the perspiring Walter, "tells me deer are plentiful in Lord Gilbert's forest." I said this with head cocked to one side and a crooked grin warping my lips. I wished to put the man at ease. The ploy succeeded.

"Aye," he grinned. "Enough that Lord Gilbert'll not miss a few... not that I'll be takin' any," he declared. "Learned me lesson."

I had no doubt of that. I had seen Gerard, old and crippled as he was, strike Walter such a blow when he learned of his son's transgression that the younger man had dropped to his knees in the road to the west of Bampton

Castle. I wondered often what other discipline Gerard might have later applied. It might have been more severe than the punishment decreed at hallmote.

"Whoso takes a deer now," Richard observed, "may keep it to himself. He'll not have to share with Thomas atte Bridge."

At the name, Walter looked away and spat upon the ground. But for Thomas, Walter might be enjoying a joint of venison yet this day. Was Walter's arrest and fine enough to put thoughts of murder in his mind? Men have slain others for less. But a year had passed since Thomas and Walter were apprehended. Would Walter's anger lay banked, like coals on a hearthstone, for a year? I did not know the fellow well enough to judge.

I retrieved Bruce from the sapling where I had tied him, and where he had made a meal of the tender new leaves. His slow, plodding gait allowed much time for thought as we traveled through Lord Gilbert's forest, past Cow-Leys Corner, to the castle. Saint Thomas Aquinas wrote that "three things are necessary for a man's salvation: to know what he ought to believe, to know what he ought to desire, and to know what he ought to do."

I would not quarrel with the scholar, but might not a man know what he ought to believe and desire and do, yet do that which he knows he should not? Saint Paul wrote that he did what he would not do, and did not do what he should. I felt great kinship with the apostle.

I knew what I should believe, and I believed it. And I knew what I should desire, and I desired it. But I was not certain that I wanted to do what I ought to do. I could count four men who might wish to hasten Thomas atte Bridge's passage to our Lord's judgment. If Walter were the felon I sought, I would not be much displeased with the discovery, but if Hubert or Peter or Arnulf were the culprit, I did not wish to know. Or if I did know, I did not wish to act upon the knowledge. Would my hesitancy lay waste my salvation? I left Bruce to the marshalsea and walked towards my home with troubled spirit.

However, my heart lifted when I saw the wisp of smoke rising from the chimney of Galen House. It was a symbol of my new status and contentment: a married man and home owner, with the right to build new as I saw fit.

Two days before Christmas Lord Gilbert had sent John Chamberlain to fetch me. I had found my employer seated in the solar of Bampton Castle, behind a table, enjoying a brisk blaze which gave pleasing warmth to his back and the small room. A sheet of parchment lay before Lord Gilbert on the table. Upon the document I saw Lord Gilbert's seal pressed in wax. He looked up from studying it when I entered.

"Master Hugh... be seated, be seated." He nodded to a chair aside his table. I obeyed.

"There is a matter we must discuss regarding Galen House," he began. "When you first came to Bampton your rent for Galen House was four shillings each year."

I nodded.

"Then I made you bailiff and provided a chamber in the castle."

I nodded again.

"Now you are to return to Galen House, as you have named it, this time with a bride."

"Will four shillings each year satisfy," I asked, "as before?" Four shillings was a bargain for such a house. In Oxford such a dwelling might command twenty shillings or more.

"Nay, Hugh. Four shillings will not do."

I am sure I appeared crestfallen at this announcement, wondering how much my rent might be increased. Lord Gilbert saw my dismay and quickly continued.

"A man need pay no rent to occupy what is his."

I did not grasp his meaning. Lord Gilbert pushed the document before him across the table to me.

"Geoffrey Thirwall has prepared this deed." Thirwall is Lord Gilbert's steward, but resides at Pembroke and rarely visits Bampton. "The document transfers Galen House to you and your heirs freehold. Do not seem so startled, Hugh. 'Tis my wedding gift to you and your bride."

This largesse overwhelmed me. I had never thought to own my own property; such a thing is reserved for gentlemen and wealthy burghers. I am neither. I was able to reply with but a stammered, "Much thanks, m'lord."

"Here," he held forth the document. "Keep it in a secure chest, Hugh, so a century from now, when we are food for worms, your great-grandson may prove ownership to some rapacious heir of mine." He laughed at his wit, but there was surely truth in the warning.

Lord Gilbert next opened a small chest upon his table and drew from it a small pouch. This he also pushed across the table to me. "Take it," he commanded.

"Our bargain, two years past, was that you would serve me as bailiff for bed and board at the castle, and thirty-four shillings each year. You will soon feed yourself, and such a wage will not keep a wife and family. I have decided to increase your salary to fifty shillings each year. Here are sixteen shillings," he nodded to the pouch, "to meet the shortage for this year. At the new year Geoffrey Thirwall will pay the new amount."

I left Lord Gilbert's presence that day with much joy, and began to move my possessions from the castle to Galen House so as to make ready for Kate.

Galen House was two stories, built of sturdy timbers, wattle and daub, with a well-thatched roof above. A chimney at the south end vented a fireplace in one room of the ground floor, which I had occupied when I lived there alone. However, once wed I required a more fitting bedchamber for my bride. With the deed stored securely and coins in my purse, I paid to have the chimney rebuilt in brick, with a second hearth in the room above, so that Kate and I might sleep warm in our bed.

Now I looked ahead at that curl of smoke and knew that Kate was preparing our dinner – although if her appetite was as it had been in the last fortnight, she would likely consume little of it.

Kate had prepared a Lombardy custard with wheaten bread and cheese. I was pleased to see her take a good portion for herself. Her appetite seemed much improved.

"How does Lord Gilbert's forest land?" she asked as we ate.

I told her of my conversation with Gerard, and Walter's response when I spoke Thomas atte Bridge's name.

"Another man with cause to strike down atte Bridge?" Kate mused.

"Aye. But for Thomas, his poaching might not have been found out."

"Oh, I near forgot," Kate exclaimed. "While you were about Lord Gilbert's business I went to purchase loaves from the baker and met Father Thomas upon Church Street. He told me to tell you that John Kellet has completed his penance and is now attached to St Nicholas's Priory, in Exeter, where he assists the almoner."

Kate saw distaste disfigure my face, as if her custard was made of rotten eggs.

"Is Kellet the priest you told me of, who betrayed the confessional and sent Thomas atte Bridge and his brother to blackmail those who confessed at St Andrew's Chapel?"

"Aye, the very man. He put an arrow in Henry's back when he thought their felony might be discovered. For this sin he lost his place and for penance was sent on pilgrimage to Compostela."

"A long journey," Kate observed.

"And dangerous. I had wished some calamity might strike him on the road. He will not show his face again in Bampton, I think."

"But he has."

I looked up from my meal in some surprise, which Kate saw. She continued: "He visited Father Simon."

"Ah... Father Simon took him in when he was a lad. Parents both dead."

"That is how he became curate at St Andrew's Chapel?"

"Aye. And betrayed his place."

"Father Thomas said he is a changed man."

"Pilgrimage and privation may alter a man's outlook. We may hope in Kellet's case 'tis so. I wonder I did not see Kellet upon the street. Is he yet about, or gone to Exeter?"

"Gone to Exeter, I think. Father Thomas said he was here but for two days, near a fortnight past."

"About the time Thomas atte Bridge was found at Cow-Leys Corner. I think I must visit Father Simon."

I found Father Simon at his vicarage, enjoying his dinner. The rotund priest has enjoyed many dinners, and employs a cook whose skills are reputed to rival those of the cook at Bampton Castle. A servant greeted me at the door and showed me to Father Simon, who was licking the last grease of a capon from his fingers.

"Good day, Master Hugh. Have you dined?"

I assured the priest that I had, and watched relief wash across his cherubic face. Some of the capon lay unconsumed upon a platter before him, reserved, perhaps, for his supper, and he worried he might be called upon to share it.

"You had a visitor some days past... John Kellet."

"Aye. But he has completed his penance. You have no jurisdiction over him."

The priest thought I yet harbored ill will toward Kellet, and would do the man mischief if I could. He was not far wrong.

"I do not seek him, but I would know when he was here. I did not see him upon the streets, nor did any other, I think, else I would have been informed."

Father Simon glanced away for a moment, then spoke: "Kellet asked no one be told of his visit. Said he wanted only to see me, an' thank me for taking care of him when he was but an orphan lad. Came one day, late it was, stayed with me two nights to rest from his journey, then set off for Exeter, where he is to serve the almoner."

"When was this?"

The priest scratched at his wispy hair. "Why? 'Twas but a visit. You cannot forbid that, even be you Lord Gilbert's bailiff."

"Too late to forbid, but I have reason to know when it was Kellet slept under your roof."

"Very well," the vicar shrugged. "He came the day before St George's Day, and set off for Exeter two days later."

"He was in the town for St George's Day? I did not see him in the marketplace."

"Nay. Said he'd seen St George slay the dragon an' rescue the fair maid many times."

"Or perhaps he did not wish it known that he was about," I asserted.

"Perhaps. He left Bampton under a black cloud, 'tis true. He spoke of his shame."

"Shame! He slew a man. Was he not in holy orders, he would have hanged by the neck before the walls of Oxford Castle."

"None saw him slay Henry atte Bridge. That felony is but your assertion."

"You doubt he did so?"

The priest was silent. This was answer enough.

"He departed for Exeter and the Priory of St Nicholas on the twenty-fourth day of April?"

"Aye, he did. Before the Angelus Bell he was off."

"You saw him away?"

"Nay. Don't rise from my bed so gladly as when I was a young man. I have the disease of the bones."

Surely the priest's corpulent form also made rising from anything, chair or bed, an irksome task.

Kellet's journey to Exeter would have taken him past Cow-Leys Corner. Did he see Thomas atte Bridge, his partner in villainy, dangling from the oak? Perhaps, if he set out very early, it was too dark to see the man.

Or perhaps atte Bridge was not yet suspended from the tree. Or perhaps John Kellet had to do with Thomas atte Bridge's place and condition that day?

If so, Kellet did not act alone. Thomas was not slung over some strong man's shoulder and carried thence to Cow-Leys Corner. Two carried him, of this I was certain, and one dropped his feet.

"Didn't know him when first he came to my door," the priest continued. "Pilgrimage to Compostela took much flesh from his bones."

John Kellet had grown fat from blackmailed venison. Did he resent Thomas atte Bridge's loose tongue, which implicated the curate in the blackmail scheme? There were others in Bampton who had greater reason to hate the priest and his betrayal of the confessional: Edmund the smith, whose dalliance with the baker's wife Thomas and his brother Henry before him learned of and used to extract items made upon Edmund's forge as payment for their silence; and the miller, whose cheating with short return on corn brought to the mill atte Bridge also knew of and exploited. These two had greater reason than Kellet, I thought, to wish revenge upon Thomas atte Bridge. Was one of them at Thomas's shoulders, and Kellet at the feet, in the tenebrous hours following St George's Day?

"Wears a hair shirt now, too, does John," Father Simon interrupted my thoughts. This was a startling revelation. The John Kellet I knew was concerned with little but his own comfort.

"You saw this?"

"Aye. Saw the hem of a sleeve hanging below his robe. I know your thoughts, Master Hugh. John Kellet is a different man, changed, as pilgrimage should do."

"It should," I agreed, "though there be pilgrims who remain unchanged. I have known such men."

"You suggest," the vicar frowned, "that a saint cannot intercede for men with the Lord Christ?"

"I am sure He hears the prayers of all men."

The priest harumphed grudging agreement as I stood from the bench to leave him. He heaved himself to his feet to honor my departure and it was then I noticed his belt. Why my eye should have been drawn to a mean cord wrapped about the fat priest I cannot say.

A plain hempen rope circled his ample belly twice. The ends of this belt fell to his knees, one length knotted three times for Father, Son, and Holy Ghost. A string of rosary beads was fastened to the cord; a cord much like that taken from the neck of Thomas atte Bridge. Priests whose purses permit fine woolen robes will often circle themselves with a mean belt to pretend simplicity and penury.

Father Simon saw me stare at the belt and peered down at it as well. The ends, dangling about his knees, were fresh-cut and unfrayed.

"Your belt is new," I remarked.

"Aye, near so."

A puzzled frown furrowed his forehead. Few men show interest in another man's girdle, especially is it made of simple stuff like hempen cord.

"The cord used to drop the bucket in my well was worn. I purchased a length of rope; some I used for the well, and some for my belt," Father Simon explained.

"Have you the length your belt was cut from?"

The request so startled the priest that he did not think to challenge such a question.

"Aye."

"May I see it?"

"A length of rope? Surely a bailiff can afford his own belt, and of better stuff than hempen cord."

"You speak true, but I seek a brief inspection. 'Tis much like the cord found about Thomas atte Bridge's neck."

"One hempen cord is much like another, and what remains of my purchase hangs in a shed in the toft."

"May I see it?"

The priest shrugged and called his servant. When the man appeared he instructed him to seek the shed and return with the hempen cord hung there. The man disappeared through the rear door of the vicarage and a moment later I heard Father Simon's hens clucking disapproval at the disturbance to their pecking.

The priest and I stood gazing at each other, awaiting the servant's return. He was not prompt. Father Simon had begun to chew upon his lower lip in frustration and seemed about to turn to the door when it swung open and the servant reappeared. He carried no rope.

"Ain't there," the fellow said, and raised his empty hands palms up.

"Bah, 'twas hanging from a tree nail," the vicar asserted, and set off for the toft.

"I know where it was," the servant said. "Hung it there myself."

I followed Father Simon into the toft. His servant shrugged and followed me. The vicar swung open the crude door to his shed, which was but half of his hen coop, and peered into the dim interior. He was evidently unable to trust his eyes, for he thrust his head forward, the better to see, and when this failed, entered the hut.

The priest appeared a moment later, anger darkening his brow. The servant's face reflected complacent confirmation of his discovery and announcement.

"'Twas there at Hocktide. I cut my new belt a few days after Easter, when the old belt frayed and finally broke where I keep my rosary. Some thief has made off with the remnant."

A look of understanding washed the frown from Father Simon's brow. "Was it the cord Thomas atte Bridge used to hang himself?"

"As you say, one hempen cord is much like another, but it may be so. What length was the missing cord?"

Father Simon peered at his servant, brows again furrowed. It was the servant who answered. "Near twenty paces long after I cut a length for the well, I think."

I did not at the moment think to ask when and from whom the cord was purchased. I should have.

Chapter 6

I was uneasy for the remainder of that day. Had I learned a thing important to Thomas atte Bridge's death? Or was Father Simon's missing rope but a minor theft, or simply misplaced? The latter explanation seemed quite unlikely. Would Father Simon and his servant both forget where a length of hempen cord was coiled?

Days grew long, so after supper Kate and I sat upon a bench in the toft behind Galen House and enjoyed the warmth of the slanting sun as it settled over Lord Gilbert's forest west of the town. I was silent, considering John Kellet and the missing rope. Kate noted my pensive mood and held her tongue for a time, but eventually curiosity overcame her – Kate does not do battle well against curiosity – and she asked of my thoughts. I told her what I had learned of Kellet, his visit to Father Simon, and the missing cord. When I was done it was Kate's turn to sink deep into thought.

While I told her of these things the servant's estimate of the rope's length returned to me. Kate followed as I left the bench, found the cord which suspended Thomas atte Bridge at Cow-Leys Corner, and uncoiled it upon the street before Galen House. It was near ten paces long. The remnant Kate discovered tossed aside at Cow-Leys Corner would add little to the length. If this was Father Simon's stolen cord, some eight paces or so, considering what had been cut for his belt, was missing.

The absent cord was found five days later. The day before Rogation Sunday, Father Simon's servant was gathering eggs and found the remnant of his master's rope coiled in the shed in its proper place. Where it had been since Hocktide no man could say. Well, some man knew, but that man was hid in the cloud of unknowing.

I learned of this discovery as Kate and I walked in the procession about the boundaries of the parish. Father Thomas, Father Simon, and Father Ralph led the marchers. I was a few paces behind the vicars when Father Simon's servant sought me out and told of his discovery. I confess my mind wandered from the prayers beseeching the Lord Christ for a bountiful harvest.

Kate and I had brought with us this day a pouch of coins, as did other more prosperous inhabitants of the town. These were distributed to the needy as we walked the parish boundary. Maud atte Bridge and her children were among those who stood beside the path with arms outstretched and palms raised.

When mass was done I sought Father Simon and while Kate returned to Galen House to prepare our dinner, I asked him about the new-found cord.

"Aye, as you were told, Robert found it coiled upon the tree nail when he gathered eggs yesterday morn."

"It was not there when he sought eggs Friday?"

"He thinks not."

"It would be well if this matter could be discussed with Father Thomas and Father Ralph," I said.

"A bit of stolen rope, now returned?"

"If you stretch it out in your toft you will find it shorter by half than when you hung it upon the tree nail at Hocktide."

The vicar squinted at me from under lowered brows. He understood my meaning. "The missing length Thomas atte Bridge used to hang himself at Cow-Leys Corner? But who then returned what was unused, and why would they do so? Did Thomas require assistance to take his own life? Hempen cord is common stuff. Perhaps this is all mere happenstance."

"Perhaps. But I would like to tell the tale to Father

Thomas and Father Ralph. They may have insight we have missed."

Father Simon agreed, somewhat reluctantly, and directed me to seek his vicarage at the ninth hour. He would send Robert to summon the other Bampton vicars.

Kate had prepared a Lombard stew for our dinner. This dish is a favorite of mine. Of course, I have many favorite dishes. When came the ninth hour I was better suited for a nap in the sun of the toft than disputing stolen rope, but I had a duty and would perform it.

I found the vicars seated before cups of Father Simon's wine at his table. The three priests eyed the cord I had brought with me as if they expected it to strike out at them like a snake.

"I have explained your wish to speak," Father Simon began, then fell silent. How much he had explained I knew not, so I began by telling of my unease regarding Thomas atte Bridge's death. I recounted the evidence, and, when I fell silent Father Thomas spoke:

"What is it you seek of us?"

"All know that Thomas atte Bridge was a disagreeable fellow," I said. "I can name many he has harmed who might have wished to do him ill."

"Murder him?" Father Thomas asked.

"Even that."

"Which of these injured folk do you suspect of having a hand in atte Bridge's death... was he not a suicide?"

"I have a theory," I confessed.

"We would hear of it," Father Thomas encouraged.

"John Kellet visited Bampton at St George's Day, quietly, and departed for Exeter the morn of the day Thomas atte Bridge was found at Cow-Leys Corner. He stayed with Father Simon two nights, and might have discovered the cord hanging in the shed."

"But he is now in Exeter, at St Nicholas's Priory. How could he have taken, then returned, the cord?" Father Simon scoffed.

"Remember I told you of the mud on Thomas's heels, and the twin gouges in the mud of the road. Two men took Thomas to Cow-Leys Corner, one at his shoulders, another at his feet. The man at his feet dropped him briefly. Perhaps Thomas struggled and the man lost his grip. Now Kellet is gone, but his partner in the crime remains among us and has chosen this time to return the unused cord, perhaps unaware that it has been missed."

Father Simon looked to his servant and spoke: "You said you would seek the stolen cord. Did you tell others of the theft?"

"Aye," Robert nodded.

"Doesn't mean John Kellet had aught to do with it," Father Simon protested.

"But the thief, whoso it was, feared discovery and restored what he took," Father Thomas answered.

"Perhaps he did not replace all of his theft," I replied.

I lifted the rope in my hand. "This is the cord from which Thomas atte Bridge dangled. Let us lay it and the returned cord out in the street, and see how long they be together."

We did so. When Father Simon's belt, the fragment found on the forest floor, and the piece cut from Thomas's neck were added to the two longer lengths, the total was twenty-one paces long.

Father Simon peered down at the segmented cord thoughtfully, his chin resting upon his left hand. His servant stood behind him.

"Near twenty paces long, you said," I reminded the servant.

"Aye; 'bout what you see here stretched out in the street."

I coiled the length of rope which had suspended Thomas atte Bridge and handed it to Father Simon.

"This is yours, I think."

The vicar made no move to accept it. I suspect he

wished no association with the dead to trouble his house.

"I have no further need of it," he grimaced. I shrugged and dropped my outstretched arm to my side. The servant followed my lead and coiled the segment which had reappeared in Father Simon's toft, shaking the dirt of the street from it as he did so.

"I'll just put this back," he explained.

Father Thomas waved a hand toward the cord in my hand. "Is it possible that Thomas had assistance in taking his own life, and his companion replaced the unused cord? If so, 'twas a grievous sin."

"That does not explain the signs that Thomas was carried or dragged to the tree, or the absence of mud upon the stool where he would have stood did he take his own life," I replied.

Father Ralph had been silent while we examined the rope segments and considered their meaning. Now he spoke:

"Kellet would have passed Cow-Leys Corner when he set out for Exeter. Did any man see him there?"

The other vicars, the servant, and I peered at one another with vacant expressions.

"Then he must have passed the place before atte Bridge was found, saw him there, and went his way. It was the herdsman who first raised the hue and cry, was it not? He made no mention of any other man there."

"What say you, Master Hugh?" Father Thomas asked. "Was Thomas long dead when he was found? You have more understanding of such matters than we."

"He was beginning to stiffen in death. He was hanging from the tree since well before dawn, I think."

"So unless Kellet arose and set off very early, he would have seen him there, even in the dark of night, as Thomas was so near the road."

"When did Kellet set out for Exeter?" Father Ralph asked of Father Simon.

"He bedded with Robert," the vicar replied, and

looked to his servant.

"Kellet slept little. I awoke twice the first night to find him out of bed."

"Men often have need to rise from their slumber in the night," Father Simon said. "I find it more so as I grow old, and Kellet is no longer young."

"First time," Robert continued, "I saw him upon his knees before the window. When he saw that I had awakened he returned to bed. Where he was the second time I awoke I know not."

"Visiting the privy, I'd guess," Father Simon said.

John Kellet out of bed and upon his knees in the middle of the night? This was indeed a revelation. Such a scene, knowing what the man had done, was difficult to imagine. Father Ralph voiced my thoughts.

"John Kellet on his knees at midnight is not credible. Probably he heard Robert stir in the night and feigned prayer."

"Why would he do so?" Father Simon objected.

"Because he was about some nefarious business he did not want known, like finding a coil of rope in your shed."

"Bah. John Kellet is a changed man, I tell you. He wears a hair shirt." Father Simon looked to me for confirmation, as if his earlier revealing this to me made of me a witness. I shrugged and said nothing.

"Why did he seek only you, and skulk about the town unknown to all others?" Father Ralph asked.

"He knows there is much ill will toward him, and did not claim it should be otherwise. He wished only to thank me for providing for him when he was a child."

"What of the second night?" I asked Robert.

"I slept soundly and did not awaken 'til near dawn."

"John said he would depart early," Father Simon added, "and would not trouble us when he did so. My cook left a loaf for him upon the table and it was half gone when I arose."

"He did not take the whole loaf?"

"Nay. But half. I told you of his changed appearance. A walking skeleton."

Robert nodded agreement.

"And you do not know when of the clock he set out?"

The vicar and his servant shook their heads.

"Did he speak of his journey to Compostela?" Father Thomas asked.

"Some. Spoke most of folk here in Bampton," the servant replied. "Said there was hardship aplenty on pilgrimage but he would not speak more of it. Asked of doings in the town since he'd been away."

"Did he ask of Thomas atte Bridge?" I questioned.

"Aye, him more than most. Wanted to know had he changed his ways. I told him not so as anyone would notice."

"How did he receive this news?"

"Seemed disappointed, troubled, like he'd expected to learn different."

"Of an atte Bridge? The father was not a bad sort," said Father Ralph, "but the sons... 'tis no calamity they are gone."

"So whoever murdered Thomas atte Bridge," Father Thomas replied, "if murder it was, has done a kindness to the town?"

"That is for God to judge," Father Ralph crossed his arms sanctimoniously. "Men must preserve order and punish evildoers."

"Some might say as that's what was done, Thomas bein' as he was," Robert said softly.

Father Ralph blew out his cheeks and looked askance at the servant for his unwanted opinion.

"One other thing," Father Simon said. "John wears no shoes. Walked from Spain barefoot. Said his shoes wore out on the way to Compostela and he had no coins to replace them. Decided to go on with no shoes as penance."

"There were such footprints in the mud at Cow-Leys Corner," I said. "Some barefoot man trod the road and stood under the limb where Thomas atte Bridge was found."

"Many poor folk save their shoes and go about barefoot when the weather warms," Father Simon asserted.

This was so. I tried to recall the day atte Bridge was found. Of all the throng gathered at Cow-Leys Corner, did any go about bare of foot? I could not remember. There were other matters clogging my thoughts that day.

"Father Simon's returned cord leaves us, I think, with a serious question," Father Thomas said. "Was the cord taken by a murderer, or an accomplice in suicide? Master Hugh, you believe a murderer, is this not so?"

"Aye."

"And you?" The priest turned to his associates.

"It may be as Master Hugh says," Father Simon offered. "But I know his mind. He believes John Kellet guilty of a felony, and will seek evidence to prove it so. It cannot be. Kellet is not the man we knew of days past. Master Hugh remembers him only as he was."

"When he did slay Henry atte Bridge," Father Ralph continued the thought, "and would have aided Thomas atte Bridge in doing murder to Master Hugh. Will a leopard change his spots? Master Hugh must travel to Exeter and seek Prior Richard. He must be told of Master Hugh's suspicion and John Kellet must be examined closely."

I greeted this recommendation with mixed feelings. I had convinced myself that John Kellet was guilty of Thomas atte Bridge's murder, and had some evidence it was so. Pilgrimage to Compostela was small penance to pay for his previous crimes, and did I not seek him and truth at St Nicholas's Priory he would escape retribution for this new felony. But I had no wish to travel to Exeter, even at a season when the weather was benign and the roads dry.

"Perhaps," I said, "a letter might be sent to the prior. He and the almoner, if told of this business, might query Kellet about his hours in Bampton."

"If he answers falsely," Father Ralph replied, "how will Prior Richard know? Kellet has served the priory for but a few days. His character is unknown there. No, a letter will not serve. You, who know Kellet and might press him if he dissembles, you must go."

"Such a journey will be a waste of Master Hugh's time," Father Simon said heatedly. "Kellet is a new man. He lives now as a penitential and mendicant. Why would he do some new felony for which he must do even greater penance?"

Father Ralph and Father Simon scowled at each other, then looked to Father Thomas, each seeking support for his opinion.

"Pilgrimage and penance may indeed change a man. I hope for John Kellet's soul it did. But you, Master Hugh, will not be convinced it is so unless you travel to Exeter and seek him. If he is yet iniquitous you may be able to discern it. Is he not, that also may be plain. If you assume his guilt in the matter of Thomas atte Bridge, you will not seek another. Then whoso did murder atte Bridge, did Kellet not, will escape punishment for his felony, in this world, if not the next. Father Ralph speaks true. You must go to Exeter, to put your own mind at ease, if for no other reason."

There was little more to say of the matter. If I did not go to Exeter, when Lord Gilbert returned at Lammastide and I had found no murderer in Bampton, my employer might be unhappy. Thomas atte Bridge was not his tenant, but died upon his land. Lord Gilbert would not be pleased to find me slothful in my duties. And if John Kellet was guilty, as I thought likely, I would not prove it so from Bampton while he served St Nicholas's Priory.

I left the priests standing before the vicarage and sought Galen House. Kate's face appeared in my mind, and you will understand why I was loath to travel to Exeter. At best the journey would take five days, and five more to return. I had not been out of Kate's presence since the day we wed. The vicars of St Beornwald's Church now required of me a fortnight away from my bride.

Kate was displeased by the vicars' decision, and spoke of accompanying me. I rejected the suggestion. I admit that the thought of leaving with her beside me, instead of leaving her behind, was a tempting one. But she was with child, and should rest at home.

"Of all those in Bampton who disliked Thomas atte Bridge, you believe John Kellet most likely his murderer?" she asked.

"Aye. He had cause and opportunity, and the deed fits his character."

"Did not others have greater cause? Peter Carpenter, surely?"

"Men may have great cause to do violence to another, but not act on it because they have not the stomach for it, or because they will not do wrong to right a wrong."

"And this Kellet would act?"

"Aye. He has done so, many times. I had lumps upon my head to prove it so."

"You spoke of two men, one at atte Bridge's head and the other at his feet, dropping his burden to the mud."

"Kellet did not do this alone. But who might have aided him? Atte Bridge had so many enemies I know not where to begin to sort through them all."

"The man would have been a friend to John Kellet before he was sent on pilgrimage, would he not? It seems unlikely," Kate mused, "that Kellet would return to Bampton and seek aid to do murder from one he did not know well."

I could not dispute her logic. To seek an accomplice among John Kellet's friends might narrow the list of conspirators. But how could I discover guilt without some proof to lay at such a man's feet, so that he might speak to charge the priest and turn justice from himself? Unwilling as I was to leave Kate for a fortnight, I was beginning to see the use of such a journey and found myself arguing

Father Thomas's position to Kate. After much persuasion, she reluctantly agreed.

"When will you depart?"

"Tuesday. I will make ready tomorrow."

"You will not go upon the roads alone, will you?"

"Nay. I will have Arthur and Uctred accompany me."

I saw relief wash across my bride's face. Since the Great Death men who seek employment are able to find it, so there are fewer brigands accosting folk upon the roads than in past days. But there are always some who would rather take what is another's than earn their own keep. Arthur and Uctred are large fellows, not tall, but well fed at Lord Gilbert's table, and seeing them garbed in Lord Gilbert's blue-and-black livery with his design across their chests, most felons would choose to allow them, and me, to pass unmolested.

Monday morning I sought Arthur and Uctred and told them to make ready to leave next day with the Angelus Bell. Uctred is a bachelor and Arthur a married man. I expected Uctred to be eager for the journey and the novelty of new lands to see, and thought Arthur would be unhappy to leave Bampton. I was mistaken. Uctred greeted the announcement with gloom, whereas Arthur seemed pleased to be away. Perhaps wedded bliss had faded for Arthur.

I left instruction with the marshalsea to have Bruce and two palfreys ready to travel with the dawn. Bruce is an old dexter and carried Lord Gilbert at Poitiers. His use was provided me as incentive when Lord Gilbert prevailed upon me to accept the post of bailiff at his Manor of Bampton. I hoped the elderly beast was hale enough to travel to Devonshire and return.

Chapter 7

Early next morn I threw a bag of my surgical instruments across Bruce's rump, and a moment later Arthur, Uctred, and I urged our mounts under the Bampton Castle portcullis. I planned no surgery in the next fortnight, but I have been so often surprised by the injuries men may do to themselves and each other that I dislike being without the tools to repair their hurts. Kate was determined to see us off, so came with me to the castle while the eastern sky was just beginning to grow light above St Andrew's Chapel. I turned in my saddle when we three gained Mill Street and was rewarded with a kiss blown from Kate's fair lips. I was determined to see my business in Exeter complete and be on my way home so soon as could be.

From Bampton to Swindon is nineteen miles. We traveled the distance easily, for the horses were rested, and sought an inn for the night. The second day we traveled longer, near thirty miles, to Trowbridge, where we found another vermin-infested inn. I wished to be in Glastonbury after three days, and near the seventh hour of the third day we saw the tor rise above the plain.

I have heard many tales of the great abbey at Glastonbury: of the graves of Arthur and Guinevere, his queen; of the thorn tree planted by Joseph of Arimathea; and of the magnificent view from the top of the tor. After three days' travel our elderly beasts were tired and lagging. I decided we would rest the horses for a day and see the great abbey and its treasures.

The gatehouse of Glastonbury Abbey is new and impressive, built but a few years past. The porter greeted us there, and sent a lay brother to fetch the hosteller when

I made known our need of shelter for two nights and provision for the horses.

We were not alone in such a request. Pilgrims swarmed through the gatehouse while we awaited the hosteller, for we had arrived on Ascension Day. All these folk could not be accommodated within the abbey precincts, or if they were, there would be no place for three more travelers.

The porter's assistant returned shortly, pushing through the throng of pilgrims. A slender monk followed in his wake. I saw the monk squint over the crowd at our horses, then peer past the swirling swarm at the gatehouse to see who it was required his aid. His eyes drifted past me without focusing. Here, I thought, is a scholar whose long hours of study, bent over his books, have rendered him blind to anything much past his fingertips.

The monk stood close before the porter, who took his arm and turned him to face me. At that close vantage I saw clearly the monk's affliction. The pupils of his eyes were milky and clouded. He suffered from cataracts.

"Brother Alnett," the porter said, "here are three fellows bound for St Nicholas's Priory in Exeter who need place to rest themselves and their beasts."

"I am Hugh de Singleton," I added, "bailiff to Lord Gilbert Talbot on his lands in Bampton. I travel to Exeter to examine a man about a death in Bampton. Arthur and Uctred accompany me."

Brother Alnett seemed to look away, but addressed me, as if by inspecting the gatehouse beyond my shoulder he could see me the better.

"We have many pilgrims here, and cannot house them all, but travelers are welcome. I will send for a lay brother to care for your beasts. Meanwhile, follow me and I will see you to the guest hall."

The monk led us past the abbot's hall and a great kitchen, where a chimney belched the smoke and fragrance of roasting flesh. Glastonbury is a Benedictine House, but I suppose the abbot had guests who required meat for their supper. Beyond the kitchen was a garden to the south and the abbot's hall to the north. On the eastern side of the garden lay a long structure, two stories tall, of dressed stone and newly built. The monk led us to the entrance of this hall.

Once we were inside the darkened corridors of the building Brother Alnett led us to our chamber as surely as if he could see clearly. I remarked on this to the monk.

"Near thirty years since I was a novice. I learned my way about the place when I could yet see well," he explained. "Now I see in my mind's eye what was when I was young." He hesitated briefly. "So I see what others see, just not in the same manner. But I do wish I might yet read. Those who can see and do not read are more blind than me, I think."

"Is there no surgeon in Glastonbury who can couch your cataracts?"

"Nay. Brother Jerome is an herbalist of great wisdom, but he knows little of surgery, and even did he possess such skill, his hand now trembles with age. A year and more past a traveling surgeon visited Glastonbury. The man claimed competence in couching cataracts. I thought to seek him, but he departed the town but a few days after he arrived. His treatment of a town alderman failed."

"Failed?"

"Aye. Went blind in the eye the fellow couched."

"What then?"

"Gone next day, when it was known about the town what happened. Of course, when a man has cataracts so cloudy as mine, he is blind already, so it matters little whether the surgery succeed or not."

"You would have sought relief from this surgeon even after his failure?"

"Aye. A woman of the town also went to him and she is pleased. Can't see so well as when she was a lass, but better than if a shroud was hung always before her face."

"Master Hugh be a surgeon," Arthur said. He and

Uctred had followed the conversation and as I had not told the monk of my training, Arthur decided it was his duty to make it known.

The monk turned to me, although was it his intent to study me for evidence of competence, the effort surely failed. The chamber was on the east side of the guest range, facing a yard which was enclosed by the dorter and refectory. Little light entered the space, even though the window was of glass. The darkness and his cataracts surely rendered Brother Alnett blind in such a place. Perhaps he turned to me of custom, behavior learned when he could yet see clearly, as an old man will turn to watch a winsome maid pass by, though the exercise will bring him scant satisfaction.

"A surgeon? I thought you were a bailiff."

"I am both. An odd combination, I know, but 'tis so."

"Do you treat men such as me for cataracts?"

"I have never done so. Such work was part of my training in Paris, but I've had no opportunity to practice the skill."

"Paris? You trained in Paris?"

"For but one year. I lacked coin for further study."

"The university there is renowned for training men who repair another's broken body. I have heard much of the new methods taught there. Tell me, do you practice in the manner of de Chauliac or de Mondeville?"

"De Mondeville... although de Chauliac has much to teach us of mending human flaws and injuries."

"But you have never couched a cataract?"

"Never. I observed surgeons at the university as they worked the remedy, that is all."

"I cannot leave the abbey to seek treatment," the monk sighed, "and no surgeon able to succor my affliction is likely again to visit. When the wandering surgeon appeared I thought 'twas an answer to my prayers... but not so."

"Master Hugh will fix most any hurt a man can have,"

Arthur claimed. "Seen 'im put a man's skull back together after the fellow had an oak tree drop on 'is head. Well... I didn't actually see 'im do it, you understand, but I see the fellow up an walkin' about regular like, him bein' Lord Gilbert's verderer."

Brother Alnett made no reply, but looked away into the dim corners of the chamber, as if there was some object there which required his study.

"I don't know when another itinerant surgeon will visit Glastonbury. I am not a youth. I fear I will go to my grave blinded, never again to read a book or watch a goldfinch flit about the abbey orchard."

I was cautious of my ability in dealing with cataracts, but Arthur felt no such reticence, as he was neither the sufferer nor the untried surgeon.

"No need to await another," he said confidently. "Master Hugh can fix you up proper as any man can."

"It would be a blessing can you do so," the monk replied.

"Even when couching for cataracts is successful," I warned, "vision is often poor."

"Ah," Brother Alnett smiled, "I do not wish to be twenty years of age again. But to read once more... I yearn for that. And Brother Andrew wears upon his nose the bits of glass and brass which allow an old man to read like a youth. If you can remove the veil from my eyes, I will seek such an aid for myself."

I did not reply for a moment. I had come to Glastonbury Abbey seeking rest, not labor. And I feared that the work asked of me was beyond my competence. I saw couching done twice while in Paris, near four years past, but had never put my hand to the work. If I should attempt the business and succeed, I might bring much pleasure to Brother Alnett, but should I fail, I would lay much distress upon him.

I told him this. When I had finished my warning the monk was silent for a time, then spoke: "One eye, then...

the worst. Work your craft upon my left eye, for that is cloudiest. Then, if you fail, I will be no more blind in my left eye than I am now. But if you succeed, then the reward will be worth the risk, and you may couch my other eye when you will."

From the corner of my eye I saw Arthur and Uctred grinning broadly at me, as if the surgery were already complete and successful. It is a good thing when others have confidence in my skill, but not so when their expectation is beyond my competence. I feared this was such a time. I thought of an escape.

"Will the abbot approve? Will he accept an unknown surgeon poking about the eye of one of his brothers?"

"We will seek him and ask," Brother Alnett said, and turned to the chamber door as he spoke. "Your companions may wait here for our return. Master Hugh, come with me."

Brother Alnett found the stairs and descended with no hesitation. In the dark passageway I was uncertain when my feet might find the last step, but not so the monk. He did not stumble upon his way, but strode firmly to the door, reached unerringly for the latch, and lifted it for our passage.

The abbot's lodge at Glastonbury is grand, as befits the head of one of the richest houses in the realm, second only to Westminster in its lands and tithes. I did pause to wonder, though, how men who had taken vows of poverty could live so well. In my youth, while yet a scholar at Balliol College, I asked this of a monk, a Benedictine. He replied that the wealth of a monastery belonged to God, not the brothers who inhabited the place. As God had no need of gold and jewels and rich tapestries, his servants felt free to use them. Cistercians take a different view.

The monks had but a short time earlier completed nones, so we arrived at the abbot's hall as he and the prior approached from the direction of the church.

Brother Alnett heard their approach, guessed who it

was, bowed respectfully, and introduced me to the abbot, Walter de Moynyngton. The abbot is a severe, thin-faced, somber-appearing fellow, and greeted me with a scowl. I did not take this personally. He seemed to me a man who received all in the same manner.

"Master Hugh," Brother Alnett continued, "has sought lodging in the guest-house, with two companions. He travels to..." The monk turned helplessly to me.

"Exeter."

"Master Hugh is bailiff for Lord Gilbert Talbot on his Bampton estate." I saw the abbot's lip curl in distaste. "And is also a surgeon, trained in Paris." The lip seemed to relax.

Brother Alnett hesitated, and the abbot turned to enter his hall, assuming, I suppose, that the introduction was done.

"He knows how to couch a cataract," Brother Alnett continued hurriedly. "Saw it done in Paris when he studied there."

All this time neither the abbot nor his companion spoke, but after this announcement the abbot turned and, with a frown, examined the hopeful face of Brother Alnett.

"You wish this surgeon to seek to clear your vision?"

"Aye, m'lord abbot."

The abbot dismissed Brother Alnett with a wave of his hand. "As you wish. You have my permit."

I bowed respectfully to the abbot as he walked past me to his hall. If he noticed he gave no sign.

Brother Alnett also bowed and turned, prompted more by the departing abbot's fading footsteps than the sight of the abbot's back.

"M'lord abbot," the monk said when he was sure his superior was beyond hearing, "is an even-tempered man. He is always angry. But he did grant permission for you to restore my sight. Will you do so? This day?"

"Nay. Tomorrow will be soon enough. I am weary

from the day's travel. My hand may not be steady, and I must sort through the instruments I have with me to see if any will serve in place of couching needles."

The monk seemed disappointed at the delay, but had borne his affliction so long that another day would seem but small abeyance.

Brother Alnett sent a lay brother with straw pallets for Arthur and Uctred. Our chamber in the guest-house had already a bed where I might seek my rest. We were served a light supper of pease pottage, maslin loaf, and ale, and because the days grew long there was enough light after supper that I could sort through my instruments for lancets and thin scalpels which might serve in place of couching needles.

The sky was yet aglow when we three took to our beds, and soon Arthur's rumbling snore filled the chamber. Uctred duly joined the chorus, adding his tenor to Arthur's bass. I reviewed in my mind's eye what I had seen of couching for cataracts while a student in Paris, planning the next morning's work. The effort was not conducive to slumber, and I heard the sacrist ring the bell for vigils before I slept.

Brother Alnett appeared at the guest-house as soon as Lauds was sung. The man was eager to undergo treatment for his affliction; more eager than I to venture the work. I have heard scholars suggest that St Paul might have suffered cataracts – the "thorn in the flesh" he prayed unsuccessfully for the Lord Christ to remove. Now I spoke a silent prayer that my hand might be guided to good success this day, and Brother Alnett's burden be lifted, even so the apostle's was not. Perhaps St Paul required a surgeon.

I chose the abbey infirmary for the work. While I had brought instruments, I had not thought to bring herbs and salves. These the infirmarer could supply, though, in truth, few are needed to couch a cataract. When the needle is applied the patient feels little pain. Nevertheless, I prepared a draught of crushed lettuce and hemp seeds mixed in a cup of ale. Brother Alnett did not need to be persuaded to drink it down.

The seeds of wild lettuce will calm an anxious man. I know not if the draught succeeded with the monk, for he seemed a phlegmatic sort anyway, but I was tempted to prepare a cup for myself.

The patient whose cataract is being couched must not be permitted to blink while the work is done. I required the infirmarer and his assistant to fix Brother Alnett's upper and lower eyelids in place, took a deep breath, and began my work.

I had among my instruments a needle, used for stitching wounds, which would serve, I thought, to couch a cataract. The milky corruption of a cataract is but a humor collected between pupil and lens, thus obstructing vision. My task was to clear this space, so that when it was empty vision might be restored. The monk's cataract was of many years and fully formed, so no medicinal treatment would avail.

I inserted my needle into the outer edge of Brother Alnett's whitened lens and worked it into the space between lens and pupil. I felt resistance when the needle touched the suffusio, for the cataract was large and firm. But because it was so it came free from its place in one whole, rather than breaking apart. When the cataract was loosened I thrust with the needle until I had worked it down and away from the pupil.

My work was done, so long as the suffusio stayed where my needle had pushed it. If it did not it would require breaking into fragments and these pieces would then be depressed. I prayed this would not be necessary, stood from my patient, and wiped sweat from my brow with the sleeve of my cotehardie. It was not a warm morning, but I noted perspiration also upon the brows of the infirmarer and his assistant. Brother Alnett seemed not so affected. Perhaps it was the lettuce seeds.

The monk blinked rapidly several times when his

eyelids were released, then turned his head to the infirmary window whence came a shaft of golden morning sun. The beam struck the infirmarer's table, upon which lay an opened book. Brother Alnett's gaze fastened upon the volume and he stood and walked to it.

We who observed were silent as Brother Alnett stood over the pages of the infirmarer's herbal. He peered down upon the book, then turned and spoke.

"The letters are much blurred, but I see them. Lenses will make them distinct and I shall read again."

The monk spoke these words with such radiance upon his face as to rival the sun which framed him against the window.

"I would learn this work," the herbalist's assistant said softly. "Yesterday Brother Alnett could not have seen there was a book upon the table; now he can read it, or near so. Will you teach me the procedure?"

"There are others at the abbey who suffer from cataracts?" I asked.

"Not presently. Brother Ailred was so afflicted, but he died last year. Had I your skill I might have lifted some part of the burden of old age from him. And if some brother suffers a cataract in the future I might ease his affliction."

I was of two minds concerning the request. An herbalist who could successfully couch a cataract would be a blessing to the town and abbey. But I knew so little of the business that I was just competent to perform the work. Could I teach another from my limited store of knowledge?

Brother Alnett heard the request. "Master Hugh travels to Exeter," he said. "When he completes his business there he has promised to again visit Glastonbury, when he will restore my other eye. You may observe and learn then."

A distant bell signaled the time for dinner. Brother Alnett led me to the guest hall, where Arthur and Uctred and nearly a hundred other guests joined me. Surely the abbey lands must be great to provide such hospitality. The hosteller left us with the promise that he would return after the meal. I had spoken of a wish to see the wonders of the abbey, and Brother Alnett was eager to display them.

Monks ate their meal in the refectory, but when we three finished our dinner the hosteller awaited, ready to show us marvelous things. Brother Alnett led us first to the great church. We entered through the north porch. Where the choir meets the crossing he displayed the tomb of Arthur and his queen, Guinevere. From Arthur's tomb the monk directed us to the south transept, where is found the great clock, pride of the abbey, if monks be proud, as they have sworn not to be. Next we saw the Glastonbury Thorn, said to have sprung from Joseph of Arimathea's rod. 'Tis surely a miracle that a tree will flower at Christmastide as well as the spring, when other, more common blooms appear.

"Our holiest place," Brother Alnett advised, "is St Mary's Chapel, for it is on this site that the old church, first in Glastonbury, was built." He led us there and indeed it was not possible to stand in the place and escape a sense of awe and the presence of God. Arthur and Uctred felt this also, and crossed themselves.

"The view from the tor is wonderful," Brother Alnett claimed. "I thought never to see the abbey from its heights again, but now I shall. I will take you there next."

The climb to the top of the tor is laborious, but worth the toil. The Church of St Michael at the top is nearly completed. What effort it took to haul the stones to the eminence! Arthur and Uctred had chattered as we began the climb, but were soon too winded to continue their prattle. At the top the magnificence of the view seemed to strike them dumb, and me as well. It was Brother Alnett who spoke: "The death you spoke of... is it a murderer you seek in Exeter?"

"Aye. The man I seek was once in league with another to blackmail those who had confessed to him their sins, for he was a priest assigned to a small chapel near Bampton. His accomplice in the felony was found hanging from a tree near the town three weeks past."

"Did not the Church demand penance of the man for betraying the confessional?"

"Aye. He was required to make a pilgrimage to Compostela, which he did, but has since returned. He is to serve as assistant to the almoner at St Nicholas's Priory, in Exeter."

"You believe this priest murdered the fellow found hanged?"

"Aye. The dead man's brother was first entangled in the blackmail, and was found dead from an arrow in the back when I was near to discovering the felony. 'Tis my belief this priest slew him to avoid his sins being exposed."

"An evil man, this false priest," the monk concluded.

Arthur and Uctred had overheard this conversation while gazing out over the town and abbey below. Now Arthur spoke: "John Kellet was always a good man with a longbow. Master Hugh couldn't prove 'e'd put the arrow in Henry atte Bridge's back, but who else would do so?"

"Kellet?" Brother Alnett turned to me with raised brows. "The priest was named Kellet?"

"Aye. John Kellet."

"He stayed three days here... no, 'twas four. I would not have thought him strong enough to draw a bow. He was near to collapse from hunger when he came to us."

"How long past was this?" I asked.

"Three weeks, thereabouts. Said he was bound for Exeter. Didn't say why. I bade him stay 'til his strength was renewed for the journey. I could not see him plainly, of course, but brother infirmarer said he was gaunt and wore a hair shirt. A holy man, we took him for."

This report troubled me. Was John Kellet so able an actor that he could take a man's life but appear pious to both Father Simon and the monks of Glastonbury Abbey?

Early next morn Brother Alnett bid me farewell and required of me a promise that I would visit the abbey again upon my return from Exeter to treat his other eye. The sun that day was warm in our faces as we traveled southward. Robins and jackdaws flitted across our way, and high above carrion crows perched in the uppermost branches of trees. From such lofty roost they watched for songbirds, and when they saw a smaller bird seeking its home they flapped from their place to swoop down and plunder the nest. Must it always be thus, that the strong take what they will from the weak? It is my duty as bailiff to see it is not so, but many who hold such a post as mine in service to great lords are much like the crows. The carrion crows do but what is their nature. Is such conduct men's nature also? It must be so, else why must the Lord Christ die for our sins? I must seek Master Wyclif and hear his opinion.

Arthur, Uctred, and I sought lodging that night in Taunton, and departed next day with multiple companions, for the inn was verminous.

Chapter 8

We reached Exeter late in the second day after leaving Glastonbury, as the sacrist rang the church bell to call the monks to vespers. St Nicholas's Priory is not so grand as Glastonbury Abbey. The latter soars over a majestic cloister, whereas at the priory a squat church presides over a mean, unadorned cloister. If the object of monastic life be to live in simplicity and humility before God, surely the brothers at St Nicholas's have an advantage over those at Glastonbury.

The hosteller at the priory is young to be a guest-master. He showed us to a chamber in the priory's west range, sent for a lay brother to care for our beasts, and spoke never a word otherwise. So I was not required to announce the reason for our visit and decided to await the new day before I approached the prior to seek permission to examine John Kellet.

Prior Jocelyn Ludlow was unavailable or unwilling to grant me audience next morn 'til after terce was sung. But the sun was warm against the stones of the guest hall, so sitting there upon a bench was a pleasant diversion. It was near time for dinner before a monk of the house announced that the prior would see me.

Jocelyn Ludlow is a gaunt, narrow-faced man. But for a different name I might have assumed him kin to the abbot of Glastonbury Abbey. His thin, pointed skull rises hatchet-like from his tonsure. This is balanced by an equally sharp nose, about which I will say little, for it is remarkably like my own. His deep-set eyes scanned me from head to toe when I was shown to his chamber. I felt as if he discerned my mission before I announced it.

I introduced myself and my task. When I was done silence followed, for the prior was speechless. I soon discovered the reason.

"John Kellet's past is known to me," he finally said. "The bishop told me of his felonies many months past. I expected a reprobate, but when the man arrived a fortnight past I found an ascetic."

"Does his work please the almoner?"

"Entirely. Too much so. Kellet is not willing to wait for the poor to appeal to the priory for aid. He goes into the town streets to seek them out, then returns with a multitude following. The infirmary is bursting with those he has found ill, and the infirmarer has near exhausted his supply of herbs and remedies. Brother almoner is at his wits' end for fear funds will be depleted. How will the priory then aid the poor? But Kellet will not desist. I do not know," the prior sighed, "what I am to do with the man. This is not a wealthy house. He seems bent on bankrupting the priory in the name of God's work."

"Kellet was once a fleshy man," I said. "I am told he is no longer."

Prior Ludlow's eyes widened at this statement. "Nay," he said. "He is all skin and bones and seems likely to blow away does a strong autumn wind come from the sea."

"He was once skilled with a longbow. I saw him place eleven of twelve arrows in a butt from a hundred paces."

"Don't know if the man could lift a longbow now, much less draw and loose an arrow."

"You think my mission foolish, then?"

The prior pursed his lips and thought for a moment before he replied. "I am not competent in the ways of murderers, as a bailiff might be, but John Kellet seems not capable of what even the bishop told me of his crimes."

The prior told me where I might find the almoner and I set off for the chamber. This was not difficult to discover, for St Nicholas's Priory is not large. I hoped I might find Kellet in company with the almoner but was disappointed. A pale, round-faced monk peered up from examining a book as I entered his chamber. He was alone. As I approached the fellow I saw that he was inspecting an account book. He did not seem pleased.

"You are Brother William, the almoner?"

"Aye." The monk stood and examined me for sign that I required alms from the priory. He seemed perplexed that an apparently prosperous visitor sought him. I relieved his confusion.

"I wish to speak to you of your new assistant."

"John Kellet? He is not within."

I could see that. "I will speak to him later. I would have some conversation with you now. I am Hugh de Singleton."

"Very well," the monk shrugged, and waved his hand to a bench. When I sat upon it the almoner resumed his place at his table. "Kellet has served here little more than a fortnight. I do not know him well. What is it you would know?"

"Do you know why he is here?"

"Aye. Brother Prior told me of his misdeeds. Is it of this you would know?"

"I know of his offenses. I am bailiff to Lord Gilbert Talbot on his Bampton Manor. I discovered Kellet's felonies."

"Then you are the reason he was sent to Compostela on pilgrimage."

"Nay. Kellet's own deeds are the reason his pilgrimage was required. I was but discoverer of his misconduct. No doubt he harbors resentment of me for finding out his sins."

Brother William's brow furrowed. "Not so," he replied. "Kellet told me all, and said 'twas well his crimes were found out, else he would likely have continued in his sins and mayhap died with them unshriven."

"Has he served you well since his arrival?"

"Hah! Too well."

"Brother Prior told me he scours the town seeking the poor and ill."

"He does, then brings them to the priory to be fed and treated. We shall be bankrupt by St Nicholas's Day if he continues."

"I am told he wears a hair shirt."

"Aye, but never speaks of it, as do some who seek a name for holy living. He lodges here," Brother William added, and nodded toward a dark corner of the chamber. There on the stone flags I saw a thin straw pallet.

"Kellet will soon return, for 'tis near time for dinner. You may see and speak to the fellow then. He will return with the halt and the lame in his train, and a few drunken fellows too, no doubt, to be fed with leavings from refectory and guest hall."

And so it was. I left the almoner when a bell signaled dinner, and had taken a place with Arthur and Uctred at table in the guest hall when a stream of dirty, tattered folk entered the chamber. At their head walked a boney figure, wearing a threadbare black robe. This garment was near worn through at elbows and knees. Why at the knees? Did the wearer spend much time at prayer? This, I was sure, was John Kellet, but had I not expected his appearance I would surely not have known him. A year past he was a fat, slovenly priest. Now he appeared a gaunt mendicant.

The man I took to be Kellet began to seat his charges at a table but was prevented by a kitchen servant. The conversation of others in the hall hid much of Kellet's discourse with the servant, but their words became heated and loud and I was able to discern some of the argument. Kellet claimed his charges were guests of the priory and so should be seated with other visitors. The servant demanded they wait for leavings at the gatehouse. The servant won the dispute, and I watched Kellet lead his motley followers from the hall as loaves were brought to the table. Arthur and Uctred looked to me with wide, curious eyes, for they knew whom I sought, they knew what John Kellet once was, and they guessed who it was they had just seen.

The priory served its guests a pease pottage heavy with lumps of pork. The loaves were maslin, not wheaten as at Glastonbury, so as to reduce the cost of hospitality, but the ale was fresh-brewed.

When the meal was done I went in search of John Kellet and found him at the gatehouse, where the hosteller had driven him and his charges. The ragged group was receiving surplus food from refectory and guest hall. I watched Kellet bustle about, making sure that all received something, and none a greater share than some other. As I watched it occurred to me that, unless he had fed in the refectory with the monks, Kellet had not eaten, for he did not take any portion of the leavings now distributed to this rabble.

While he saw to his flock Kellet was too busy to observe others, but when all were fed and even the scraps consumed he paused to look about him and saw me standing in the gatehouse. I think at first he discounted what his eyes told him. He glanced in my direction, then back to his hungry companions. A heartbeat later I saw him stiffen and jerk upright. He turned cautiously and stared at me across the shabby assembly. A moment passed while our eyes met. He then bowed slightly to me and resumed his work. His eyes did not again meet mine until the last of his ragged collection had drifted away down the street.

Kellet could not enter the priory without passing before me. I thought my position might, if he had a guilty conscience, cause him to hurry off toward the town on some pretended business. I was somewhat disappointed when he walked toward me and made no effort to escape a confrontation. This seemed not the act of a guilty man.

"Master Hugh... you are far from home."

"As are you."

"Aye, and you well know why 'tis so, but here is now my new home, and I am well content. Why do you visit St Nicholas's Priory?"

"You cannot guess why I might seek this place?"

"You have business for Lord Gilbert in Exeter and seek lodging?"

"Aye, you speak true on both counts."

Silence followed. Kellet seemed unwilling to ask of my business, and I sought some sign from him that memory of a recent felony caused him distress. I saw no such token, and if he was curious about my presence in Exeter he hid it well.

"The bailiff of Bampton Manor must be about Lord Gilbert's business," said Kellet finally.

"Aye. There has been a death, and I seek knowledge of it."

"In Bampton? Who has died?"

"Thomas atte Bridge."

Kellet was silent for a moment. When he spoke his words startled me.

"I thought so," he said softly.

"You knew of this? How so?"

My suspicion, I thought, was about to be confirmed. I imagined Kellet about to confess. I should have considered his remark more carefully.

"Shall we go to the almoner's chamber?" he asked. "I would like to know more of this."

"As would I," I said, and turned to enter the cloister, from which enclosure the almoner's room was entered.

Brother William looked up from his accounts book as Kellet and I entered. "Ah, you have found John."

The remark needed no reply. The almoner looked from me to Kellet, saw a scowl upon my face, and remembered some duty which required him to be elsewhere.

"I have business with Brother Prior," he said, then turned to me. "You may speak privily here."

I motioned for Kellet to seat himself upon the almoner's bench, but remained standing. I had learned in past interrogations that a guilty man, when forced to raise his eyes to an accuser, may be more likely to admit his crimes.

"Why did you say, 'I thought so,' when I told you of Thomas atte Bridge's death?"

Kellet sighed, then spoke: "'Twas dark an' I could not see who it was hanging as I passed by."

"You saw Thomas atte Bridge hanging from a tree at Cow-Leys Corner?"

"Aye. Thought that's who it was."

"Father Simon told that you were two nights in Bampton, yet no other but his servant saw you."

"Not so. Thomas atte Bridge saw me."

"Before you and some other did murder at Cow-Leys Corner?"

"Nay," Kellet said sharply. "I did him no harm."

"When, then, did atte Bridge see you?"

"The night before St George's Day, when I was new come to Bampton. I rose in the night and sought Thomas."

"Why?"

Kellet looked to his bare, boney feet before he replied. "I wished to confess my sin against him and his brother."

"Henry?"

"I slew Henry with an arrow, and it was my thought to betray those who confessed to me at St Andrew's Chapel. I sought Henry, then Thomas, to blackmail them on my behalf and share the spoils. For these sins I sought forgiveness from Thomas."

"What did Thomas reply?"

"He laughed. Said I'd done him a favor, putting a shaft in Henry's back."

"How so?"

"He'd been encroaching upon Emma's furrow since, taking as his lands those which were Henry's."

"Where did you have this conversation?"

"In the toft behind Thomas's cottage. I disturbed his hens, so he'd think mayhap a fox was at them. Thought the cacklin' would draw him out, an' it did so."

"And this was the night before St George's Day? Not

St George's Day?"

"Aye, it was."

"So Thomas harbored you no ill will?"

"No more so than against any man. He and Henry disliked all. This was why I sought them when I yet lived in my sin. I knew I would find willing conspirators."

"You sought Thomas atte Bridge, to confess a sin against him, but you would willingly have seen me dead in the churchyard of St Andrew's Chapel and helped to bury me. You saw no need to seek my forgiveness while in Bampton?"

Kellet studied his feet again. "I should have done," he said to the floor, "but I thought you would be angered to learn that I was about, and I wished no more trouble from a vengeful bailiff."

Kellet had thought I would not forgive his evil done to me, so to avoid my scorn he did not seek me. Was this so? Would I have denied him forgiveness had he asked? I fear so, for my dislike of a priest who would have seen me murdered and who betrayed the confessional was great. Is this also a sin, to refuse forgiveness, even for such evil deeds?

"Tell me of departing Bampton and what you saw at Cow-Leys Corner." I was not yet convinced of Kellet's truthfulness, and thought to seek some contradiction between his words and what I knew of Thomas atte Bridge's death.

"I wished to be away from Bampton, beyond Clanfield, before any were upon the streets, so I arose well before dawn. Father Simon's cook left a loaf for me, as I had told of my plan. I took part of the loaf and set out.

"The moon had not yet set, and by its light I saw a form hanging at Cow-Leys Corner while I was yet fifty paces or more from the place. I hurried to the tree, but the man was dead."

"You did not recognize Thomas atte Bridge?"

"His face was dark and swollen, and well above me.

But I thought then 'twas him."

"You sought no aid?"

"To what purpose? He was a dead man. And I was too much the coward to face the questions which would come did any know I had returned to Bampton."

"You are certain he was dead?"

"Aye. I touched his arm. It was cold. He was dead long before I found him."

"And you would not call the hue and cry?"

"'Twas near dawn. The sky to the east was growing light. I wished to be gone, and I knew that soon there would be folk upon the road."

"You were once fat with indulgence, but are now but skin and bones. Was pilgrimage so arduous?"

"No more than should be."

"Should be?"

"What favor from God if a penance be easy?"

"You found God's favor?"

"Aye. I did not seek it, at first, but found it, as the Lord Christ found me."

"How did He do so?"

"I set out for Compostela in foul mood, angry at all who crossed my path. I had traveled as far as Gascony when I fell in with a Franciscan who also traveled to Compostela. I wished no companion but he persisted and I came to accept his presence. He told me later he saw my wrath and knew the Lord Christ had put me in his way."

"You journeyed to Compostela with this friar?"

"Aye. There were other pilgrims on the way, but none wished to join with me, so black was my temper."

"And this friar chose to walk with you even though other more amenable companions were at hand?"

"No matter how sour my words, I could not drive the friar away. When I was silent, so also was he. When I spoke, he listened and rarely answered. Not at first. Before three days passed he knew all."

"And he did not desert you then?"

"Nay. He opened to me the Scriptures. I had thought my sins so great that no deeds of mine, no pilgrimage, could wipe them away. In this I was correct, the friar said. No man can earn heaven."

"'Why this pilgrimage, then?' I asked the fellow."

"What did he reply?"

"It was of no value to save my soul, he said."

Kellet was silent, again staring at his dirty, emaciated feet. "The Lord Christ died for my sins," he said, "so I, and all men, might find salvation, did we believe and follow His commands."

"And this you now believe?"

"Aye."

"But you seek to earn God's favor now by helping the poor and denying yourself. You wear a hair shirt."

"The shirt will not save my soul from God's wrath. I wear it but to remind me of what I owe to the Lord Christ. It is His death, the friar said, that was in place of my own. I live now not to win salvation, for such is mine already, but in respect to the commands of the Lord Christ, who taught that we must care for the poor."

"And you traveled to Bampton to show others of your change of heart?"

"Nay. Such would have been prideful. I wished to confess and seek forgiveness of those I had wronged: Father Simon and Thomas atte Bridge."

"But not me?"

"I should have, I now see. I might have saved you a long journey. But I was fearful of your wrath. No man wishes to anger the bailiff of a powerful lord, can he avoid it."

Had I been so harsh that even a man reformed of past transgressions would fear to face me? I did not think myself so frightening. Perhaps a bailiff needs to create a sense of apprehension in those who might violate the law. Can I better govern Lord Gilbert's manor if I am feared or loved? Surely John Kellet and Thomas atte Bridge neither feared nor loved me when they thought me dead and plotted my burial outside the church wall at St Andrew's Chapel a year past.

"Thomas atte Bridge was dead and cold when you passed Cow-Leys Corner?" I said, returning to my inquiry.

"He was."

"You were about when all good men are to be abed, behind closed and barred doors. Did you see any other man upon the road?"

"None other. Thomas was cold. I saw the stool he stood upon to hang himself overturned near the tree, where he kicked it."

"You thought him a suicide?"

"Aye. Was he not? A moment past you charged me with his death."

"Thomas atte Bridge did not take his own life," I replied. I did not offer why I believed this was so, and Kellet did not ask. He found me trustworthy; more so than I found him.

"When you spoke to atte Bridge in his toft, did he seem ready to take his own life?"

"Nay. Why encroach upon Emma's furrow did he not plan to harvest the crop he would plant there?"

"Yet when you saw him dead, at his own hand, as you thought, this did not puzzle you?"

"Thomas was ever unpredictable and hasty in his judgments... especially had he too much ale of an evening."

"You thought him dead of his own hand in drunken insensibility?"

"Aye, something like that."

"You did not consider that there are those in Bampton and the Weald who might wish to do him harm?"

"Him, and me also, but such a thought did not come to me then."

"Atte Bridge died at the end of a hempen cord taken from Father Simon's shed," I announced.

Kellet looked up to me from the bench, his eyes wide.

"This is sure?" He appeared a man whose carefully plotted tale was about to be undone.

"Aye, as sure as can be. The cord was gone, then returned a week past, missing the length found with the corpse at Cow-Leys Corner."

"I was here, in Exeter."

"When the cord was returned, aye, but not when it was taken. One man did not haul Thomas atte Bridge from his toft to Cow-Leys Corner and there hang him. There is evidence that two did so. The man who took the rope from Father Simon may not be he who returned the unused portion."

Kellet was silent again. I thought, nay, I hoped, that he was a guilty man devising some tale which might deflect suspicion, some tale I might catch him up in. My only option, if Kellet were innocent as he claimed, was to return to Bampton and discover there a felon.

"So you believe me guilty of the crime," Kellet said softly, "along with some companion. Who in Bampton remembers me so fondly they would do murder with me? I am disliked there by all men, as much as Thomas atte Bridge was."

I could not argue the point. But to agree with Kellet would be to deny his guilt, to admit that my journey to Exeter had failed, and further, would require of me forgiveness of the man's crimes against me. Forgiveness is costly, but not so dear as anger and hatred and resentment. These three had taken me to Exeter, with a bit of suspicion added. My mistrust of Kellet would linger, I knew, but I saw that my wish for evidence of his guilt over any other man was due to desire as much as to evidence.

Father Simon had told me John Kellet was a changed man, but was I? Kellet surely needed to transform his life, although I yet held suspicion of whether or not he had truly done so.

Men who knew John Kellet a year past would agree about the man's need to reform. What of me? Did I seek guilt where it would be most convenient? There was evidence to direct my suspicion to Kellet, but when I learned from Father Simon that he had amended his ways, I wished not to believe it so. If Kellet was indeed a changed man, I could not assign another death to him, as I wished to do.

Kellet had not asked for my forgiveness, so he said, because he was fearful I would not grant it. Must I now ask his forgiveness for doubting the transformation in his life? I did not do so, and now, some weeks later, as I write of these events, my heart is troubled.

There was little more to learn from John Kellet. If the man was a murderer, I had found no way to prove it so or coerce a confession from him, although I admit that when I left the almoner's chamber I had not given up all hope that somehow he might be discovered guilty of Thomas atte Bridge's death. I did not wish to return to Bampton a failure, nor did I wish to see some friend of mine hang for avenging themselves upon Thomas atte Bridge.

I wished justice to strike John Kellet for his past sins. What of my sins? For those, I desired the Lord Christ to have compassion and show mercy. May justice and compassion live together? If so, how may a bailiff blend the two, or is such the work of God only?

I did not wish to agree with Father Simon, but my conversation with John Kellet left me with few options. If Kellet was not a man transformed, he was a better actor than any I had seen perform upon the streets of Oxford or Paris.

I found Arthur and Uctred and told them we would begin our return to Bampton next day. For what remained of this day I had another goal: I wished to see the cathedral.

The Church of St Peter is a wondrous structure, as are all great cathedrals. I have worshipped in the abbey church at Westminster, at Notre Dame and St Denis in Paris, and at Canterbury. I am always filled with wonder to do so. Is the awe I feel due to the magnificence of God, or the works of man? Perhaps man's soul magnifies the Lord Christ in his works.

Early next day Arthur, Uctred, and I set out for home. I did not bid John Kellet farewell. I should not have behaved so meanly, but I was yet distressed that the most convenient felon had eluded me.

I turned in my saddle as the road crested a hill above the valley of the Exe to gain a last view of the cathedral rising majestically over the town, then set my face toward home and Kate.

Toward the ninth hour of the next day we again halted before the gatehouse of Glastonbury Abbey. I was not pleased to lose a day of return to Kate, but I had promised Brother Alnett to deal with his other cataract, and to demonstrate the procedure to the infirmarer's assistant. And 'tis true enough that our three elderly beasts would appreciate a day of rest.

The hosteler was pleased to see me, and announced that he had sent to London for eyeglasses. "From Florence," he said proudly, "where the best are made, 'tis said by all."

Next morn after terce I couched Brother Alnett's cataract-clouded right eye, with the infirmarer's assistant peering intently over my shoulder. He needed a more proficient tutor, but in the breech I must serve. I pray, if the man is called to couch a brother's cataract, he may meet with good success though his instruction may have been wanting.

Chapter 9

Three days later, Whitsunday, shortly after the sixth hour, we weary travelers passed Cow-Leys Corner and the oak where Thomas atte Bridge died. I was dolorous for my failure at Exeter. To revisit the scene where my disquiet began reduced the joy I felt at returning to wife and hearth.

I left Bruce at the marshalsea and made my way past the mill to Church View Street and Galen House. Kate seemed much pleased at my return, and after an embrace set about preparing a feast to celebrate the event.

She disappeared into the toft and a moment later I heard a chicken squawk. Kate reappeared with a capon dangling from her hand. My dinner had taken its first step toward my belly.

While she plucked and cleaned the fowl, I announced my intention to scrub away the dirt of road and inn. I have a barrel, sawn in half, which I keep for the purpose. From the well I brought several buckets of water which I poured into iron kettles and set upon the hearth, near the fire. As Kate had placed more wood upon the blaze to prepare for roasting the capon, the water in these pots was soon warm enough for my purpose. I emptied the kettles into the barrel, stripped off cotehardie, chauces, kirtle and braes, and immersed myself in the soothing bath. While I soaked, Kate set the capon to roasting, then took my cotehardie to the toft where she noisily pounded the dust from it.

I was soon garbed in clean braes, chauces, kirtle and cotehardie, and enjoyed a stomach full of roasted capon. To conclude the meal, Kate had prepared some days past a chardedate, expecting my imminent return. The dates and honey were a delightful welcome home.

I would not seek another journey to Exeter, or any other place, but returning home to Kate's embrace made the hardship of travel fade. Memories of the road stretching before me, Bruce's jouncing gait, the verminous inns, the failure to discover a murderer, all these were blotted from my mind as the sun fell below Lord Gilbert's forest to the west.

Kate's appetite had returned. Next morn, as we shared a maslin loaf, she told me the gossip of the town.

"There was a marriage three days past," Kate announced between bites of her loaf. "Edmund the smith wed Emma atte Bridge."

So the town smith married the widow of a man who had blackmailed him a year past. This was no business of mine. Edmund was Lord Gilbert's tenant, not a villein. He could wed as he wished. And Emma atte Bridge was a tenant of the Bishop of Exeter and no concern of mine.

"You have not spoken of John Kellet since your return," Kate remarked. "Did he do murder when he visited?"

"I think not."

"Your face and mood speak disappointment."

"If Father Simon's judgment is true, and Kellet be a changed man, I must seek a murderer among our neighbors."

"What of your judgment?" she asked.

"I fear Father Simon is correct."

"You fear?"

"Aye. I will be doubly cursed when I find who murdered Thomas atte Bridge. I will send some acquaintance to the gallows, and his fellow townsmen will blame me for the death. Whoso he may be, he – and his companion, for more than one man dragged Thomas atte Bridge to Cow-Leys Corner – is considered by most to have done a commendable service to Bampton and the Weald."

Kate hesitated before she replied. "Will you abandon

the search? All men think atte Bridge took his own life. None would fault you for admitting agreement."

"None but myself. And you? Would you think well of me did I quit the search for a felon, or would I forfeit some small part of your esteem?"

"You will continue, then?"

"What else may I do? Justice belongs to all."

"Even those who deny it to others?" Kate mused.

"It must be so. What is justice but truth with its sleeves rolled up, ready for labor? If only those who have always done justly, who have always spoken truth, deserve justice, who, then, is worthy?"

"Then you must do as your conscience requires. If you succeed, and find a murderer all the town would prefer remain concealed, and we are then hated in this place, we may return to Oxford. A good surgeon will not lack bread for his babes."

Kate had grown fond of Bampton. She told me so but a fortnight after we wed. I thought she might miss the bustle of Oxford, but she claimed not so. It was easier, she declared, to find friends in a small town than in a city, where folk seem too occupied to concern themselves with others. So to advise removing to Oxford spoke more than the words alone might mean. Here was Kate's admission that I must pursue justice no matter where the path might lead.

But where did the path begin? It is difficult to conclude a journey at the proper destination if one cannot find where to begin. I saw before me several roads, but which must I follow?

I left Kate with an embrace and sought the Weald. To reach Maud atte Bridge's hut I must cross Shill Brook. I have passed this way many times, but the flowing stream, any flowing stream, always seizes my eye. I stood upon the bridge, observing the clear water pass beneath the span. But this wool-gathering would achieve nothing. I turned from the pleasant scene to my disagreeable duty.

Maud's oldest lad answered my knock upon her door.

When Maud heard my voice she appeared behind the youth in the smoky gloom of her hovel. I had spent time drawing and heating water to help rid myself of stink and vermin. I did not wish to do so again, so bid Maud speak to me on the street before her hut. I was sure the place harbored more life than Maud and her children.

"You came to me a month past, sure that Thomas did not take his own life," I began. The woman made no reply.

"You said he heard the hens disturbed – perhaps by a fox, so went to chase away the animal, and you did not see him alive again."

"'At's right."

"And you said this happened the night of St George's Day?"

"Aye. We was abed when Thomas 'eard the ruckus."

"Are you sure this did not happen the night before St George's Day as well?"

"Well, it did so then, aye. 'Twas two nights the hens was vexed. 'E was found dead after second time... day after St George's Day. 'Ow'd you know that? Thomas come back first time. Said as how he'd run off a fox. 'At's why he thought the beast come back next night."

I was about to tell Maud there was no fox, at least not the first time her hens were troubled, but chose to hold my tongue. Maud was no adversary in the business, but her wagging tongue might reach a man who was.

I thanked Maud for her time and left her scratching her head before her hut. She was puzzled that I knew that Thomas had visited his toft twice, when she had not told me of the first event. She was not stupid. She would soon deduce that some other person knew of her disturbed hens, and this person had told me of it. She would want to know who this might be, assuming the man, for a man it would surely be upon the streets late at night, would know who had slain her husband. Indeed, the fellow might be the culprit. I expected her to call at Galen House before the day was done.

Kate believes that a man must have no secrets from his wife. Whether the opposite is true I know not. When I returned to Galen House she placed her needle and fabric upon our table and asked of Maud and of my visit.

I had told Kate little of John Kellet, so drew a bench aside her chair and related my conversation with the man. I told her of his nocturnal visit to atte Bridge's toft the night before St George's Day, and his claim to have seen the corpse suspended at Cow-Leys Corner before dawn as he departed Bampton.

"You believe he spoke true?" Kate asked when I had concluded the tale.

"Aye," I replied reluctantly.

"Someone heard him, then," she said. "Someone who plotted against atte Bridge heard, or learned of, John Kellet's late visit and used the same deception to draw him from his house."

"So it seems."

"Was it then Arnulf Mannyng who slew Thomas? He lives in the Weald, but a few doors from Maud. He might have heard the hens from his house, and thought to see were his own fowls endangered. When he saw how readily atte Bridge might be drawn from his house, perhaps he decided to use the same deceit to get him into the dark of night."

Kate's solution was plausible, but hardly enough to accuse a man. If Arnulf was the felon I sought, I must find some evidence of it, for I had none.

"Perhaps," I replied, "some other man Thomas atte Bridge had harmed, Peter Carpenter, mayhap, lay in wait in the dark near Thomas's hut, seeking some way to draw him forth. While he hid, seeking vengeance, John Kellet appeared, rattling a stick upon the hen coop. When such a man saw how easily Thomas could be persuaded to leave his house, he worked the same ruse next night."

Kate pursed her lips, perhaps unhappy that I had so swiftly dispensed with her conclusion. But Kate is not one to hold a grudge.

"You think whoso bothered the hens the second night knew of John Kellet doing so the first night, and decided to try the same trick?"

"Aye, upon that we agree. But who it was I cannot guess."

"I wonder if there might be some way to draw the man out... or the men, as it seems two have done the murder?"

"Perhaps. I will think on it."

"We will think on it," Kate smiled, and returned to stitching a new cotehardie. The one she now wore would not serve by autumn, and Kate is a woman who plans ahead.

Edmund Smith, like most who labor at his trade, is a strapping fellow, broad-shouldered and with forearms as large around as the axles under Lady Petronilla's cart. He is no friend. I caught him out a year past in dalliance with the baker's wife, when he was caught up in the plot between Kellet and the two atte Bridge brothers. I had stopped the blackmail against Edmund, but also ended his dissolute behavior with the baker's wife. For this he did not thank me.

Edmund's forge is upon Bridge Street, near to the marketplace. After a dinner of pease pottage improved by the remains of yesterday's capon, I set out to visit the smith. I knew of no recent conflict between Thomas atte Bridge and Edmund, but the smith seemed to me a man capable of nursing a grudge. He also seemed an impetuous sort. Would he nurse his wrath for a year before striking down a foe?

I found the forge cold. Edmund was not at his work this day. I set my feet once again to the Weald and found the smith at Emma's hut, repairing the door. This door swung on hinges Edmund had made, then given to Henry atte Bridge to purchase his silence in the matter of the baker's wife. Edmund looked over his shoulder as I approached, then bent again to his task.

"I am told congratulations are due," I began.

"Why must you be told of it?" he replied sharply.

"I have been away a fortnight on Lord Gilbert's business. Do you make your home here now?"

The smith had lived alone in a crude shed behind his forge.

"Aye. Can dwell where I like... I'm a free tenant, as you well know."

"Surely, so long as the vicars of the Church of St Beornwald agree. Emma is tenant of the Bishop of Exeter, and whoso lives with her comes under their authority as his agents."

"Emma needed a man about the place. Couldn't pay 'er rent. Vicars don't care does she wed or not, so long as the bishop gets 'is coin."

"Hmmm. And now Maud is facing like misfortune."

"We all got troubles. Maud'll have to do as best she can. No concern of mine."

"Did Thomas atte Bridge's death please you?"

Edmund looked away from his work and studied my face. "I 'eard the talk, how some think 'e din't hang hisself. No matter to me. Did 'e take 'is own life or did another do away with 'im, the town is well rid of 'im."

I had been standing close enough to the smith that his odor was overwhelming. I doubt the fellow has bathed since I came to Bampton two years past. Whenever I was in his presence the stink was the same. Emma must surely have faced ruin to accept the fellow. I backed away a step to relieve my offended nostrils.

"What does Emma think of such gossip? I saw her in dispute with Maud some weeks past. Does Emma have opinion?"

"Ask 'er," Edmund shrugged, and returned to his work.

"I will. Where may she be found?"

"In the toft."

I found Emma and two of her children drawing weeds

from a patch of cabbages and onions. She arose from her knees at my approach and brushed a wisp of graying hair back from her brow with the back of her wrist. When her children also looked up from their work she barked at them to continue. This they did with alacrity, glancing to me from the corner of an eye while they toiled.

"You have now a husband to lighten your labors," I began.

The woman made no reply, as if my assertion was so foolish that no response was required. The stray locks once more dropped across her forehead and she again brushed them back under her hood, then stood with hands on hips and silently awaited what more I might say. A visit from a great lord's bailiff often draws such a response from folk. Her stance, I think, was due to apprehension, and apprehension due to ignorance. She did not know why I had appeared in her toft, nor what I was about.

"You had a quarrel with Maud some time past, here in the toft," I said.

"Hot of temper is Maud," Emma replied.

My experience of the two women was that Emma better fit such a description, but I saw no reason to voice the opinion. "What disturbed her?" I asked.

"Not a matter for Lord Gilbert's bailiff... we of the Weald sort our troubles with the vicars."

"And has the quarrel been settled? The vicars have rendered judgment on the issue?"

"Uh, not yet."

"Have they been asked?"

"The matter is resolved. No need to trouble 'em."

"And what was the result?"

"Not your bailiwick," she muttered.

"Maud's husband died upon Lord Gilbert's lands. There is some question as to the manner of his death. So when I see his widow in conflict with another, I make it my business. What was your dispute with Maud about?"

"Me an' Edmund had naught to do with it."

I thought this a strange response. "I made no such accusation," I replied. "Why do you fear I might do so?"

"Folk be talkin'. Sayin' you don't think Thomas did away with hisself."

So gossip had prepared this ground before I cast a seed. Why, I wondered, did the woman seem startled to hear from me what she had already learned from others? And how had the rumor got loose in the town? Father Simon's servant, perhaps?

"Did your words with Maud have to do with the death? Does Maud make accusation against you or Edmund?"

"Nay, wasn't about that." The woman fell silent, and looked away, across the crude fence which separated her toft from Maud's. "Since Henry was kilt in the forest Thomas has been plowin' into my land. Wouldn't have done so was Henry alive to say him nay. Maud hired plowmen, an' told 'em to widen the furrows, as Thomas was doin'."

"You challenged her about this?"

"Aye."

"To what end?"

The woman was again silent for several moments. "Edmund told 'er plowmen where they must stop. Maud was angry."

"Is the plow-land in dispute land that Henry had of the bishop for many seasons, or is it of the land he gained when his father died?"

Emma again seemed startled, and I guessed the answer before she spoke. "'Twas of his father's land. Henry was oldest, so was to have it. Thomas was resentful. An' when Henry was slain 'e saw 'is chance to gain what was mine."

"It may belong to neither," I advised, and was rewarded with another surprised expression. "Your father-in-law possessed the land as dowry from his second wife, Alice's mother, so I have learned. Henry seized land which should have gone to Alice."

"Not so," Emma declared. "Henry was due the land. Was it not so, the vicars would have denied him."

"Perhaps they should have done. No bailiff is assigned to direct the bishop's lands in the Weald, as you know. The bishop expects the vicars of St Beornwald's Church to do the work. But they are more concerned with masses and keeping God's house than maintaining order in the Weald."

"Who says 'tis so?"

"Evidence will be presented when the vicars call hallmote, I am told."

Emma snorted in disgust and turned back to her cabbages. I left her to her work and set out for Bridge Street and home.

I had but finished my supper when a rapping upon Galen House's door drew me from my table. As I expected, Maud had been thinking upon what I had told her and now stood in the evening shadow at my door.

"G'day, Master Hugh. A word, if I may."

I invited the woman into my surgery. Through the open door I could see Kate bustling about in our living quarters, with an ear cocked, I was sure, to the conversation beginning in the other chamber.

"'Ow'd you know Thomas went out to see to the hens two nights?"

"The man who drew him out the first night told me."

"Man? Wasn't no fox, then?"

"Nay, nor was there a fox the night of St George's Day."

"Then the same man who come the first time murdered my Thomas," Maud declared. "Why'd the man call him out in the dark of night first time? Did 'e try then to slay Thomas an' failed?"

"He said not. He wished to speak privily to Thomas, to apologize."

"Apologize? For what? Doin' 'im to death next day?"

"Nay. It was another who troubled your hens St George's Day. The first man wished to seek forgiveness of past transgressions."

Maud's eyes widened as I spoke. She knew of Thomas's multiple offenses against others, or at least some of them, but was at a loss to remember trespasses against her husband.

"Who was this, then, what came to our toft at midnight?"

"That you need not know. The man did not slay Thomas. I have spoken to him and know of his words with Thomas. You must trust me. I will seek whoso murdered your husband, but some things about the search you may not now know."

Maud's expression said plainly she was not pleased with this response to her visit, but she knew better than to dispute with Lord Gilbert's bailiff, even was she a tenant of the Bishop of Exeter.

"You'll be about finding 'im out, then?" She sought confirmation that Thomas's death, now fading in the memory of most townsmen, would remain fresh in mine.

"I seek the felon each day," I assured her.

Maud seemed pleased with my promise. She curtsied, which is not a necessary honor for a mere bailiff. Perhaps she thought that as a supplicant in my home such deference might advance her cause and would cost nothing.

I spent the rest of the evening on Lord Gilbert's business, but my mind was more devoted to the confusion of death at Cow-Leys Corner than overseeing the care of Bampton Castle and Manor in Lord Gilbert's absence at Pembroke.

Days grow long and nights brief after Whitsuntide. There was yet a glow in the northwestern sky, beyond the Ladywell and Lord Gilbert's forest, when Kate and I sought our bed. The day had been warm with the promise of summer, but the eve soon cooled and I closed the window of our bedchamber.

Kate is a light sleeper, so heard her hens while I was asleep. She elbowed me to wakefulness and when she was sure I heard, whispered to me of the disturbance in the darkened toft.

"The hens are troubled... a fox, you think? Or has the man who murdered Thomas atte Bridge visited us to draw you into the dark?"

"Not a very inventive fellow," I whispered in reply, "to employ the same ruse he tried before... a man intending me harm would seek some new method. 'Tis a fox in the toft, I think. I will see to it."

"Take care," Kate said softly, rising upon an elbow as I drew on chauces and kirtle.

"A fox," I reassured her. "No man would try a second time what he had worked in the past."

I must learn to listen to Kate's admonitions. I stumbled down the darkened stairway, yet unsteady from an abrupt awakening. I unbarred the door to the toft and stepped into the darkened enclosure. A waning moon was just rising to the east, but Galen House blocked its light and the toft was in deep shadow. Kate's hens seemed quieted. I thought, did a fox disturb them, the animal was probably now away, perhaps with the neck of a hen in its jaws to feed a litter of kits. I would count the fowls in the morn, to see were any taken.

I turned to re-enter Galen House as the blow fell. This perhaps preserved my life. Some shape, darker than the shadows of the toft, leaped toward me and before I could recoil I felt a sharp pain in my right arm, between elbow and shoulder.

My attacker grunted with the effort of his strike, and I yelped in pain. 'Twas most unmanly. Kate had already opened the shutters to see what I might be about, and when she heard my cry she shouted for explanation.

I had fallen to my knees. From this position I could see my assailant's shadowy form crouching to deliver another blow. But when Kate shouted from the window he looked up to her, hesitated, then turned and ran from the toft and disappeared beyond Galen House toward Church View Street.

I put my left hand to my right arm and felt there something warm and wet. I was stabbed. My arm was not the target, I think. My attacker had aimed to put a blade into my back, but when I turned to re-enter Galen House he did not see clearly the movement for the blackness of the place and so plunged the knife into my arm. I did not know who this assailant might be, but I knew who it was not.

As I stood in the dark, stupefied by pain and the sudden attack, Kate burst through the door. She cast about for a moment, then found my white kirtle in the shadows of the toft. The garment had helped my assailant find me as well. She spoke as she approached.

"Was a fox here? Did you frighten it away?"

"Nay. I am stabbed in the arm," I replied. "You spoke true. Whoso murdered Thomas atte Bridge wished to end my pursuit."

Kate took my left arm in her hands while I clutched my right. Together we entered Galen House. "What must I do?" she asked.

"Light a cresset... no, two. We must see how badly I am pierced, and you must have light to stitch me whole."

"Me?"

"Aye. I cannot do the work with but one hand, and you are skilled with needle and thread."

Kate found and lit two cressets from coals yet smoldering upon our hearth and set them upon our table. With Kate's assistance I removed my kirtle. The garment was rent and blood-stained, so could be little more damaged. I inspected my wound, then pressed the kirtle against the cut to staunch the flow of blood. 'Twas then I saw that the blade had passed through my arm, leaving a wound to be sutured on both sides, and made a small puncture between two ribs as well. No knife for use at table made the wound, for such a blade would not be long enough to enter my ribs.

Whoso attacked me had driven a large dagger home with much force. I think I was not intended to survive the cut, and had it been delivered against my back, I surely would not have. Not for the first time I questioned the wisdom of accepting Lord Gilbert's offer to become his bailiff. What some men will do for money.

I wrapped the blood-soaked kirtle about my arm while Kate went to fetch my instruments box. I should like to have bathed the wound in wine, but there was none in Galen House. Wine could be had at the castle, but the gate was closed and portcullis down at this hour. Much shouting and pounding upon the gate would be required to rouse Wilfred. I felt in no fit condition to walk there, and would not send Kate. My assailant had evaded the beadle's watch to enter my toft at such an hour, and might yet be upon the streets. Kate must sew me up as she found me.

Kate returned with the box, opened it, and found needle and silken thread. Threading the needle was small challenge for Kate, even in the dim flame of a cresset, but I thought I saw her hand quiver slightly as she drew the silk through the needle's eye.

With my left hand I pressed the sides of the wound together, then set Kate to her work. She may have trembled while preparing needle and thread, but when she plied the needle upon the wound she was all fierce determination and her hand was steady. I saw in the light of the cressets Kate's brow furrowed and her lips drawn tight in concentration. I wished as small a scar as possible, so instructed Kate to make many tiny stitches. She nodded silently and bent to the work. Twelve stitches later she had closed the larger of the lacerations upon my arm. I dabbed a few remaining drops of blood from the wound, then raised my arm so that she might repeat the process upon the wound under my arm. As this injury was smaller, and would be invisible to most folk, I told her five stitches would suit. The work was soon completed.

There remained but the small gash across my ribs,

where the point of my assailant's dagger had blessedly stopped short after puncturing my arm. Kate closed the wound with three small stitches, brushed a stray wisp of hair from her forehead, and raised her eyes to mine.

"I know," I admitted. "You warned that the visitor might not be a fox."

"You think it was he who slew Thomas atte Bridge?" she asked.

"Who else have I angered recently? I think Sir Simon Trillowe is snoring in his bed in Oxford at this hour, and I know of no other who holds a grudge against me."

The cressets provided little light, but I thought I saw Kate blush as I spoke. Sir Simon had sought Kate's favor, and lost, which defeat he had taken badly and plotted to do me much harm for interfering with his suit.

"Could you see who it might have been?"

"Nay, but I know who it was not."

Kate peered at me from under raised brows, awaiting an explanation.

"Hubert Shillside is left-handed. The man who came upon me in the toft held his dagger in his right hand. He would have driven it into my back, but I turned as he swung, intending to return to the house and my bed. This he did not see for the darkness, but my kirtle was white and so he had a fair target for his stroke."

"If the man is the same who murdered Thomas atte Bridge," Kate mused, "then Shillside is innocent of the death."

"Just so. I must take care he never learns I once considered him."

"He was determined that you see atte Bridge's death as a suicide. Was he guilty that would be a sign… that he wished to turn you from a path which might lead to him."

"Well, he was not, and my heart is eased."

I yet held the torn and bloody kirtle in my hand. The hour was now well past midnight, and I shivered from the cold and the realization that, but for good fortune or the hand of God, Kate might now be a widow. She saw me quiver, took my left arm and pressed it close to her cheek. I felt a dampness there. Kate had begun to cry. She was strong when duty required it of her, but now the crisis was past and her mind could wander through the event and other potential outcomes, she yielded to the emotions which came upon her.

My assailant's dagger, as I believed, had glanced from the bone of my upper arm as it passed through to my ribs. The ache I first felt grew to a pain which throbbed fiercely. Kate sensed this, I think, and drew her damp cheek from my shoulder.

"You have herbs and potions for others when they are hurt," she said. "I will pour a cup of ale and you must take a dose of your own remedy."

I searched through my instruments chest in the dim light of the cressets and found pouches of pounded hemp seed, ground seed of lettuce, and willow bark. When Kate returned to the table with a cup of ale I poured a large measure from each pouch into the brew and drank it. De Mondeville, whose teaching I follow, taught that wounds heal best when left dry and uncovered, with no ointment applied, but in my chest I had a vial of oil of St John's Wort, which can dull pain and help cleanse a wound in the absence of wine. This oil I applied to my cuts.

When in the past I had prepared such a concoction for patients who had done themselves some injury, or upon whom I worked some surgery, I had assured them the potion would alleviate some of their distress. Perhaps I lied. Kate and I climbed the stairs to our bed, where I lay through the remainder of the night, unable to sleep and reviewing in my mind the attack. Kate's rooster announced the dawn but had no need to awaken me. Nor Kate. Each time I turned in our bed she peered at me closely. I assured her twice that an arm wound was not likely to send me to meet the Lord Christ, but I would have been more certain of this had I been able to bathe the cuts in wine before Kate worked the needle upon them.

When the Angelus Bell rang from the tower of St Beornwald's Church I left my bed. If I could find no rest in the night it was sure I would find little in the day.

Kate arose before me, and when I appeared at the base of the stairs turned to observe me with worried expression. Evidently my appearance did not calm her fears. Her forehead remained lined and her lips were pale and drawn.

I smiled a greeting. This had little effect upon her features. I pretended hunger and sat at our table, where Kate had readied a loaf and a wedge of cheese. I managed to stuff a sizeable portion of the bread and cheese past my lips and saw that this brought Kate more comfort than any words I might employ to assert my health. I am seldom found without an appetite no matter the circumstance, which Kate knows.

Kate saw how cautiously I moved and suggested a solution. She had in her chest a length of linen, left from some past stitchery. This fabric she brought to me, measured and cut a section, and fashioned a sling for my aching arm. I had decided against such an aid, for I intended soon to go upon the streets and did not wish to advertise my wounded condition. The sling brought such relief, however, that I reconsidered.

Chapter 10

At the third hour I left Galen House, right arm supported in Kate's sling, and sought John Prudhomme. The beadle lived on Rosemary Lane, near to Peter Carpenter, and it was his custom to rise late from his bed as his duties enforcing curfew kept him from slumber when other men lay snoring upon their pillows.

The beadle was not at home. I found him tending to a field of dredge between St Andrew's Chapel and Shill Brook, where he had a yardland of Lord Gilbert. Weeds in John's furrows were few, but even few were too many for the fellow. He looked up from his labor as I approached, and I saw his eyes dart to my wounded arm.

Had the beadle seen any man upon the town streets after curfew he would have told me of it, as was his obligation. So I did not expect to learn from him a name, but I hoped he might recall some event or sight out of the ordinary.

"You have injured your arm," he said by way of greeting.

"Aye. Well, I did not... some other did so."

A puzzled expression furrowed John's brow. I did not leave him in confusion, but explained my wound and asked if he saw or heard anything uncommon to a May evening.

John scratched his head and considered the question. "'Twas quiet, as always," he replied. "Only man I was likely to find on the streets after curfew was Thomas atte Bridge, as you know, for I reported 'im to you often enough. Now 'e's in 'is grave the town is more peaceful, like, of a summer's eve."

I had held little hope that the beadle could provide

the name of someone prowling the streets after curfew, so was not much disappointed with his reply.

"I'm obliged to watch an' warn 'til midnight," he continued. "Was some fellow on the streets after that, who'd know of it?"

"I assign you no blame, John," I assured the beadle. "'Tis as you say... the attack came in the dark of night, midnight or past. If you hear of any man speak of prowlers in the night, tell me straight away."

Prudhomme assured me he would do so, and I left the fellow to his crop and weeds. He seemed agitated that some miscreant had been prowling the streets he was to see cleared, as if the man had done injury to him rather than to me. John would be alert for any odd events for the next weeks, I knew, and for this I might sleep more securely. So I thought, until I returned to Galen House.

Kate stood at the open door, awaiting my return. I assumed her worried expression had to do with concern for my injury. Not so.

"Come to the toft," she whispered when I was near the open door. "See what I have found there."

I followed Kate through the house and out the door to the toft. She turned to her left, walked a few paces, then halted and pointed to the soft ground near a shaded corner of the house. I saw there an object which at first I could not identify.

A length of broken branch near as long as my arm and as thick through as my wrist lay on the earth beside Galen House. At one end of this stick was wrapped many turns of hempen cord, much like the rope used to hang Thomas atte Bridge. In the dark and confusion of the night neither Kate nor I had seen this club.

"What is it?" Kate asked. "And how has it come to be here?"

I picked up the stick with my good left hand and with this closer inspection knew what it was I held. Bits of earth stuck fast to the wrapped cord at the end of the branch. I lifted the winding to my nostrils, and touched it with my fingers. They came away greasy.

"A torch," I replied. "Someone has made a crude torch of this broken branch. The cord wound about the end has been soaked in tallow."

"A torch? Did the man who attacked you last night plan to light it so as to see what he was about?"

"Nay, I think not. He carried flint and steel so as to light this, I think. Then it was his plan to toss it to the thatching above our heads. Whoso carried this into the toft wished to burn Galen House down upon our heads as we slept."

"But… the hens? Did he not wish to draw you into the toft to attack you?"

"I think not. The hens saved us. The man made some sound we did not hear, but the hens did, and were vexed. When I opened the door to the toft the fellow saw he was found out. 'Twas too late then to do as he intended. Piercing me with his dagger was not part of his plan, I think."

"Would a man murder two to save himself?" Kate asked.

"Who can know what a man might do if he believed his life forfeit?"

"But Hubert Shillside was not responsible?"

"Nay. I would not have believed such a deed of him, but as he is left-handed he is eliminated from suspicion."

"And the others? Peter Carpenter? Arnulf Mannyng?"

"I do not wish to believe it, although I know little of Mannyng. Would Peter murder you in your bed to silence me? I cannot think it of him."

"A carpenter works with chisels," Kate said. "Perhaps the blow which pierced your arm was delivered by a hand which held a chisel, not a dagger."

"You do not know the carpenter," I protested.

"Perhaps you do not know him either, or not so well as you believe."

"Must I suspect all men of wishing me ill?"

"Are all men pricked by evil?"

"Aye, soon or late. Else why did the Lord Christ die in our place?"

"You take my point, then," Kate replied with a wry smile.

"Aye. Trust no man. Is this a way to live?"

"Perhaps, until you discover who it is who wishes you... us to die."

My eyes fell to the mud of the toft. Kate and I had trod the place twice, but among the footprints there was the mark of a man who would have slain my Kate to halt my pursuit of him. The print of Kate's tiny foot was clearly discernible among those made by two men. Of the male footprints one set was long and narrow, the other shorter and broad, with a higher heel. The narrow marks were mine. The man who assailed me in my toft wore shoes seemingly made to increase his stature. Would a carpenter or tenant farmer wear such shoes?

I left Galen House and sought Roger Waleton, Bampton's cobbler. Roger is a sociable fellow, much given to conversation, which he can continue while repairing a man's shoes or making new. I found him alone, stitching a sole to the upper portion of a boot. He was eager for a visitor, but not so pleased when I requested he leave his shop and accompany me. The boots he toiled over were to be readied for a customer on the morrow, he explained. And what, he asked, had I done to my arm?

I explained to the cobbler that some unknown assailant had stabbed me and left behind footprints in the toft behind Galen House. I told Roger that I wished for him to view the marks made in my toft, for the imprint seemed unusual, and I hoped he might be able to identify the owner of the shoes, did he recognize the footprints as made by work from his own hand.

Roger willingly then left his bench and walked with me to Galen House. We passed into the toft and Kate appeared at the door, having heard our conversation as we approached. I pointed out the imprint of my attacker's footsteps and the cobbler put hands on knees and bent to peer more closely at the muddy print.

I saw Roger reach out a finger and gently prod the footprint, then move to another print to inspect it.

"A horseman," he said. "The heel is meant to catch a stirrup. See here, just before the heel, something has worn a cross groove into the leather of the sole. A stirrup, I think."

"These are not heels to make a man appear taller than may be?" I asked.

"I think not... 'though they be some higher than most. These prints were made by the boots of a horseman."

"You are sure of this?" I asked, bewildered.

Roger chewed upon his lower lip before responding. "Sure of it? Nay, but 'tis likely."

"Have you made boots like these?"

"In times past, for knights an' squires who serve Lord Gilbert... but 'tis a waste of leather to make a heel quite so tall as that which left this mark. Such a heel would not much help a rider keep 'is seat, an' might hinder 'im when 'e walks about."

I thanked Roger for his opinion, and when he left the toft I turned to Kate, who had heard all while standing in the door.

"What man who bore a grudge against Thomas atte Bridge owns a horse?" she asked.

"Hubert Shillside does not. Peter Carpenter owns a runcey to draw his cart. I've never seen him atop the beast. Arnulf Mannyng may, but if he does possess horses they will be for plowing, not for riding."

"There must be some other man atte Bridge angered," Kate said thoughtfully. "A man you do not suspect of murder, but who has learned of your doubt that atte Bridge took his own life, and believes you in pursuit."

"And wealthy enough to own and ride about upon

a horse. A short, wealthy man, who may wish to appear taller than he is."

"Perhaps not," Kate objected.

"What? The man does not own a horse?"

"I meant that he may not be short. Gentlemen may be as vain as any lady. The villain may be as tall as you, yet wish to be thought taller yet."

Kate ended her conversation abruptly, wrinkled her nose, then darted for the door and disappeared into Galen House. I followed, and found her at the hearth, where she drew an iron pot from the coals. The contents of the pot, my dinner, had boiled over and the scent told Kate something was amiss.

Small harm was done. Kate had prepared coney in cevy, which was so tasty I nearly forgot the pain in my arm. I attempted to bring food to my lips with my right hand, but gave up the experiment and consumed my meal left-handed. I laced another cup of ale with hemp seeds to complete my dinner, then moved to the toft and sat upon a bench there in the sun to consider my wound and the man who made it. The hemp seed did its work. I sat with my back against the warm west wall of Galen House and was soon drowsing under the effect of the sun, the herbs, and a full belly.

I spent several hours pursuing nothing but my own comfort. This I only partially achieved. A man may more readily advise patience and endurance who has never suffered pain. I will be more tolerant of the ill and injured who seek my care henceforth.

Kate's hens clucking about my ankles and the renewed throbbing of my arm drove lethargy from me and at the ninth hour I entered Galen House to prepare another cup of ale with hemp seed. Kate halted her work to observe the procedure, then came to me and clasped her arms about me, careful to avoid my aching arm.

"What are we to do this night?" she asked. "Mayhap the villain will return and this time succeed in burning us in our bed."

I had considered the possibility, but had not wished to alarm Kate while I thought on it. "Would a man who failed in his purpose try again so soon after discovery?" I asked, speaking more to myself than Kate.

She provided the response: "One so filled with anger or hate or fear, whatever it was drove him to the attempt last night, will not think clearly."

I agreed with my bride. The thought brought much unease. But if such a felon was so driven as to make another attempt, perhaps the man might be surprised at his work and apprehended. The position of bailiff to a great lord often brings with it onerous obligation, but also some privilege. I told Kate I would assign three grooms from the castle to watch, hidden in the toft, so as to seize any man prowling about Galen House after curfew.

At the castle I found Arthur and told him of his duty for the night. I told him to seek two others to accompany him, and arrive at Galen House at sunset. With three keeping watch, one might sleep while two kept vigil. I would spend part of the night with the grooms, although with my aching arm I would be of little use in apprehending a felon should one appear.

I next visited John Thatcher at his home and workshop on Broad Street and made provision for Arthur to remove from John's yard several armloads of reeds which, when strewn upon the mud aside the hen coop, would keep the sentinels dry and hidden in that dark corner of the toft.

Arthur was at my door before the sun had set, and had with him Uctred and Anketil Mere, a youth new to Lord Gilbert's service who was fleet of foot. I saw the lad win a footrace a few months past. If someone bent on mischief approached Galen House this night, and escaped Arthur's bear-like grasp, Anketil would surely run the man to ground. I was well pleased.

The reeds were dry. They rustled and crackled with each movement of the men who sat upon them. Arthur, however, understood that the plan was not to frighten the arsonist away, but to capture him. He sternly bade his companions to remain immobile. I left them there, alert and eager for complete darkness. This was sport, a rare game in the dullness of ordinary castle life when Lord Gilbert was in residence elsewhere.

I climbed the stairs to our chamber, where Kate was already abed, but not asleep. She asked was all prepared and I assured her it was. I did not disrobe. If the grooms surprised a man in the toft I wished to be upon him quickly. I left open the chamber window, so I might hear plainly even a slight sound from the toft, and left my dagger upon a stand where I might seize it quickly.

I slept fitfully, and when I lay awake I could sense that Kate was also alert. When the night was young I sometimes heard the rustle of reeds through the open window as one of my guards shifted his position, but soon even this sound ceased. Either Arthur and his companions had disciplined themselves to some fixed position or they had fallen to sleep. The thought did not bring me rest. Once in the night I heard a snore, but this was quickly silenced as a more wakeful watcher delivered an elbow to the sleeper's ribs. I was reassured that at least one of the three, if not fully awake, at least slept as fitfully as Kate and I.

When I saw dawn begin to lighten the east windows of our bedchamber I left the bed and stumbled down the darkened stairs. Uctred and the youth were awake and watching, while Arthur slept. When Uctred saw me leave Galen House he stood, stretched, and spoke: "No visitors this night. Arthur was that displeased. Took the first watch, 'e did. Said as how a man bent on mischief wouldn't want to wait overlong to be about it. Likes a bit of a scrap, does Arthur."

This observation was true. Arthur is a good man to have standing by one's side in a brawl. His enjoyment of such a contest is probably due to the fact that he is generally victorious. It is difficult to appreciate a fight if one is usually vanquished.

Uctred's words woke Arthur. He and Anketil stood, stretched, and brushed dust and bits of broken reed from their garments. As they did so Kate's rooster left the hen coop, cocked a curious eye in our direction, then announced the dawn.

No man had sought my life this night, and I thought Arthur and his cohorts might think they had been summoned to Galen House to spend a cold night on a fool's errand. Not so. Arthur was apologetic that no felon had appeared, and voiced unwillingness to abandon the watch.

"You'll be wantin' us again this night, I 'spect?" he said through a great yawn. "A man who'd trouble hisself to try an' burn down another's house don't seem to me likely to give over the plan so easy."

Uctred and Anketil nodded in agreement, although the youth seemed less enthusiastic than his elders. He had probably not contemplated such a turn of affairs when he joined Lord Gilbert's service. Most likely he envisioned a life of comfortable work in the castle, with a warm bed to greet him at close of day.

It seemed to me that if I could apprehend the man who wished to burn Galen House, I would also find the man who had dragged Thomas atte Bridge to Cow-Leys Corner and suspended him there from an oak limb. Why else would any man be so driven to destroy me, my house, and Kate? I saw no reason to prowl the town seeking a murderer when it was possible, was I patient, the man would come to me. Perhaps not this night, as he had refrained from the attempt in the past night, but soon or late my prey would seek once again to halt my search for him and silence me. Then Arthur, Uctred, and Anketil would be ready.

When I began the search for Thomas atte Bridge's murderer I was dismayed to think I might discover the felon among friends. Then I hoped John Kellet was the guilty man, for he was no friend. Now I sought a man who had taken one life and would have destroyed two more to preserve his secret. The fellow might have been a friend in times past, but no more, and when I found who it was I would suffer no displeasure at his meeting a noose.

I bid my three protectors good morn with the injunction that they were to return again at dusk to wait and watch. I spent the day trying to avoid moving my arm, which had become an angry red where Kate's needlework bound the flesh together. Little pus issued from the wound, which some would consider an ill thing, but I hold with Henri de Mondeville that no pus from a wound is preferable even to laudable pus.

Arthur, Uctred, and Anketil yawned the next four nights away, hidden in the dark aside the hen coop in my toft. No man disturbed their vigil. When dawn broke on Trinity Sunday I sent the grooms to the castle with an admission that the surveillance was a failure and they no longer needed to seek Galen House at dusk.

My arm no longer ached so fiercely, so this day I drank a morning cup of ale without the herbs. We took no loaf to break our fast, but after quenching a thirst prepared ourselves for the day.

As for Whitsuntide, white is the color for Trinity Sunday. Except for my kirtle I own no white garments, but Kate drew from her chest a long white cotehardie which she kept for such occasions. Dressed in my grey cotehardie and black chauces I felt a crow aside a swan. I was not alone. When the village was gathered at St Beornwald's Church it was the womenfolk who were attired in honor of the occasion, in garments carefully preserved for such a holy day.

Kate had prepared let lardes for our dinner this day, and after we ate we joined others who gathered in the marketplace for mystery plays. That God has become three – Father, Son, and Holy Ghost – is surely a mystery. This mystery will be revealed when the Lord Christ returns, and perhaps the mysteries of who murdered Thomas atte Bridge and attempted to burn Galen House will be disclosed then as well. My progress at solving these two puzzles was so scant, any solution seemed likely hidden 'til the end of the age.

So while the players told the story of the Bible and God among men I fretted about my failures, standing at the fringe of the marketplace crowd. Kate noted my joyless demeanor and asked was my arm troubling me again. I shook my head, and I think then she understood my unease. She took my arm, my good left arm, and entwined her arm in mine. Thus we stood while the players concluded the account, a story all knew and had heard before, but 'tis useful to be reminded. Men forget the sacrifice the Lord Christ made in their behalf. Duty and worry and such cares as are common to all press upon folk, so they neglect their obligation to the Savior.

My own thought accused me, for while the players told their tale I considered felons and how I might find them out. I devised no answer, and took little joy in the players' work. 'Twas a misspent afternoon.

Monday morn, after a maslin loaf and ale, I set out for the Weald and Maud atte Bridge's hut. I dispensed with the sling this day, the ache in my arm being much reduced. I lingered at the bridge over Shill Brook. The flowing water is unchanging, whenever I halt in my business to observe it, yet the scene seems ever fresh. The brook is the same, but the water coursing 'neath the bridge is new. So it is with the realm. King and nobles and commons may change, but the kingdom endures. May it always be so.

Late spring is a thin season of the year for most tenants and villeins. Last year's grain harvest is near gone, and the new crop two months from the scythe. Pigs slaughtered in the autumn have, by early June, usually been consumed by all folk but those uncommonly frugal of flesh in the pot in the winter past.

So I was not surprised when I found Maud tending a kettle of barley pottage upon her hearth. No scent of pork came from the pot. The thin gruel would be her family's only meal for this day and many more like it, but for the occasional egg from her fowls. I felt some sorrow for the widow and her state. She lived now without beatings, but which, I wondered, was more trying – bruised ribs or an empty stomach? The woman looked up from her pot as my shadow darkened her doorway, open to the air and morning sun. She could see only my form, for the brightness behind me, but guessed who it was who called.

"'Ave you news of who slew my Thomas?" she asked as she stood from her smoky hearth.

"Nay. I know little more than when we past spoke. One thing I have question about, which brings me here this day. Did Thomas have business with any gentleman, or wealthy burgher… some bargain which may have gone bad?"

"Business with a gentleman?" Maud scoffed. "Why'd 'e be dealin' with such like?"

"I have reason to believe whoso slew Thomas is a horseman."

Maud's hands had been upon her hips as she spoke. At this news they dropped to her side and I saw her eyes widen.

"A horseman? Thomas 'ad no truck with such folk. He'd nothin' a gentleman would wish to buy, an' no coin to purchase what a rich man might sell."

Maud's logic was excellent, but how else to explain the boot-print in my toft? The man who sought to end my investigation was no poor man. He rode a horse, and often enough that the stirrup had worn a groove into the sole of his boot.

"The man I seek may not be of great wealth," I explained. "But he has the means to keep a horse."

Maud was silent, her eyes narrowing in thought. "Two, three years past, I'd near forgot. Thomas an' Henry had business with a knight of Cote. Lived in the manor house there."

"What was this business?"

"Don't know. Thomas din't say. Kept things to hisself."

"Was Thomas satisfied with his dealings with this knight?"

"Oh, aye. 'Eard 'im an' Henry laughin' 'bout it once."

When men like Henry and Thomas atte Bridge find humor in business with another, it is sure the other man has suffered in the bargain. Cote is not a rich manor. An injured knight there might fit the pattern I saw developing.

I bid Maud good day, and left her at the door to her hovel. Two of her children had appeared as we spoke, and watched suspiciously from behind her skirt as I departed.

I was but a few paces along the path when the sound of a horse and cart behind me caused me to turn. Arnulf Mannyng approached. Sacks, perhaps full of surplus grain he was taking somewhere to sell, filled the cart. This left no room for the man, so he rode upon his beast upon a crude saddle. Leather straps hung down from this saddle, and from them simple iron bars were bent into stirrups. I waited at the side of the track for Mannyng to pass, and waved a greeting as he did so. When the man turned from me back to the road I stole a quick glance to his feet. His shoes had heels, to be sure, but they seemed to me no higher than need be, and surely Arnulf did not ride the horse so often as to wear grooves in the soles. Or did he?

Cote is little more than a mile to the east of Bampton. I decided I would this day call on Sir Reynald Homersly, knight of the Manor of Cote. I knew little of the man but his name, but as Cote was too humble to support more than one manor, Sir Reynald must be the occupant of the manor house there.

At the castle I sought Arthur and Uctred and told them that, after their dinner, they would accompany me to Cote. I might have had a groom of the marshalsea prepare Bruce and two palfreys, but the distance to Cote is small, and I was uncertain how my wounded arm would receive Bruce's ponderous gait. I required Arthur and Uctred to arm themselves with daggers. Was Sir Reynald the man who pierced me, he might be displeased to see me before his door. Arthur and Uctred, in Lord Gilbert Talbot's blue-and-black livery, daggers at their belts, might temper his discontent.

I might have enjoyed a pleasant stroll through the late spring countryside but for some worry about my reception in Cote. We were the object of turned heads, as strangers usually are, when we passed through Aston.

Old manor houses now are often torn down and replaced with new, but not so at Cote. Sir Reynald's home was but a larger reflection of Galen House. It was built of timbers, wattle and daub, with a well-thatched roof. The house did possess two chimneys. A wisp of smoke drifted from one which vented the kitchen hearth.

Few folk were about, which was no surprise, as there are few folk in Cote to be anywhere. The village was much reduced when plague struck seventeen years past, and again when the pestilence returned five years ago.

Arthur and Uctred stood respectfully a few paces behind me, caps in hand, as I rapped my knuckles upon the manor house door. A moment later the door opened to the music of ungreased hinges, and an elderly female servant stared dumbly through the opening at me.

"Is Sir Reynald at home? I am Hugh de Singleton, a neighbor... bailiff to Lord Gilbert Talbot in Bampton."

The woman seemed to hesitate, then replied, "Aye. 'E be 'ome, as always. I'll see can 'e speak with you." The stout woman left us at the door and disappeared into the dark interior. She was not well trained in the art of receiving guests. Perhaps her normal duties lay elsewhere, or the house was unaccustomed to receiving visitors.

A few moments later I understood what the woman meant when she said "as always". I was shown into a room at the rear of the house, where a man sat propped in a chair. One leg extended straight out upon a cushion, covered with a wrap, as the chamber was on the north side of the house and cool. The fellow looked to be of some forty or fifty years, although age can be difficult to determine with the ill and maimed. A woman of similar age sat upon a bench near the chair, and stood when the old servant ushered me into the room.

"You seek my husband," she asked, and looked to the pale form propped in the chair.

If this was the man who murdered Thomas atte Bridge and attempted to burn Galen House, he had surely suffered a sudden illness and rapid decline.

"Aye, what illness has overcome Sir Reynald?"

"Injury, not illness. My husband was riding about the manor, seeing to plowing and such, when a hare startled his horse. The beast threw him. He broke a leg, and was in much distress."

A tear appeared at the corner of the woman's eye as she completed the tale. I turned to Sir Reynald and asked when this mishap had occurred.

"Four days past Easter," he replied.

The man had been confined to bed and chair more than a fortnight before Thomas atte Bridge died, and surely had not run from Galen House a week past.

Arthur, standing behind me in the door from the corridor, then spoke: "Master Hugh be a surgeon. Deals with broke legs and such."

"I've heard so," Sir Reynald replied.

"Was a physician or surgeon brought to set the break?"

"Aye. The herbalist at Eynsham Abbey came. Put reeds about my leg and tied them tight, then set all in plaster. Said I was not to walk about 'til June."

"Does the break pain you?"

"For a fortnight it was troublesome, but no longer. Did you call from Bampton to ask of my leg?"

"Nay. There is a matter in Bampton which requires sorting out, and I thought you might assist me."

"I know little of matters in Bampton. I have troubles enough here in Cote."

"Did you, two or three years past, have business with

Henry and Thomas atte Bridge?"

I saw Sir Reynald's lip curl as I spoke the names. I needed no further answer, but received such anyway.

"Aye. Scoundrels. Cote has suffered much from plague. When it first struck I was a young man. I watched my family perish, and most of the village also. I alone remained of my father's house, so I became lord of Cote Manor when I was but twenty-four.

"We had no priest to shrive the dead. Father Oswald was among the first to perish. Four years passed before the bishop found another vicar. Then five years ago plague visited us again. Mostly children of the village it was who died this time. Amecia," he looked at his wife, "and I lost our youngest son. But Cote lost also some adults, so that now I have few tenants and much land lies fallow.

"So three years past, it was, I hired Henry and Thomas to plow on demesne land. They were to give me three weeks in February and March. But after a few days at their labor they asked for their wages and came no more. Said they could not spare more time from their own holdings. Next day a calf was missing from the barn."

"You believe they took it?"

"Aye. Couldn't prove so. They came in the night, knowing the lay of the place, and made off with the calf, so I believe. Cote has no beadle. Since plague none has been needed."

"Did you inquire in Bampton and Aston about the stolen beast?"

"Aye. None saw them with it. 'Tis my belief they took it to Witney or Eynsham or Brize Norton or some such place an' sold it."

"They will not trouble you more," I replied.

"I heard that Henry's dead. What of Thomas?"

"Dead also. Found hanging from an oak at Cow-Leys Corner, to the west of Bampton."

"Hanging? Did the scoundrel take his own life?"

"So some believe."

"But not you, eh? Else why would you seek knowledge of me, who was injured by the knave? When was he found?"

"The day after St George's Day."

"I'm not sorry the rogue is dead," Sir Reynald admitted, "but you can see I'm not the man who slew him, though if some fellow did do away with the rascal, I wish him well."

There was no reason to inspect the knight's riding boots. He could not have murdered Thomas atte Bridge, nor could he have run from my toft a week past. I apologized for disturbing the peace of Sir Reynald's home.

"'Twas no imposition," he smiled. "You brought me a good report."

"That Thomas atte Bridge is dead?"

"Just so. When I am able next week to rise from this chair I will have double reason to rejoice."

Arthur and Uctred heard the conversation from their place in the passageway which divided the house. As we left the place Arthur offered an opinion, a thing he was never reluctant to do. "Seems lots of folks had reason to wish ill upon Thomas atte Bridge, an' if they didn't do 'im harm they're not regretful someone else did."

To solve the puzzle of who murdered Thomas atte Bridge I needed to eliminate men from suspicion for the deed until but one possible felon remained. Instead I was discovering more folk Thomas had wronged. How many more such men might I find?

I thought on this as we three retraced our steps through Aston and back to Bampton. The day was far spent when we entered the town. I released Arthur and Uctred, saw them off to the castle, and walked through quiet streets to Galen House. I had departed the town with high hopes four hours earlier; now I was again frustrated in my pursuit of a murderer. And my arm ached.

Kate is well able to renew my mind and cause aches and pains to fade. Perhaps it is well that the law gives women so little power, as God has given them so much. She had removed her cap, and allowed her hair, the color of an oak leaf in autumn, to fall to her shoulders. A respectable matron wears her hair up, and Kate is respectable, but I like her hair as it was that evening when I returned to Galen House.

"What have you learned?" she asked. I had told Kate where I was going and what my purpose was.

"That Sir Reynald suffered a broken leg at Hocktide and could not have attacked Thomas atte Bridge or fled from our toft."

"Oh," she replied quietly. "Well, an empty stomach will not help solve the puzzle. I have mortrews and a maslin loaf, and ale fresh brewed from the baker's wife."

The meal was simple but toothsome. I have enjoyed great feasts at Bampton Castle and Goodrich, but few meals there were so delectable as this plain fare taken across the table from my beloved Kate.

"You have become quite shaggy," Kate teased when the meal was done. I had grown a beard last autumn after three days in Oxford Castle dungeon. Rather than shave the stubble when Lord Gilbert saw to my release, I chose to allow the whiskers to grow, being persuaded that my appearance was improved by having as much of my face covered as possible. But this beard I kept trimmed short, until an injured arm made it difficult to comb and trim the whiskers.

I managed to lift my tender right arm, and protested that the work required to trim my beard would provoke much discomfort should I lift and hold my hands to my face with comb and scissors. Kate rolled her eyes to the excuse, having less sympathy than she might. So I challenged her to take up the task, under my instruction, and make me presentable by her own hand. To my surprise, she accepted the invitation.

I retrieved scissors from my instruments chest, found my comb, and moved a bench to the toft with my good arm. I sat in the warmth of the setting sun and instructed Kate in the use of scissors and comb against beard. She had barely begun when I heard her exclaim, "Hah!"

I felt a sharp tug against my chin and a moment later Kate held a whisker before my eyes. It was white.

"I have wed an old man," she laughed.

"'Tis but a mark of wisdom."

"Then the more I discover the more likely you will be to discover who murdered Thomas atte Bridge and tried to roast us in our bed."

"We may hope this is so."

The trimming of my beard continued with no further discovery of silver whiskers and no damage to my neck. Or, if Kate did find more pale whiskers, she held her peace about it.

Chapter 11

Three days later was Corpus Christi. All who owned red garments wore such in the procession. Kate donned the deep-red cotehardie she had worn a year and more past when I first saw her at her father's shop in Oxford. I am unlikely to forget the event or the gown. The vicars of St Beornwald's Church led the march, taking turns holding aloft the host before the throng as we passed through Bampton's streets. Master Wyclif takes a contrary view of this holy day, although to avoid angering the bishops he does not make his opinion known to any but those who are like-minded. Only in the Third Lateran Council of the past century, he points out, was it decided that the bread and wine of the mass became the flesh and blood of the Lord Christ when blessed by a priest. Was it possible, he asks, that bread and wine did not change in their nature until the past century? Or did they do so from the beginning of Holy Church, but no one thought to notice? I must admit that I see wisdom in his position. I do not fear to write this. The bishops are unlikely to read my words and will think me too insignificant to trouble with even should they do so.

Had the man found dead at Cow-Leys Corner been some upright townsman, I would have been more diligent in pursuing the felon who took his life. But Thomas atte Bridge's death was no more mourned in Galen House than under any other roof in the town. Each day which passed found me with fewer thoughts on how I might find the man responsible for atte Bridge's death, and also with less interest in doing so. It is to my chagrin I admit this. Life in Bampton continued, pleasant summer days were upon us, and if the town knew I sought a murderer and had failed to discover him, no man seemed remorseful of my failure, not even me.

So long as I moved my arm slowly and made no contact with any object, my wound no longer gave discomfort. Twilight yet illuminated the windows of our bedchamber the night of Corpus Christi when I fell to sleep, untroubled either by my lack of success in finding a murderer or by a punctured arm.

I was startled from my slumber, however, when from the window we had left open to the mild June air came an unintelligible roar, then a shout that someone should halt. Kate and I sat upright in unison, and I then leaped to the window as the bellowing faded. Whoso created the tumult had passed from the toft to the side of Galen House and seemed to be making for the street, all the while bawling out that some other man must halt. Kate's hens then also added to the racket.

It is sure that when a man hurries to do a thing, the doing will take him longer than if he was at leisure. I hastened to pull on chauces, don kirtle and cotehardie, and find my shoes in the dark. While I scrambled about the chamber Kate added a shriek or two to the shouting without. I thought dawn might come before I was dressed and able to investigate the uproar. It did not.

I remembered to arm myself with my dagger, then plunged down the steps in the dark, managing to bounce against the wall upon my right arm. Pain is nature's way of telling a man not to repeat some action. I slowed my pace, reached the ground floor with no further insult to my arm, unbolted the door, and ran into the street. It lay silent before me in the starlight.

I walked 'round the house to the toft, alert should some assailant wait there to pounce, but as there was little moonlight I could see nothing there amiss. I caught movement from the corner of my eye and saw Kate leaning from our bedchamber window.

"Is it you, Hugh?" she whispered, sensing rather than seeing me, I think.

"Aye."

"What mayhem is there?"

"Nothing. No man is here to be seen or heard, and no mischief done... perhaps when day comes we may learn different, but whoso was here a moment ago did no harm that I can see."

"Two were here," Kate reminded me.

"Aye. Some fellow woke us crying out for another to halt."

"'Twas me," a voice replied from behind me.

"Who is there?" I demanded.

"Arthur," came the reply, and it was then I recognized his voice.

"What are you about, here in my toft so late at night?"

"Watchin', to see did some man make another bid to burn Galen House."

"I released you from the duty."

"Aye, but after I thought on it for a few days I decided to return an' watch, to see did the villain make another attempt. Should've told you."

"How many nights have you spent in my toft awaiting the felon?"

"'Bout a week. Was ready to give it up, thinkin' the man had forsaken the idea, then he come back this night."

"A man appeared this night? Are you certain he meant harm? 'Twas not just some drunken fellow who escaped John Prudhomme's notice?"

"Nay. I was near to sleep on them reeds you put by the hen coop when I saw a flash an' 'eard somethin'. Woke me right quick, it did, an' I knew what the fellow was about. Strikin' flint against steel, 'e was, an' tryin' to be quiet about it so's hens wouldn't hear an' raise a fuss.

"Them reeds is dry, an' when I stood to chase after the man 'e 'eard 'em snap an' took to 'is heels. Hens 'eard me rise an' began to squawk, too."

"That is when you woke us?"

"Aye. Yelled for the man to halt, but I can't run as when I was a lad. Took out down Church Street, 'e did, an' I followed as far as Broad Street. Too dark to see for sure, but 'e went through the marketplace, I think, an' last I seen 'e was off toward St Andrew's Chapel."

"Not toward the Weald?"

"Nay, I think not."

Here was a puzzle. If it was Peter Carpenter who sought to burn Galen House, he would have run down Church View Street to seek safety at his home. If Arnulf Mannyng was the man, he would have sought escape across Shill Brook and to the Weald. Neither man would have gone east, toward St Andrew's Chapel. Then again, to confuse a pursuer, perhaps they would.

"Whoever the man was, he will not return this night. You may return to the castle and your bed."

"Wilfred won't like bein' turned out to open the gate an' raise the portcullis," Arthur replied. "Had a cozy place made in them reeds. Think I'll just stay right here, an' you've no objection. I'll speak to Uctred and Anketil. They can join me tomorrow. Anketil will run the fellow down, an' that's sure."

"'Twill not be needed," I said.

"What? The man tried twice to burn you an' Mistress Kate in your bed. He'll not give over without another try."

"Perhaps, but now he knows some watcher may lie in wait for him in my toft he'll not approach the business from here again."

"Think 'e'll try to toss a torch on your roof from the street?" Arthur asked skeptically. "No place there to hide hisself. 'Course, does 'e return some night when there be no moon, an' wear black clothes, he might stand in the open an' no man see 'im 'til 'e strikes flint against steel again."

"If he does," I said, "there will be no one here to burn."

"How so?"

"Kate and I will remove this day to my old chamber in the castle. I'll not risk again her safety, nor my own. If some fellow wishes to kindle a flame on the roof of Galen House he will do so with the place empty."

I left Arthur in the toft and climbed the stairs to Kate.

"I heard," she said when I entered the chamber. "We will abandon Galen House?"

"Aye. Arthur and Uctred and Anketil might spend a fortnight or more in the toft to no purpose. Then, when we think the arsonist frightened away, he may return, biding his time until we have relaxed our guard."

"But what of Galen House? Will you permit it to be destroyed?"

"Not if I can prevent it. But I will not rest easy any night with you sleeping under this roof. We will make our home in the castle 'til whoso wishes me dead and silenced is discovered."

"You will be more diligent in seeking who slew Thomas atte Bridge?"

"I must… else we will make our home in my bachelor chamber at the castle, which is no fit place for a man with a wife."

"And soon to have a child," Kate reminded me.

"Aye," I smiled. Kate heard the pleasure in my voice and drew me to her there in the dark chamber. Returned to our bed, we lay in each other's arms 'til sleep once again came to us. A house may be lost and replaced. A beloved wife, once gone, is forever so.

At dawn I found Arthur yet faithful at his watch. I told him to return to his wife and rest until mid-day, then, after his dinner, bring a horse and cart from the marshalsea, and several more grooms, to move Kate and me and our possessions to the castle.

I did not wish this transfer to be concealed. If the town knew of it, whoso wished my death might no longer seek to burn Galen House, knowing I was no longer resident there. My absence might save me, Kate, and the house.

Kate and I spent the morning preparing our goods for removal to the castle. We consumed a last meal – last for a short while, I hoped – at Galen House and were ready when the clop of hooves and creak of axle told that Arthur was at our door.

Many folk passed Galen House while the grooms were at their work. Some halted to ask what I was about, as I had wished, and I told them of our removal to the castle. By the time the cart returned for a second and final load I had told the tale to a dozen folk or more. Soon the wives of Bampton and the Weald would bend every ear with the news. Any who did not hear of it from them would learn of the business from their husbands. This, I was sure, would preserve Galen House from future assault. This was not my first mistaken assumption, nor will it, I think, be my last.

My old chamber off the Bampton Castle hall was too small for Kate, me, and our possessions. Our bed, two chests, a table, a bench, and two chairs filled the space. Another bench, our cup board, and my bath barrel I left in the hall. When Lord Gilbert and Lady Petronilla returned at Lammastide this would no longer serve, the hall being put to Lord Gilbert's service. But by that time I hoped to have discovered who wished to end my life and my pursuit of a felon. I was sure that by finding one man I would solve two mysteries. Then Kate and I could return to Galen House and a peaceful life. Certainly Galen House would await our return unmarred now it was known we no longer inhabited the place.

Hubert Shillside I could discount, as my attacker was surely right-handed. But Peter Carpenter, Arnulf Mannyng, Walter Forester, and Edmund Smith remained as potential murderers. I could not envision Peter or Arnulf attempting to silence me if to do so would harm Kate. Fear, however, may drive a man to do what he otherwise would not consider. My thoughts of Walter and the smith were not so benign. They seemed less likely than Peter and Arnulf to concern themselves with an innocent victim of their vengeance, but seemed also less likely than the others to have wished harm to Thomas atte Bridge. Edmund had reason to resent Thomas and the blackmail he did, but it seemed to me the smith would not have delayed revenge for more than a year. Edmund never seemed a patient sort.

I had seen Arnulf ride a horse, and this he did often enough that he owned a saddle, crude as it was. But did he possess a dagger with such a long blade as the one which pierced my arm?

Peter Carpenter also possessed a horse, but would own no riding boots. He would have chisels among his tools as well as a dagger of some sort, and the injury done my arm could have come from a chisel as well as a dagger. The wound was caused by a thrusting stroke rather than a slash.

And what of Edmund? Like Peter, he would own no shoes suitable for stirrups, but he was a smith, and could at his forge make any weapon he desired.

Kate and I sought our bed as darkness fell upon the castle, secure behind gate and portcullis from him who sought to do us harm. I lay abed considering Arnulf, Peter, Walter, and Edmund, but before sleep came I found reason to dismiss all four. Was it possible there was another man in Bampton or the Weald whose hatred of Thomas atte Bridge washed beyond that miscreant to engulf me?

I woke before the Angelus Bell with the same thought occupying my mind. If some man I did not yet suspect murdered Thomas atte Bridge, and sought my life to preserve his own, I must devise some way to learn of him. I decided that after I broke my fast I would seek Father Thomas de Bowlegh.

Since my return from Exeter I had spoken but briefly to the vicar. I am like most men, I believe. I see little merit in reviewing my failures with another. This may be mistaken behavior, but conceit often interferes with wisdom. I had traveled to Devon seeking a murderer and, as Father Simon predicted, I found instead a walking skeleton who was not at all the man who once served as curate at St Andrew's Chapel. That earlier John Kellet might have taken the life of another from spite, but it was difficult to envision the new Kellet doing so. Nor could I see Kellet with the strength to subdue Thomas atte Bridge and carry him to Cow-Leys Corner, even with the aid of another.

I found Father Thomas at his vicarage, preparing to cross the lane to the church for nones.

"Master Hugh," he greeted me with a sober expression. "A good day to you... although my wishing will not make it so, I fear. I have heard of your removal to the castle."

"And you know the cause?"

"Aye. 'Tis an evil thing, that a man would seek to burn another man's house. There has been little rain the past fortnight. All roofs are dry. Set alight one roof and half the town might burn to ashes."

Concern for my own danger had obscured the plight of the town should Galen House have caught fire. Would Peter Carpenter have done such a thing? His house and shop are but two hundred paces from Galen House. A conflagration begun there could engulf his property. But perhaps he did not think of that in his determination to end my probe of Thomas atte Bridge's death, if he was the guilty man, which I increasingly doubted.

"Since St George's Day, when Thomas was discovered at Cow-Leys Corner, have you seen any man joyful of his death?"

The vicar chewed upon his lower lip and pondered the question before replying. "I've seen no man sorrow for it. Thomas had done injury to many folk."

"Including me," I smiled ruefully, and rubbed my skull where atte Bridge had twice delivered strokes in darkened churchyards which raised knots upon my pate. As I rubbed my scalp I thought I could yet detect the lumps left there by his blows.

"Aye," Father Thomas agreed. "There are those who think you had better reason than most to see Thomas atte Bridge buried in unhallowed ground."

I had not considered this. While I sought a murderer, and my search became known in the town, there were those who saw me as a likely source of vengeance against the dead man. I must be doubly careful in my quest, else in accusing another, could I find cause to do so, folk might believe I was seeking to deflect suspicion from myself.

"If you hear of any man more pleased than most that Thomas atte Bridge no longer vexes the town, I would know of it."

"You will not give over pursuit of a murderer, then, even after so many weeks with no success? Surely the trail now grows cold... and remember, many yet believe there was no murder, but suicide."

"Aye, many believe so. But you have heard my evidence."

"Aye," he sighed. "And so, like you, I believe a murder done. But if you quit the search few will think the worse of you for it. Most wish that nothing but a suicide happened at Cow-Leys Corner."

"The man responsible for Thomas atte Bridge's death is the one who seeks to burn me in my bed, so I believe."

"Oh," the vicar replied thoughtfully. "The fellow must think you close on his trail, then?"

"He is mistaken. I could select ten men at random upon Bampton's streets and find eight Thomas atte Bridge had wronged."

"Aye," Father Thomas chuckled wryly. "And the other two would have suffered at his brother Henry's hand."

"Do you know Sir Reynald Homersly, of Cote Manor?"

"Aye."

"He is another Thomas atte Bridge wronged."

"At Cote? How so?"

"Three years past he hired Henry and Thomas to

plow. Said they worked but a few days, then sought their pay and came no more. Complained of no time to labor upon their own strips in the Weald. Next day a calf was gone from Sir Reynald's barn."

"Sir Reynald believes Thomas and Henry made off with it?"

"He does. Could prove nothing."

"How does the Lady Amecia? She was sorely grieved when plague took their youngest lad five years past. 'Tis well Sir Reynald's older lad is well."

"She seemed well enough. Sir Reynald has an older son?"

"Aye. Can't recall the lad's name. I remember he was sent off to be squire to some knight of Oxfordshire and learn the arts of a gentleman. Near old enough now to be knighted, I'd think."

"His father will find use for him when he returns to Cote."

"Unless he attaches himself to the retinue of some great lord. Some would prefer to be a small fish in a great sea, like London, than a large fish in a pond like Cote."

Father Thomas spoke true. Nobles are fond of exhibiting their power with the number of knights in their train. Cote would offer a young knight little compared to life serving a powerful gentleman. Perhaps Sir Reynald's son had made his choice, and that was why he was not spoken of when I visited Cote.

I enjoined Father Thomas again to keep ears alert for any who spoke gleefully of Thomas atte Bridge's death and turned to leave the vicarage when he called out to me: "'Twas the sheriff... Sir John Trillowe."

"Who?"

"Sir Reynald's lad. I remember now. He is squire to Sir John. As Sir John was dismissed from that post, he'll need fewer retainers. Likely the lad will return to Cote when his service to Sir John is ended."

I agreed, and considered this information while I

returned to the castle. My path took me past Galen House, now dark, its shutters closed, its chimney cold. If I walked past the house each day its condition would, I thought, inspire me to greater labor to find the man who slew Thomas atte Bridge.

After dinner at the castle, which, according to Arthur, was much improved now that Lord Gilbert's bailiff once again took meals in the hall, I spent the afternoon seeing to business of the manor. Some obligations cannot be set too far aside, even to seek a murderer.

I lay abed that night considering where I might seek truth. That I must redouble my efforts if I wished to return to Galen House was sure. But would my toil bring success? A man may spend much of his life seeking truth, yet not find it unless he search for it where it may be found. No hunter's effort will find a stag in the castle marshalsea; no tenant's labor will harvest oats in a field planted to barley. To find the truth of Thomas atte Bridge's death I must seek it where it may be found, else all my struggle will be in vain.

This was not a reassuring thought to propel a man to restful slumber.

Next morn I awakened to the distant sound of the Angelus Bell from the tower of the Church of St Beornwald. The tolling of the bell did not cease, however, but continued; a slow, mournful repetition. Someone was near death, and the passing bell warned all to pray for the soul of him who was departing this life.

I did not take time to break my fast, but dressed hurriedly and with a word to Kate of my intention left the castle to seek news of who it was dying in Bampton. None of Lord Gilbert's tenants or villeins had been ill, that I knew of, but several are aged, and death may come to any man, no matter his years.

I found Father Ralph and his clerk on Church View Street. He was returning to his vicarage, he told me, having been called to the Weald to shrive Philip Mannyng.

Mannyng was the bishop's tenant, so I had no duty in the matter, no heriot to set, but I thought it appropriate to visit the Weald and express sympathy to those who mourned. I found Philip's family crowded into the house when I arrived. Amabil was silent. She had mourned her husband for many days as he lay fading from life in his bed, so had few tears remaining, I think. Arnulf also was silent, but his thoughts were transparent. He strode about the room, fists balled at his side, and when he noticed my arrival spared but a brief nod to me before he resumed his pacing. His brow was deeply furrowed, and his lips drawn tight against his teeth.

Was Arnulf angry regarding his father's death? Or was his stalking and unwelcoming scowl but the way of a man in sorrow? I did not know Arnulf well enough to interpret his moods. It seemed to me he viewed my presence with distaste, but why? I had nothing to do with his father's injuries or his death, and had provided soothing herbs to help the old man in his pain. Was the son bitter that I now sought one who had murdered the man who injured the father? Was Arnulf that man? His expression said this might be so.

Words at such a time are often insufficient. And many words are no more suited to the moment than few. To speak the appropriate words and no more is a skill. Some folk believe that by speaking many words a few in the bundle might be found to suit the occasion. I am not such a one. I expressed condolence to Amabil and Arnulf with few words. Amabil replied with thanks, but Arnulf simply nodded and continued his pacing. This was not convenient for him or others, for the house was small and crowded with family and neighbors. Arnulf seemed not to notice, and the mourners made way for him as he traversed the room.

I bid Amabil good day – an affectation of custom, for surely it would not be – and left the house. The day had dawned cloudy, and now rain began to fall as I returned to the castle.

Rain continued throughout the day and night, so when mourners began the procession from Philip Mannyng's house in the Weald to St Beornwald's Church the streets were deep in mud. Arnulf Mannyng was one of four men who carried Philip upon his bier at the head of the procession, immediately behind the three vicars of St Beornwald's Church. All who walked behind the corpse seemed clear-eyed and walked without lurching. The wake must have been a quiet and solemn affair.

I had another motive beside honoring a good man on his last journey to the churchyard. I wished to see the prints Arnulf Mannyng's shoes might make in the mud of street or churchyard. Too many mourners followed the corpse to see what marks Arnulf's shoes made in the street. His footprints were obliterated by those who came behind.

I moved to stand close to Arnulf when he and his companions set down their burden in the lych gate. But again the press of other folk made it impossible to see what mark his shoe made in the mud.

At the churchyard, after the funeral mass, I found a place behind Arnulf and so was able to examine his footprints in dirt freshly excavated from his father's grave. His heels made no deep impression, and I saw no groove across the sole. It was as I thought when I saw him a few days past upon his beast. He was not accustomed to riding a horse, and his equipage for doing so was crude and seldom used. Unless Arnulf possessed other shoes or boots, he had not been in my toft. Most men of his rank own but one pair of shoes, and if they have another it is likely they will be rough, wooden-soled and made for work in the fields. I did not know whether I should be pleased at the discovery or not.

Hubert Shillside, John Kellet, and Arnulf Mannyng I had absolved of Thomas atte Bridge's death, although I was prepared to be mistaken should I learn some new thing which might lay murder at the feet of one of these, especially some new thing of John Kellet. Peter Carpenter,

Walter Forester, and Edmund Smith remained of those I knew to have reason to desire vengeance against Thomas atte Bridge. Would any of these attempt to stop my inquiry by burning Kate and me in our bed? Did they wear shoes meant for a knight? Would Peter burn a house so near his own the flames might spread and consume him as well? Did he possess a dagger? Or would he be so enraged that he would pierce me with a chisel?

I could not answer "aye" to any of these questions. I sought truth in the wrong place. It was not to be found in Bampton, I decided, but in Cote. Sir Reynald could not seek to silence me, but he had a son who might. Sir Reynald might have provoked this son to revenge against Thomas atte Bridge and to my destruction. Why he would do so I could not tell. Would a man fan the coals of a grudge into flame after three years? Would even a hot-headed youth kill to avenge a stolen calf? Would he seek to end my search for him when I had given no sign that I suspected the knight? Indeed, when the first attack came against Galen House, I knew nothing of the man.

Next day the rain had ceased. The sky was bright blue and dotted with clouds scudding west to east in a brisk wind. It was a good day to travel. I told Arthur and Uctred they would accompany me to Cote again that day, and to make ready to set out after dinner.

Sun and wind had dried the roads, so we arrived dry-shod at Cote. As we entered what remained of the plague-stricken village I saw a cotter hoeing weeds from his patch of leeks and onions. I halted, cleared my throat to warn the fellow of my approach, for his back was to the road, then entered his toft. He stood erect, leaning upon his hoe, and stared suspiciously at me as I drew near. Strangers entering isolated villages often bring such a response.

I smiled to put the fellow at ease. This seemed a failure. His expression did not change, and he seemed to grip the hoe the tighter.

"Good day. We come from Bampton. Can you tell me

if Sir Reynald's older son is yet in Cote, or has he returned to Oxford?"

"Geoffrey?"

"Aye, Geoffrey." Now I had a name, which before I had not.

"Ain't seen 'im in years."

"I heard he had returned from Oxford for a time." This was a lie. May the Lord Christ forgive me.

The cotter scratched himself, smiled wryly, then replied, "Nay. Not been seen in Cote since before my Matty perished."

"Matty?"

"Me wife. Took ill two winters past. Young Geoffrey went off to Oxford summer afore that. Three years it'd be now, near."

"And he's not returned?"

"Did once, I heard. I din't see 'im, but word gets out. Sir Reynald wanted 'im to return to Cote when 'e was knighted. Geoffrey had other plans. Manor house servants said as there was hard words. Geoffrey ain't been seen in Cote since, far as I know."

"You are sure of this?"

"Aye. Was 'e to return, the village would know of it."

"He was sent off to Oxford to serve as squire to the sheriff, was he not?"

"Aye, but sheriff had little use for more retainers, so 'twas said, so Geoffrey become squire to sheriff's son."

"Sir Simon?"

"Uh, aye. Believe that was 'is name."

I thanked the fellow for his conversation and returned to the road. Arthur and Uctred had remained there, but the toft was humble and so close were they to the cotter, they had no difficulty hearing the words exchanged.

"That squire what you patched up back before Christmas, after him and Sir Simon was sliced up on the Canditch... suppose that was Sir Reynald's lad?" Arthur asked.

I did so suppose, and had the same thought which Arthur voiced. If Sir Reynald and his son had a falling out near three years past, and the youth had not been seen in Cote since, it was not likely the lad would strike down another who had wronged his father, nor would he know of my pursuit of the man who did. And if he did not slay Thomas atte Bridge, he had no cause to stop my search for the felon who did so. Geoffrey Homersly did not try to burn Galen House.

I saw no reason to approach the manor house at Cote to confront Sir Reynald concerning his son. The man endured enough sorrow, I thought, without my adding to it. I turned to the west, my face warmed by the slanting sun, and Arthur and Uctred fell in silently behind. I was left with but two men Thomas atte Bridge had wronged who might have done him to death: Walter Forester and Edmund Smith.

Walter worked regularly with sharp tools, and might have plunged one of them through my arm. And Walter, with his father and brother, would use horses to draw carts full of timbers and firewood from Lord Gilbert's forest. Would he occasionally ride upon a beast, so as to put cross-grooves in the soles of his shoes from stirrups? That seemed improbable.

I had searched for truth in Bampton and found none. I searched for it in Cote and found none. Or rather, the truth I discovered brought no solution or satisfaction. Perhaps the truth I sought might be found in Alvescot. I resolved to visit there again next day.

All men seem more imposing when astride a horse, even if the beast be a humble palfrey. Bruce is aged, to be sure, but he was once Lord Gilbert's finest dexter. I chose to travel to Alvescot upon the old horse, so left word with the marshalsea that I would require him on Monday at the third hour.

Chapter 12

King Edward requires that all the commons be proficient with the longbow, and Lord Gilbert has placed upon me the responsibility for seeing that his tenants and villeins are not found wanting should war with France resume. Perhaps I should write "when war with France resumes."

On the Wednesday before Corpus Christi I had tacked a notice to the church door that the following Sunday there would be archery practice and a competition.

So the day after my abortive journey to Cote, after the mass and a convenient interval for dinner, families began to gather at the castle forecourt. I assigned two grooms to bring the butts from the castle storeroom, had in my pouch six silver pennies for the competition, and required of the castle butler a cask of fresh ale to quench the thirst of the competitors.

The day was yet windy, so archers were sorely tried when they attempted to place their shafts in the target from much beyond sixty paces. Much good-natured banter was provoked by arrows gone astray in the breeze. By the twelfth hour the ale was gone, the pennies awarded, the butts returned to the storeroom, and my mind – freed for a time from thoughts of murder and flames – returned to ways I might root out a felon.

I felt no need to require Arthur or Uctred to accompany me when I mounted Bruce on Monday morn and set out for Alvescot. Walter, was he guilty of Thomas atte Bridge's death, would cause no tumult before his father and brother.

The warm sun and brisk breeze had in three days so

dried the roads that Bruce raised dust rather than clods of mud as he plodded his way toward Cow-Leys Corner. I reined the old horse to a stop at the oak where Thomas atte Bridge had dangled near six weeks past, and studied the tree. The halt puzzled Bruce. He stamped a great hoof, impatient to be on his way.

What did I expect to learn from Walter Forester? If I asked him plainly had he to do with Thomas atte Bridge's death, he would surely deny it. He might be speaking truth, or he might speak falsely. How might I know? What could I ask of him that might lead to the fellow incriminating himself? I had proof of nothing, only suspicions. The King's Eyre does not deal with suspicion but with fact. I had none. If Walter would not confess to the felony, I could offer no sure evidence of his guilt.

I had no reason to wish Walter guilty for, unlike John Kellet, the man had done me no harm. If John Kellet did not do the murder, nor Geoffrey Homersly, nor Walter Forester, I was left to sort out a felon among friends.

There was also Edmund Smith, but if he did harm to Thomas atte Bridge he had felt no haste to work his vengeance. And if he was guilty I had no more evidence than for Walter Forester. Six weeks I had contended with my ignorance. Ignorance seemed triumphant.

I turned Bruce and set him plodding back toward Bampton and the castle. Wilfred the porter was doubtless surprised to see me return so soon after departing, but a good porter pays little regard to the coming and going of his betters. That they wish to come or go must be enough for him.

Kate, however, required explanation.

"You are going to lay aside the pursuit of a murderer, then?" she asked when I explained my sudden return.

"Unless some new information, some new gossip or rumor, comes to my ear, I know not what more to do."

Kate did not respond, which was a clear sign she had no better idea than I as to what I might next do. If she has such notions she is not hesitant to speak them for my benefit.

Sleep did not come that night. In the past, when I was a bachelor bailiff for Lord Gilbert, residing in the castle, if I experienced a wakeful night I would prowl the castle parapet, considering the issue which robbed me of sleep. It was near midnight when I crept from my bed this night to walk again upon the parapet. I tried to quit our bed without disturbing Kate, but I believe she slept uneasy as well, for she sat up and asked, when she understood I was drawing on my chauces, what I was about.

I told her, hoping she would not volunteer to accompany me. She was soon to become a mother, and must have rest, and I wished to consider my failure alone. Bad enough to be ineffectual, but to be so in the eyes of one's beloved is doubly distressing. I was relieved when she murmured a drowsy response and drew the bedclothes up to her neck.

Wilfred and his assistant were snoring in their chamber in the gatehouse. I heard them in duet through the door which Wilfred leaves open in all but the harshest weather so he may be more easily awakened in the night should need arise to open the gate and lift the portcullis. I thought for a moment to wake the porter and tell him what I was about, so that should he leave his bed and find some shadow atop the castle wall he would not raise an alarm and disturb the sleep of others. But the rumbles and snorts from his chamber convinced me that discovery from that quarter was unlikely. I passed by the door and mounted the steps to the parapet.

I completed a circuit of the castle wall and was beginning a second when I saw a glow in the sky to the east, over the willows which line Shill Brook and the mill pond. My mind was fixed upon the death of Thomas atte Bridge so the orange tint did not at first register upon my thoughts. 'Twas the moon, rising to the east, so I assumed. But on the north parapet, as I walked west I saw a sliver of new moon hung above Lord Gilbert's forest.

My thoughts fused abruptly and I spun about to look to the east. The glow above the trees was brighter, and I knew what it must be that caused it, yet I prayed as I ran that it be not so.

I plunged down the parapet steps, burst through the door to the porter's chamber, and shouted for the fellow to awaken. He did so with much spluttering. When I knew him to be alert and ready for instruction I told him there was fire in the town. He and his assistant must awaken the grooms in their quarters, and all must attend the blaze at once with rakes and hooks and buckets. But first he must open the gate and portcullis that I might leave the castle.

I ran through the forecourt in the dark to Mill Street, thence across Shill Brook. When I came to Church View Street I was joined by three others, for the cry of "Fire!" had spread quickly through the town and many converged on the scene. Galen House was ablaze.

Flames leaped from the thatching, and already men were attacking the roof with hooks, attempting to pull the flaming reeds to the ground where they might be more easily extinguished, and to prevent the flames from consuming the entire structure. If the thatching be pulled down the frame of Galen House might be saved.

This was not to be. The thatch was too dry. Although there had been rain but three days past, the summer sun had dried the reeds and they burned readily. Flames rose high into the night sky and sparks settled upon the roofs of neighboring houses. It was well the conflagration came when all was dark. Did any sparks alight on the thatching of a nearby house the glow was quickly seen. Men placed ladders upon such dwellings and took buckets of water from the well to splash upon these new threats before they could grow and consume another house.

Galen House could not be saved. Daub cracked in the heat and fell away. Wattles then caught fire, and after that the beams of the house were kindled. I shouted over the roar of the inferno that men should leave Galen House, which many were already doing for the intense heat, and seek out sparks which might set other homes ablaze.

As I spoke I felt soft hands upon my back. Kate had come. I turned to her and saw the tracks of tears upon her cheeks in the orange glare of the blaze now consuming our home. There was nothing to be done but to comfort each other, so that is what we did. Clasped in each other's arms we watched as the beams supporting the upper floor of Galen House collapsed. As they fell a fresh shower of sparks and embers erupted into the sky. By this time the entire town was witness to the conflagration, I think, so any brand which fell where it might ignite another house was immediately found and extinguished. Small boys darted about Church Street and Rosemary Lane, as far as Broad Street, reporting to their elders when any sparks yet unextinguished were discovered.

The night was short, and the eastern sky ere long became pale. Soon the rising sun illuminated the scene of devastation before us. A pile of blackened beams, many yet ablaze and smoking, lay where once Galen House had proudly stood. My new chimney stood tall and unmarred at the south end of the smoldering heap; all else was ruin.

Kate and I had wordlessly watched the flames consume Galen House. What was there to say? When the sun lighted the scene she finally spoke: "Will you now continue your search for a murderer?"

I did not answer straight away. This question was in my mind since the hour I realized our home was ablaze. Was there a man in Bampton or the Weald who did not know we had abandoned our home and resorted to the castle for safety? Many had seen the cart transfer our goods to the castle, and I made clear to many why we had changed our abode. Was town gossip so weak that some, after near a week had passed, did not yet know of it?

This was not creditable. If the murderer wished to burn Galen House even if I no longer resided there, he must desire some vengeance beyond preventing his discovery. Destroying my empty house would not destroy me or cause a halt in my search for a felon.

Perhaps the man who set fire to Galen House was not of Bampton, so could not know I had changed my dwelling-place. Did Geoffrey Homersly do this thing? I could think of no other who might wish harm to both Thomas atte Bridge and me, and who might be from some distant place where my move from Galen House was not known.

"I must," I finally replied to Kate. "Else we may never rebuild this house. As soon as we do the felon will burn it again."

"Even if we reside in the castle?"

"Even so. Unless Thomas atte Bridge's murderer is from some far place he will know Galen House was empty this night. Setting it ablaze could do me no injury, yet he burned it."

"You believe this is so?" she asked. I saw tears once again leak from the corners of her eyes.

"Nay. I think our home was burned by some man who thought we slept this night under its roof."

Kate turned to inspect the charred beams and ashes which were once a home and shuddered.

I required of Kate that she return to the castle. This she was loath to do while I remained on Church View Street, but I convinced her that she could do little but stir the ashes. Her most important work this day and for many months to come was to give life to our babe. I would search the rubble, when it cooled, for anything of value we might have left behind when we removed to the castle, or for any clue which might identify who had done this thing. While I stood before what had been our door Hubert Shillside approached.

"'Tis well you had foresight to abandon the place," he observed.

"Aye. But I thought to save my house by leaving it. A man could not murder me by burning my vacant house."

"Should'a kept watch a few days longer," Arthur muttered, joining the conversation. "But who would've thought the knave would seek to burn an empty house?"

"Who wishes revenge upon you, Hugh?" Shillside asked.

"A bailiff makes few friends," I replied, "but I can think of none I have injured so much this would be their response."

"But it must be so. Else why burn the place if you were not meant to die in the flames?"

"Perhaps I was."

"You think the felon unaware you were abed in the castle?"

"Aye."

"Well, whoso the villain may be, he might have destroyed half the town seeking harm to you. Do you discover who has done this, it will go hard for him when he is brought before hallmote."

Arthur had wandered away while we spoke. He found an unburnt rafter, pulled from the roof when it was hoped the blaze might be checked. With this he began to probe the cooling ashes of Galen House for bits of iron, nails, hinges, and anything of worth which the fire might not have consumed. Shillside and I joined him, poking about the edges of the blackened beams which once supported a fine house. It was yet too hot to enter the center of the pile. How little effort it takes for one man to destroy the hopes of another.

Six grooms joined us in sifting the ashes. I did not wish to spend the day waiting for the pile to cool, so set four to work with buckets, hauling water from the well to toss upon the embers. Each bucket produced an upwelling of smoke, ash, and steam, but after an hour of this work the results of each new bucket of water became less dramatic as the remains became soaked.

Near mid-day I led the grooms to the castle for our dinner. We reeked of smoke, but as it was my intention to return and finish the work of picking through the ashes after the meal I did not demand the men change their apparel. Washing of sooty hands and faces must serve.

Nothing of value remained of what had been Galen House but for scraps of iron and the new chimney. The bricks were well made and the mortar strong and neither suffered great harm from the heat. My face, hands, chauces, and cotehardie were black with ashes and soot when I gave up the search and returned to the castle with Arthur and the others. All were black as me, for none stinted in the work. I was some relieved that nothing was found in the ruins, for that meant that Kate and I had been thorough in removing our possessions. Unless we had overlooked some burnable object, in which circumstance, who would know?

After a light supper I sent to the castle kitchen for a dozen buckets of hot water. I filled my barrel with these and soaked away the soot and stench. Even so, my clothes were so saturated with the odor of burnt wood that our chamber reeked. We could not clear the room of the smell until my clothing was gone. Kate bundled the lot while I soaked, and took the sack to the scullery for washing next day.

I resolved next morn to travel to Oxford and seek Geoffrey Homersly. I would first learn where he stabled his horse, and discover if the beast's stall had been vacant the night Galen House burned. I found Arthur and told him what I intended, and that he and Uctred would once again accompany me, then sent word to the marshalsea to prepare our mounts after dinner. I told Kate that my intention was to return the next day, or in two days at the latest. She, meanwhile, I asked to remain within the safety of the castle. Kate would be curious about what remained of Galen House.

Perhaps the cook realized that my mood was sour and so attempted to improve my disposition with a meal. For dinner that day he prepared mussels in broth, parsley bread and roasted pork. I was not much hungry when I sat in the hall to begin my meal, but the pleasant fragrance as the dishes were placed before me soon set my stomach to growling. I had eaten nothing that day to break my fast.

Arthur, Uctred, and I went straight from the hall to the marshalsea, where our beasts were ready for travel. Kate blew a kiss as I rode Bruce under the portcullis. I hoped she would heed my direction to remain within the castle precincts. Perhaps Geoffrey Homersly, or whoso sought my life, might yet lurk in some hidden place about Bampton. If the man would burn my home to injure me, he might also strike at my wife. I nearly drew Bruce to a halt at the thought. As it happened I need not have troubled myself with worry. Not with that worry, anyway. Other worries would soon prove trouble enough.

From Aston we traveled the north road through Yelford and Hardwick. We neared Sutton when I saw a figure approaching upon the road. The man strode furiously, his head down, as if he mistrusted the way and thought to keep it under close observation lest he stumble.

I gave the man little more thought until we were nearly upon him. He had heard the fall of horses' hooves and the squeak of our saddles and so moved to the verge to make room for us to pass. Horses usually mean knights, and such folk dislike moving aside to make way for the commons. Their dislike is often translated to action, which the common man who does not step from the path will rue.

I was nearly upon the traveler when he looked up, to see, I suppose, was he far enough aside to clear the way. I thus looked into the face of my father-in-law, Robert Caxton. I yanked upon the reins to halt Bruce, and Caxton was so startled at my appearance that he stumbled and nearly fell headlong. I soon discovered why this was so.

"You… Hugh!" he exclaimed. "You are not dead? And Kate? Is she… I was told…"

"Dead? Nay. I am well, as is Kate. Why would you think otherwise?"

"I was told so but this morn."

"You were told falsely, but an attempt was made two

nights past to murder us in our beds. I would hear more of this."

I dismounted so I could speak more readily to my father-in-law, and asked what he had been told, and when, and who it was who brought him the news.

"This morn," he began, "I had just raised the shutters and opened the shop when a young gentleman entered my door. I thought he sought parchment or ink. He was no scholar, but wore the garb of a wealthy young burgher or knight.

"I bid him good day, and he replied that it was indeed, for some, but not for me. His words were a mystery to me. I asked, 'How so, good sir?'

"'You have a daughter, wed to the bailiff of Bampton Manor?' he said. 'Is this not so?'

"'It is,' I answered.

"'Word has come this day that your daughter and her husband have perished. Their house burned night before last, and none escaped the flames.'

"I asked the fellow how he knew this. He said 'twas spoken of by many."

"Did the gentleman visit your shop to make a purchase, or was it only to give you this sad account?"

"He made no purchase... turned and was gone after he made his report."

"Do you know the fellow? Have you served him before?"

"Seen him about Oxford. Think he may have done business with me, but 'twas a long time past. What of Galen House? Did it burn, as the man said?"

"It did, and whoso set it afire thinks Kate and me dead in the ashes and ready for a place in the churchyard."

"Set it afire? But... why would a man do such a thing?"

"Come, ride behind me. You have walked far and fast, and Bruce is a sturdy animal. We will speak more of this while we travel to Bampton. You will see Kate well enough, and in six months' time she will make of you a grandfather."

Caxton's somber expression was gladdened at this report. I mounted Bruce and gave a hand to my father-in-law to assist him up behind me.

"I did not wish Kate to go to the churchyard without me there to mourn her," he said, "or if she and you were already in the ground I thought to pay the vicar to pray for your souls."

"We are both safe," I said. "I moved Kate and our goods to the castle, because there had already been other attempts to set fire to our house. I thought this would preserve it. Who would destroy it if I no longer lived under its roof?"

"Who indeed?"

"Some man who knew not we had changed our residence," I replied. "Or someone so filled with malice that he would do me harm in any way he might."

"Why would a man be so spiteful?"

I explained to Caxton the death of Thomas atte Bridge, and told him of the many folk in Bampton and the Weald he had harmed. Yes, and in Cote, also. I spoke of my belief that the attacks upon Galen House were an attempt to murder me and thus halt inquiry into atte Bridge's death. I told him that my mind was to travel to Oxford this day and seek Sir Simon Trillowe's squire, to learn, if I could, had the youth been absent from Oxford two nights past.

By the time Bruce ambled past St Andrew's Chapel, Robert Caxton knew all. I wonder if he was now less pleased about his daughter's choice of husband than he once seemed. If so, he spoke no word of it.

Kate was astonished to see her father, and nothing would do but to repeat his tale of the visitor – for customer he was not – who had told Caxton of our deaths. While he enlightened her I considered his account and came to a conclusion regarding the matter. I was very nearly correct.

"The man who burned Galen House is from Oxford,"

I said when his report was done. "This is why he did not know we were abed in the castle when he set it alight. He did not desire vengeance, he wished to do murder."

"And believes he has done so," Kate added solemnly.

"Indeed."

"Who is the man?" Caxton asked.

"I believe it must be Geoffrey Homersly. He resides in Oxford, had reason to murder Thomas atte Bridge, and is squire to Sir Simon Trillowe, who has little love for me or Kate."

"How may this be proven?" Kate asked.

"When I set out for Oxford after dinner it was my thought to find Homersly and observe him as he goes about his day. He will accompany Sir Simon much of the day, but soon or late he will visit a stable where his horse is kept. A silver penny or two may persuade the keeper of the mews to say if Homersly's horse was absent the night Galen House burned."

"Perhaps it was this Homersly who visited my shop this morn?"

I thought at the time this was likely so.

"When the fellow told you of Galen House burning, was he pleased or sorrowful?"

"He was not distressed. Now I think back upon it, the report seemed agreeable to him."

"I will seek Arthur and Uctred and tell them to make ready to leave again for Oxford in the morn. You may sleep in a guest chamber this night. We will sort out this business, and should the youth not wish to admit his felony, Arthur and Uctred are brawny and a scowl from them will persuade him to confess all."

We broke our fast early next morn with a wheaten loaf, cheese, and ale, and before mid-day passed Osney Abbey and crossed the Thames at the Hythe Bridge. We stabled our horses at the Stag and Hounds. My father-in-law insisted he had room and enough above his shop for us all to sleep.

Arthur knew Sir Simon Trillowe. After a dinner of roasted capon at an inn on the Canditch I sent him and Uctred to prowl the streets and watch for the knight. If they found him they would follow to see where he dwelt, then report to me at the castle.

I set off for the castle. Sir Roger de Elmerugg, newly made Sheriff of Oxford, was a friend of Lord Gilbert and had been of good service in the matter of Master Wyclif's stolen books.

Chapter 13

The stone-walled passageways of Oxford Castle are familiar to me. I went unhindered to the clerk's anteroom, where I found several other men waiting also to see Sir Roger. I introduced myself and my office and told the clerk I sought audience with the sheriff upon Lord Gilbert Talbot's business. Although I, a mere bailiff, did not outrank the prosperous burghers who were before me, Lord Gilbert surely did. I hoped such announcement would gain me quick access to Sir Roger, and I needed but little of his time.

At the mention of Lord Gilbert the clerk, who until that moment seemed unimpressed of my appearance and office, became more alert. When I had done with my appeal he rose from behind his table, cracked open the door behind him, and in a low voice delivered my request.

I heard a chair scrape against the flags of the sheriff's chamber and a moment later Sir Roger appeared in the narrow opening. His eyes were crinkled in a smile beneath his shaggy brows.

"Master Hugh. Lord Gilbert requires some service? Come in... come in." He drew the door wide. "How may I serve Lord Gilbert?"

I caught a glimpse of unhappy scowls upon the faces of those who had awaited Sir Roger's pleasure from before I entered the anteroom. My request would not take long, and when I entered his chamber I saw no other man there. Sir Roger was engaged in some business which prevented him hearing the pleas of his petitioners. It was not my request which restrained him from attending to their needs. I felt less guilty.

"Good to see you again, Master Hugh. Are you well?" Sir Roger clapped a meaty hand across my back as he pointed me to a chair. "Be seated... be seated. Is all well in Bampton? No, of course not. Foolish question. You would not seek me was it so." The sheriff dropped his brick-like body into another chair, then continued. "How may I serve Lord Gilbert?"

I explained the cause of my visit, relating the death of Thomas atte Bridge, the destruction of Galen House, and my suspicion as to the felon who worked these evil deeds.

"Geoffrey Homersly, you say? Squire to Sir Simon? Don't know of the lad, but I see Sir Simon about often enough, and a youth accompanying him. Must be this Homersly. Sir John departed Oxford when I replaced him and now resides on his lands near Abingdon, so it is said. Thought Sir Simon might accompany his father... wish it was so. The man is naught but trouble."

I was eager to learn what difficulties Sir Simon might have created for the sheriff, but Sir Roger did not explain. "Has one ear lower than the other now, has Sir Simon," Sir Roger grinned. "That'd be your doing, I suspect."

"He should thank me he has two ears. Odo Grindecobbe nearly sliced the one from his skull. 'Tis not simple work to sew an ear back upon a man's head. I received no instruction on the technique in Paris."

"When he is not strutting about the town with his cronies Sir Simon resides at the Fox's Lair. The squire probably takes a room there as well. You know the place?"

"Aye."

"If the squire is guilty of the evils you suspect of him," Sir Roger continued, "he may resist being taken. And Sir Simon may assist the lad. He'll have no wish to make your life easy. Have you men with you to arrest the fellow?"

"Two grooms from Bampton Castle. Robust fellows. Arthur was with me here in Oxford last autumn."

"I remember the man. Would make a good sergeant.

The three of you could surely take one man, and him a youth, but if Sir Simon resists you, and has companions with him, the task might be beyond you. I'll assign two sergeants to accompany you. Come," he said as he arose from his chair, "I'll see to it."

Those in the clerk's anteroom who sought audience with Sir Roger looked up in dismay as he strode through the chamber. Before he could reach the door, Arthur and Uctred burst through it, saw me and the sheriff, and Arthur said, "Found 'im. Takes a room at an inn called 'The Fox's Lair'." Arthur, Uctred and I followed Sir Roger through a narrow passage, then down a stairway. A short way from the base of these steps Sir Roger pushed open another door. In this room several men sat alertly, in repose, but seemingly ready to be thrust into motion abruptly. Two of them were.

"John, Humphrey," Sir Roger addressed two of the sergeants. "Here is Master Hugh de Singleton, bailiff for Lord Gilbert Talbot at Bampton. He seeks a felon in Oxford. You will accompany him and his men, and arrest the miscreant should he attempt to flee."

John and Humphrey sprang to their feet as the sheriff spoke. They were men of considerable size, although should Geoffrey Homersly attempt to flee they seemed unlikely to overtake the youth in a foot-race. Such an eventuality would leave me to deal with the squire alone, for neither Arthur nor Uctred was likely to show a turn of speed either, and Homersly, was it him who burned Galen House, had already escaped Arthur. When the two sergeants approached I saw in their faces the marks of men accustomed to combat. One man wore a scar, long healed, across a cheek. The other owned a nose which had, at some time past, been broken and clumsily set, or not set at all. This beak turned down and to the left as it departed his brow. That both men seemed acquainted with conflict and were willing to see more reassured me.

"When you find this Homersly, bring him to the

castle. Being nigh the dungeon has a way of loosening a man's tongue," Sir Roger laughed.

The Fox's Lair is beyond the river from the castle, near to Rewley Abbey. I did take lodging there once, after Lord Gilbert made me bailiff. The bill convinced me that I must seek other lodging when in Oxford. To my good fortune Master Wyclif has offered a guest chamber at Canterbury Hall when such need arises.

The inn is larger than most, new-built but a few years past, on land outside the city walls, where other, more ancient structures would not cramp its bulk. It is constructed of timbers, the spaces between on the ground floor filled with brick, in the new fashion, the upper story of whitewashed wattle and daub. Four chimneys vent the many fireplaces. Glass closes all the windows. Sir Simon and his squire occupied a pleasant inn.

The entrance to the Fox's Lair is centered in the ground floor. The first story covers this entry, and gates there may be closed at night to bar entrance to the courtyard. The yard is bounded upon three sides by the inn, and the stables close it in the rear.

The porter peered out at us as we passed his closet. He stood, but a better look at the size and determined expressions of my companions apparently convinced him we should be permitted to pass unchallenged. I told one of the sergeants to wait at the gate, then entered the courtyard.

We were nearly across the enclosed yard of the inn when I saw a youth appear from a stall. He carried a bucket, which he took to the well, and when he had filled it, retraced his steps. I motioned to my escort and together we followed the youth into a darkened stable.

The lad had just finished pouring water into a trough when he glanced up and saw four shadows blocking the light at the entrance to the stall. Because our faces were in shadow he mistook who approached.

"Do you require your beast, Sir Simon? You did not

say… I would have had him readied but you spoke no word."

The youth spoke nervously, as if he feared displeasing Sir Simon. This, I knew, was not a difficult thing. I had done so easily. And Sir Simon's wrath was to be feared, especially so by a stable boy who had no great lord to protect him from the irascible Sir Simon, as had I.

"Oh," the lad said abruptly. He had stepped closer to the stall entry and saw it was not Sir Simon who stood before him. "Do you seek a horse, sir?" he said. "This beast belongs to Sir Simon Trillowe. The inn owns others you may employ be you lodging here."

The youth seemed slightly less fearful since he saw it was not Sir Simon who stood before him, but, although my slender form is not likely to cause unease in others, the three beefy men who stood behind me surely would.

"Sir Simon has a squire," I said. "Does the fellow also keep a horse in this stable?"

"Uh… aye."

"Two nights past," I asked, holding out a silver penny to the lad, "did Geoffrey Homersly require his horse?"

The stable boy peered over my shoulder into the yard, as if he sought assurance that no other man observed our conversation. When he was satisfied none took note of the interview, his hand grasped the coin, quick as a cat on a mouse.

"Aye," he whispered. "Gone all night."

"Did he say where it was he traveled?"

"Nay. Went off with Sir Simon an' come back at dawn."

With Sir Simon? I was dumbstruck. Would Sir Simon have aided the destruction of Galen House? Why not? He had no love for me.

The stable boy suddenly glanced over my shoulder, said, "I must be about my tasks," and picked up his bucket for another journey to the well.

As he set off a voice came from the yard. "Stephen, Sir

Simon wishes his horse made ready at the twelfth hour."

I turned and saw a well-made young man of about twenty years striding across the yard. It was clear he spoke to the stable boy, now hurrying to the well with his bucket. So this, I decided, is Geoffrey Homersly.

The squire was not so tall as me, but well formed. He had pale hair, like his mother. I recognized him, for six months past I had cleansed his wounds and soothed his bruises when he, along with Sir Simon, was attacked near the Oxford Northgate by men who thought they assaulted me and Arthur.

Homersly turned from the stable boy to observe me and my companions. I thought I saw a spark of recognition flash across his face, but perhaps not. He had seen me only once, so far as I knew, at the Augustinian Friars' infirmary, and was not in good health at the time.

"Geoffrey Homersly?" I asked, and strode toward the young man. My burley companions followed.

Sir Simon's squire looked to me with narrowed eyes. No doubt he wondered what I was about, emerging from the stall which housed Sir Simon's beast. "Aye. Do I know you?"

"In a manner of speaking. I patched you and Sir Simon last autumn, when men set upon you in the Canditch."

"You... you are Hugh de Singleton?" he said incredulously.

"Aye. Does my presence here surprise you?" I guessed my presence anywhere but St Beornwald's Churchyard would surprise him. "We must speak. There are unresolved matters..."

Before I could complete the words the squire bolted toward the gate. I set out in pursuit, but he had a head start and was fleet of foot. Arthur and the others lumbered after. A horse and cart appeared in the gate, the cart loaded with sacks of oats for the beasts of the stable. This vehicle so blocked the passage that the squire was forced to slow his pace and attempt to squeeze between cart and wall. A moment later the sergeant I had left at the gate, who saw our thundering approach, had Homersly by the arm.

I thought Sir Roger's advice wise. Castle walls are intimidating, especially so to those who fear they might be introduced to the gaoler do their answers to certain questions not satisfy.

I required of the sergeants that they keep Homersly in close restraint, and with me walking before and Arthur and Uctred behind we crossed Castle Mill Stream Bridge and entered the castle. I took the wide-eyed squire to the sheriff's anteroom, now cleared of all who sought audience with Sir Roger, and told the clerk to announce my return to the sheriff.

If there is a thing more intimidating than the cold stone walls of Oxford Castle, it is Sir Roger's brows when they unite in a frown. Such was his expression when he flung open the door to his chamber in response to his clerk's words. Geoffrey Homersly seemed to shrink from squire to the size of a page before my eyes.

"Is this the fellow?" Sir Roger barked. Without waiting for an answer he spoke to his sergeants. "Wait here." Then, to Homersly, "Master Hugh and I need answers from you… enter."

The sergeants released the squire with a shove which propelled him toward the door to Sir Roger's chamber. He staggered and would have fallen had not the door-frame been close for him to grasp and steady himself. When the sergeants released him they stood with folded arms. Homersly glanced from his place, gripping the doorpost, then entered the chamber, seemingly pleased to be released from the grip of the sergeants. They were men unaccustomed to treating miscreants gently.

I followed Homersly into the sheriff's chamber and Sir Roger slammed the door behind us. Still scowling, the sheriff pointed to a bench and with a nod of his head indicated that Homersly should sit. The youth seemed grateful to be able to do so.

"Where did you and Sir Simon go two nights past that you required your horses?" I began.

"Uh... two nights?"

"Aye. Why would you need horses past curfew?"

"You must be mistaken."

"Not so. I have good information that you and Sir Simon were gone the night, and did not return 'til dawn."

"Who says so?"

"No matter who, so long as his word is true."

"Mayhap it is not," the squire countered.

"Mayhap. But he who says so has no reason to deceive. You do."

"Why would I do so?" Homersly protested.

"Because you thought to do murder, and burned my house to perform the deed."

"Not so," he said with some heat.

"Was it not you who two nights past rode with Sir Simon to Bampton and threw a torch to the roof of my house?"

"Nay."

"Then tell Master Hugh where it was you went," Sir Roger growled.

"I did not enter Bampton," the squire insisted.

"I did not ask where you did not go," the sheriff replied with some menace. Homersly surely noted the tone. His face grew pale.

"I will send the sergeants to bring Sir Simon," Sir Roger announced. "It seems reasonable that since you left the inn together, and returned together, that you traveled through the night together as well. Perhaps Sir Simon will wish to tell us what you do not. No doubt, wherever you journeyed, Sir Simon will place blame for destroying Master Hugh's house upon you. Who is to be believed: a mere squire, or a knight?"

This introduced a new and unwelcome thought to Homersly. I saw his eyes flicker about the chamber, as if seeking some previously hidden means of escape. But there could be no flight from either the chamber or Sir Roger's suggestion.

"'Twas Sir Simon," the squire blurted.

"What?" I asked. "Sir Simon accompanied you?"

"Nay. 'Twas not that way. I accompanied Sir Simon."

"To Bampton?"

"Aye. Near so. Sir Simon stopped near a small chapel to the east of the town and bade me remain there with the horses. He went on afoot."

"How many journeys to Bampton in the night did you and Sir Simon make?" I asked.

"Three."

"What transpired on these nights?"

"The first two times Sir Simon ran back to my place and urged me to mount quickly, as did he, and we galloped away."

"Did he tell you what he intended?"

"Nay. Not 'til the third night."

"Two nights past?" Sir Roger asked.

"Aye. Sir Simon was in no hurry the third time when he returned to the chapel. When I asked if we were to be off he said, 'Nay,' and watched the sky over the town. Soon flames lit up the sky. This seemed to satisfy Sir Simon. He then instructed me to mount my horse and together we rode through the night back to Oxford."

"Did you ask Sir Simon what meant this glow in the night sky?"

"Aye, I did so. When we were well on our way from the town."

"What was his reply?"

"He laughed and said a lass who made sport of him would regret it, did she live."

"A lass?"

"Aye."

"So it was Sir Simon's plan to burn my house? Not yours?"

"Why would I wish to burn your house? I knew you only as the surgeon who bathed my wounds and stitched Sir Simon's cuts."

"Sir Simon did not tell you whose house he intended to set alight?"

"Nay."

"Do you remember Thomas atte Bridge?"

"Thomas who?"

"Atte Bridge."

Homersly was silent, thinking. "Nay," he finally replied. "Should I?"

"Your father hired him and a brother to plow some years past."

The squire shook his head. "I remember my father speaking of finding workers. Don't remember that he named 'em."

"Did he speak of their theft?"

"Ah... were they the thieves who made off with the calf?"

"Your father believes so."

"If he spoke their names, I do not remember."

"And you say 'twas Sir Simon's plan to set my home ablaze?"

"Aye."

"Why, again, would he do so?"

"His friends made sport of him, mocked him because a maid chose another, a bailiff, Sir Jocelin said, over him."

"So he wished to kill the lass?"

"I did not know his intent," Homersly pleaded. "I would not have accompanied him had he told me his plan."

"For a third visit? You did not ask what he was about the first two attempts?"

Homersly did not immediately respond. "Sir Simon does not appreciate questions from his inferiors," he finally said. "He says, 'Come,' and I come."

"We will see how he likes questions from his betters,"

Sir Roger said, then arose from his chair and approached the chamber door.

He opened it and called to the two sergeants who remained with Arthur and Uctred in the anteroom. "Return to the Fox's Lair and find Sir Simon Trillowe. Place him under arrest and bring him to me."

"He required the stable boy to have his horse ready at the twelfth hour," I added. "It is nearly that hour. If you make haste you will have him before he may depart the city."

"Take Master Hugh's men with you," the sheriff advised. Arthur and Uctred sprang to their feet and followed the sergeants from the room.

Sir Roger then spoke to his clerk. "Bring the warder."

To me he said, "We'll allow this squire to spend a few hours in the dungeon. Might serve to aid his memory and loosen his tongue, do we need more from him."

The warder must have been close by. He appeared nearly as soon as Sir Roger finished his explanation, and a moment later he dragged Homersly from the chamber. As the squire disappeared into the passageway he continued to object that the destruction of Galen House was none of his doing. I began to believe him, as did Sir Roger, I think, but there might be more knowledge to be prized from the fellow and some hours of contemplation in the stink of the dungeon might help bring it forth.

A castle valet appeared in the anteroom just then, and announced to Sir Roger that his supper awaited.

"Excellent. Master Hugh, you will join me. Perhaps when we are fed Sir Simon will have been found and will be awaiting examination."

Sir Roger's cook prepared an excellent meal. The sheriff's stout frame gave evidence that this was not uncommon. I was so sated after two removes that I could consume little of the third, and ignored the subtlety. Sir Roger noted, and asked if I was ill. It was nearly so, but this was not the cause of my failed appetite but the result of my eager consumption of the first two removes. I hoped the coming confrontation with Sir Simon would not add to my indigestion.

It did.

I followed Sir Roger into his clerk's anteroom and over his shoulder saw Arthur, Uctred, the two sergeants, and a furious Sir Simon Trillowe. I think at first he did not notice me, the sheriff being so constructed as to block the view of any behind him.

"What means this?" Sir Simon roared as he turned to face Sir Roger. I saw then the result of my surgery six months past. The scar upon his cheek was pale, no longer red and fierce, as are fresh wounds. His beard covered much of this blemish, but his left ear stood from the side of his head like a pennon in a gale. The fleshy organ was not lost to him, as I feared it might be when I sewed it to his head in the infirmary of the Augustinian Friars, but my needlecraft had left the appendage standing abruptly from his skull. He was no longer symmetrical. Rather than thank me for preserving his ear, I suspected he was irate at its appearance. This proved true.

Sir Simon should thank me for more than saving his ear. Pride is a great sin. With such an ear extending from the side of his head it will be difficult for the man to feel pride in his appearance. Of course hate is also a grievous sin. Perhaps my labor caused Sir Simon to exchange one sin for another.

Sir Roger strode to his chamber door without answering. It was then Sir Simon saw who it was who followed behind the sheriff. The knight's mouth opened and closed spasmodically, but no words came forth. Sir Simon surely believed me dead in the ashes of Galen House. Perhaps he thought he saw the ghost of the man he had burned alive.

Sir Roger opened his chamber door, nodded to Sir Simon and growled, "Enter." A man would no more argue with Sir Roger when he speaks so than with an alaunt snarling at his throat. Sir Simon glared at me, his surprise now become anger, and did as he was commanded. I followed.

Sir Roger seemed short of vocabulary. His next utterance was, "Sit." He pointed to the chair Geoffrey Homersly had recently occupied. I, having a fine command of language, knew to keep silent. Sir Simon remained standing, intimidated, but not cowed enough to place himself in an inferior position.

"What means this imposition?" he finally spluttered. "I'll see that my father learns of this."

"Your father," Sir Roger rejoined, "is busy convincing King Edward that he did not do fraud when he occupied this office."

Sir Simon made no reply.

"I am told you travel the roads of Oxfordshire at night. Where is it you go when good men lie abed?"

"Who says so?" Sir Simon snorted.

"Two who have no reason to deceive."

Again Sir Simon made no reply.

"Your silence means agreement, I think," Sir Roger growled. "And there is no need for you to tell us what you have been about. We," he nodded to me, "know all. Are you surprised to see Master Hugh standing here, fit and unburnt?"

Sir Simon glowered sullenly in my direction but I cared little for his black look. I would have accused him also but Sir Roger needed no assistance. I held my tongue and awaited a propitious moment.

The sheriff circled Sir Simon and peered intently at the knight's misshapen ear. "Do the maids approve of your new ear? You should thank Master Hugh you have two. Had I been he I'd have lopped it off and completed the job that abbey servant began."

Sir Simon's expression said clearly he did not agree.

"The King's Eyre will meet again in a fortnight. I think you will remain a guest here in the castle until the court decides what to do with you. Burning a man's house and attempting his life might be cause enough for the scaffold, I think."

Sir Simon had faced us haughtily until these words. I saw him blanch and unconsciously put a finger to his gentlemanly neck.

"Two weeks in the dungeon will give you leisure to consider your sins and prepare your soul to meet God. He may be more lenient than the judge. Lord Gilbert Talbot is a man of influence, and he sets great store by this bailiff of his, as I know. A word from him to the judges of the King's Eyre and their finding will not go well for you."

All this time Sir Simon made no protest of innocence. At the sheriff's last words I saw his Adam's apple bob as he gulped at the thought of Lord Gilbert's involvement in the matter. He had seen my employer shape the decision of a court once before.

"Describe your house in Bampton, Master Hugh. What was it this scoundrel burnt?"

"Galen House was two stories," I began, "of oaken timbers, wattle and daub. Two rooms below and two above, with a newly thatched roof. Had it been otherwise, were the reed old and rotting, this miscreant might not have succeeded in setting it alight so readily. And a new brick chimney also, with fireplaces above and below."

"Hmmm," Sir Roger pondered my description of the house. "The chimney may be of use. All else is ruin?"

"Aye."

"To rebuild such a house will cost… what would you say, Hugh? Eight pounds?"

I was about to agree, when Sir Roger continued before I could speak: "Nay. Should the chimney need to be pulled down 'twill be nine pounds or more, I think."

Sir Roger turned again to Sir Simon and lowered his brows in a scowl. He understood, I think, how effective the expression was. Sir Simon stared back at him, but arrogance was gone from his open-mouthed features.

"Ten pounds, I think," the sheriff said. "Bring to Master Hugh ten pounds so he may rebuild his house and I'll not charge you before the King's Eyre."

"I... I have not ten pounds," Sir Simon protested.

"Your father does. I will release you to his custody. Leave the castle, go to the inn, claim your horse, and ride to Abingdon. If you do not return by the ninth hour tomorrow with ten pounds I will send sergeants to convey you hither and you will see out the next fortnight in the dungeon."

Sir Roger spoke with conviction. I felt certain that there must have been in past months other disputes between the two knights which the sheriff now saw means to settle. If doing so rewarded me with ten pounds to rebuild Galen House, I was pleased to be of service.

"Then, after you place the coin in Master Hugh's hand you will leave Oxford and not return for a year... no, two years. Neither do I wish to learn that you have been seen about Bampton."

"But," Sir Simon stammered, "where am I to go?"

"I would make a suggestion," Sir Roger said balefully, "but those who go there are sent by a greater authority than mine. Now begone! Remember, tomorrow at the ninth hour, in this place, we will meet again."

Sir Simon gave me one more glance, fraught with hostility. If Sir Roger saw he did not comment. I thought then that I had not seen or heard the last of Sir Simon Trillowe. Even should he obey the sheriff's commands, two years would pass swiftly.

Sir Simon stalked from the chamber with as much dignity as he could muster, and when he was gone Sir Roger turned to me and grinned. The corners of his eyes crinkled beneath those massive brows, which I saw could express mirth as well as wrath, although in truth Sir Roger's brows are most capable when displaying choler.

"What of Geoffrey Homersly?" I asked when Sir Simon had departed.

"What is it you wish? You believe he had part in the

plot, or was he obedient to Sir Simon's demands?"

"Sir Simon is a hard man against those beneath him in rank," I suggested.

"Aye. A rabbit before his betters, a wolf to those inferior. What is your desire?"

"Leave him for a night in the dungeon, then tomorrow send him to his father in Cote. And tell him also he may not reside in Oxford for a year, nor set foot near Bampton. His father was recently injured and requires assistance on his manor. The youth will be well served doing useful work rather than following some rogue knight about Oxford."

"Very well. It will be done."

Chapter 14

T he night was again spent in my father-in-law's upper chamber. The evening was warm, so Caxton left open the windows. Any who violated curfew would have heard from the openings a quartet of snores, grunts, and snorts. I slept little, partly because of the racket, and partly because of thoughts I could not escape.

Sir Simon was the man who had plunged a dagger into my arm, and would have driven it through my back but for my good fortune. My supposition that these attempts upon my life were designed to bring an end to my search for Thomas atte Bridge's murderer was now proved wrong. Sir Simon knew nothing of Thomas atte Bridge, and from Geoffrey Homersly's testimony Sir Simon's wrath was turned against Kate as much as to me. I had come to Oxford convinced that Homersly was responsible for all. He was responsible for none.

I turned on my pallet and entertained more pleasant thoughts. I would soon return to Bampton with ten pounds in a pouch, enough to rebuild Galen House. Indeed, enough to build better than the house Sir Simon burnt.

Arthur, Uctred, and I consumed a leg of lamb and bowls of pease pottage at an inn on the Canditch for our dinner next day, then made our way to the castle. Several men awaited the sheriff's pleasure in the anteroom, but Sir Simon was not among them.

The clerk was instructed, I think, to notify Sir Roger when I arrived. So soon as I entered the chamber the man sprang to his feet and hurried to the door. Sir Roger appeared a moment later, ushering some petitioner from his presence. When the fellow had departed the sheriff motioned me to enter his chamber.

"I expect Sir Simon at any moment. If he arrives past the ninth hour he knows I'll see him in the dungeon."

"What if he does not return?" I asked.

"Then the devil take him... after I've done with him. He'll come."

"With ten pounds?"

"He is his father's youngest son, apple of his eye, 'tis said. Such a lad can do no wrong. Sir John will fume a bit, but he'll not withhold ten pounds if the sum will keep his lad from Oxford Castle dungeon, or a gallows."

"Would the King's Eyre send Sir Simon to the scaffold even though he failed to murder me and Kate?"

"Likely not. Sir John has displeased the king, to be sure, but he has yet some influence. Sir Simon knows this, but he does not know how much authority his father yet commands. Would you risk your neck on such an uncertainty? For ten pounds?"

The question required no answer, nor was there need for one. We heard voices in the anteroom and a moment later the clerk's face appeared at the door.

"Sir Simon Trillowe is arrived, sir," he announced.

Sir Roger opened the door between his chamber and the anteroom. Sir Simon stood stone-faced before the clerk. Behind him were two others. I recognized one: Sir Jocelin Hawkwode. Sir Jocelin had suffered some from his association with Sir Simon, but evidently not enough to cause him to end the relationship.

"You have Master Hugh's coin?" Sir Roger asked abruptly. Sir Simon took half a step back as the sheriff approached him.

"Aye," Sir Simon muttered, and produced a leather pouch of great size.

Sir Roger looked to his clerk. "Count it," he ordered. To Sir Simon and his cohorts he commanded, "Sit, 'til Master John has made sure the amount."

Sir Simon dropped the purse heavily upon the

clerk's table and sat sullenly while the clerk dumped the contents upon his board. I saw groats and pennies, some half-pennies, and golden gleams indicating Sir Simon had included many nobles in the heap.

Sir Roger and I stood while the clerk ordered the coins into piles, each with its like, then scratched upon parchment with his quill the number in each mound. He rubbed his chin, reviewed his count, then said, "'Tis two pence short, Sir Roger. Here is nine pounds, nineteen shillings, and ten pence."

The sheriff glared at Sir Simon as if the knight had robbed a widow of her last two farthings. Sir Simon turned to Sir Jocelin and muttered something I could not hear. Sir Jocelin reached for his purse, produced two pennies, and after peering up at Sir Roger to be sure his standing from his bench would not be taken amiss, quickly thrust the coins toward the clerk. Master John placed them with their brothers, then proceeded to count the piles again. There were sixty-two nobles, and perhaps four dozen groats. All else were pennies and half-pennies, with a few farthings. The coins made a considerable heap, gleaming dull silver and gold upon the table.

"Ten pounds," the clerk affirmed. Sir Roger, who had stood all the while with his arms folded across his chest, observing his clerk's work, turned to Sir Simon. "Two years. Do not be found in Oxford or near Bampton for two years. It will go hard for you should you defy me. Now, begone from Oxford before nightfall."

Sir Simon managed a weak scowl in my direction, but otherwise seemed eager to do the sheriff's bidding. He was immediately upon his feet and with Sir Jocelin and his other companion disappeared into the corridor beyond the anteroom. I heard their rapid footsteps fade as they descended the steps at the end of the passage which led to the ground floor and the castle yard.

"Come," Sir Roger said, and waved me before him into his chamber. From a window in that room we watched as the three knights entered the yard, took the reins of their horses from grooms, mounted, and spurred their beasts through the gatehouse into Great Bailey Street.

I was pleased to see Sir Simon's back disappear past the gatehouse, and hoped he would heed the sheriff's warning. Perhaps in two years' time his ire would cool and his companions no longer bait him regarding Kate and his misshapen ear. Mayhap he would discover some other lass, one who would not mind a jutting ear, overlooking the deformed appendage for his better qualities. Of these I was unaware, but there must be some, else Kate would not have one time considered the man. I must ask her some day. Then again, perhaps not.

We bid Sir Roger good day, and I took my leave of the sheriff with much thanks. The leather purse hung heavy from my hand, and attracted some attention as we walked the Canditch to Holywell Street and Caxton's shop. Arthur noted this scrutiny and when we arrived at the stationer's bid me wait there with Uctred while he retrieved our horses from the stable behind the Stag and Hounds.

"Seen too many folk eyin' the purse," he explained. "Won't do to have you about the streets. Even in day there be folk willin' to risk their neck for a takin' like that."

I thought Arthur's advice of merit, and while he was gone asked my father-in-law for a length of cord. This I tied under my cotehardie and fastened the purse there, hidden. I appeared then as a young man too much given to his trencher, but when I was seated upon Bruce the bulge would be little noted.

June days are long. The afternoon sun warmed my face as our beasts passed Osney Abbey, but we would reach Bampton before night fell. I was somewhat relieved for this, for although we were three men armed with daggers it would yet be well to be off the roads before darkness overtook us. Several times I turned in my saddle, uneasy that some miscreant might have seen my pouch and collected a band of ruffians and be even now in pursuit.

But not so. We met few men upon the road, and none caught us up. Perhaps the lack of travelers was due to the season. Soon after we passed Osney Abbey we saw families at work haymaking, singing at their labor. Men had swung their long-handled scythes since dawn, and were surely weary, but warm, sunny days must not be lost. Behind their husbands and fathers women and children followed, prodding and turning the hay with forked sticks so it might dry evenly.

There is no rest for tenants and villeins. When the meadows have been cut 'twill then be time to shear the sheep and plow fallow fields once more.

Fatigue etched men's faces as they swung the scythes, but there was joy there also. Rains had been plentiful, but not so much as to rot the hay in the fields. If there was no deluge until the hay was dried and stacked there would be abundant winter fodder. More beasts might be kept this next winter, for fresh meat come the lean days of April and May. No wonder the laborers smiled as they toiled.

Shortly after the twelfth hour we crossed Shill Brook and turned our horses into the Bampton Castle forecourt. Kate, sitting upon a bench in the sun, awaited me there and was ready with questions of how matters stood with Geoffrey Homersly.

I dismissed Arthur and Uctred, told them to see the horses to the marshalsea, and instructed Arthur to seek the cook and tell him Kate and I required a light supper in our chamber.

While we supped on slices of cold mutton, bread, cheese, and ale, I told Kate of events in Oxford and placed before her Sir Simon's purse. She stared at it with troubled expression.

"'Twas he, then, who stabbed you," she said, glancing to my arm.

"Aye. And this eve you have more work. The wound has healed and 'tis time to cut the stitches free."

"You suffer no more discomfort?"

"None."

"It was me Sir Simon wished to slay, was it not?"

"Both of us, I think."

"But I rejected his suit and made of him a laughing-stock before his companions."

"And it was I who won you from him. He had ample reason to resent both of us. No matter; Sir Roger has ordered him from Oxford for two years, nor is he to come near Bampton."

"Will he obey?"

Kate's lovely face was clouded with concern. The sheriff's commands did not bring her much comfort.

"Sir Roger threatened the scaffold did he disobey."

At this the lines upon Kate's brow relaxed. She softened more at my next words.

"Tomorrow I will seek Peter Carpenter and Warin Mason and make plans to rebuild Galen House. There is enough coin there," I nodded to the purse, "to build a house with a fireplace in each room and chimneys at either end."

"That will be well," she smiled. "Our babe will be born in November, when winter will be nearly upon us."

We had nearly finished our meal when Kate spoke again. "What will you now do in the matter of Thomas atte Bridge?"

I had asked myself the same question since speaking with Geoffrey Homersly. I had no good answer.

"Many men had cause to wish him harm, but when I seek to assign the death to one or another I find reason to exonerate rather than blame."

"Is that what you seek?"

"What I seek?"

"Aye. Do you seek guilt of some men, as Geoffrey Homersly, but innocence of others? What a man seeks, I think, he will often find."

"I cannot tell," I admitted. "There are men who, are they guilty of murder, I would rather not know of it, and others, did they slay Thomas atte Bridge, I would have little distress for their penalty."

"Such are my thoughts," Kate admitted.

"I have no strategy whereby I might find a murderer," I sighed. "I intend to set myself to rebuilding Galen House, which thing I can do, and dismiss the death of Thomas atte Bridge. The matter has vexed me long enough. Mayhap, in time, some new clue will appear, or some guilty man will let his tongue slip."

"If that does not happen," Kate asked, "will you be content to leave the matter unresolved?"

"I do not know of all the mischief Thomas atte Bridge did in his life. What I do know is vile enough. Perhaps his death was justice for some evil he did, and if I found who took his life, and hallmote or the King's Eyre send the man to the scaffold, that would be the greater injustice."

"Do you say this because you believe it so, or to salve your pride that you have not found what you sought?"

"I do not know," I replied. "I do know that my wound has been stitched long enough." I arose from my place at table, brought forth scissors and tweezers from my instruments chest, doffed cotehardie and kirtle, and set my arm before Kate. She snipped the sutures with as much skill as she had employed creating them, and I thought then she might make a fine assistant. Mayhap I should instruct her in some rudimentary surgical practice so if some man injures himself while I am distant she might offer aid until I return.

I woke early next day, before the Angelus Bell or the poulterer's rooster could summon other castle folk from their beds. I had dreamt of beams and bricks and rooftops, and was eager to spend Sir Simon Trillowe's purse on a new Galen House.

I sought first Peter Carpenter. He walked with me to the pile of cold ashes which had been Galen House, and I explained to him what I wished him to build. I would have a house somewhat larger than Galen House had been, of posts and beams. The spaces between timbers on the ground floor I would have filled with bricks, in the new style. For the upper floor, wattle and daub, whitewashed, would suit. I would have two windows, of glass, in each room, and Warin Mason I would have build another chimney to match the one which yet stood sentinel over the acrid stink of what once was my home.

"And for the roof," I concluded, "I will have tile."

"No more will a man set thatch alight and burn your house, eh?" Peter agreed.

"Nay. Does some felon seek my life in future, he will need to devise some new way."

Peter told me he would assemble workmen and set to work with his horse and cart hauling away the debris this very day, as he had few other obligations before him. I next called upon Warin Mason and found him hoeing weeds from cabbages in his toft. I told him of the brickwork I wished him to do, and the fellow seemed pleased to leave the hoe to wife and children and set his hand to masonry.

No tilers reside in Bampton. I thought Warin might know of such a man in some greater town. He did, and promised to send for the fellow.

I took dinner in the castle and while we ate I told Kate of my plans. She seemed much pleased at the new house I described. Glass windows particularly caused her cheeks to glow and her eyes to sparkle. I entertained a brief worry that my plans might be beyond Sir Simon's contribution, but I could not disappoint Kate after making much of her forthcoming residence.

Late in the day I sought a groom of the marshalsea, ordered Bruce made ready, and set off for Alvescot. I found Gerard limping about his wood yard, where were stored beams and poles cut from Lord Gilbert's forest.

"You'll want elm for the beams what'll be upon the ground," Gerard said when I told him of my plans. "Oak an' beech'll do well for the others. Tiles is heavier than thatch, so for rafters you'll need stout poles. I got enough, I think, dryin' in the shed there."

I left the verderer with the understanding that Peter Carpenter would soon call upon him with a list of the timbers needed. Gerard assured me that the wood yard held all Peter would need, and a few glances about the place in the fading evening light told me he spoke true.

Bruce had carried me near to Bampton when I saw, a great way ahead of me, a figure standing in darkening shadows beside the road. As I approached I saw that a man was flinging something about at Cow-Leys Corner. The fellow glanced up from his work, saw me while I was yet far off, and immediately fled. Bruce lumbered up to the place where the man had been busy and I reined him to a halt, curious about what I had seen. From atop the horse my eyes discerned nothing of interest, but surely there must be something here, I thought, else why the fellow's actions and hasty departure when he discovered he was seen?

I dismounted and searched among the foliage at the verge. The place, I noted, was where Thomas atte Bridge had been buried near two months past. And then I found what had been cast about the grave.

Entrails lay scattered there, near to the wall which enclosed Lord Gilbert's meadow. I could not identify the beast from which the guts had been torn, but surmised a goat had perished so the ritual I had observed from a distance could take place. Many believe that spirits will not rise in the dark of night to vex the living if the entrails of a goat be strewn about the burial place.

Was there some man of Bampton who feared the ghost of Thomas atte Bridge? Why else undertake to keep his spirit below the sod? Who might so fear a ghost? The murderer? I mounted Bruce and prodded him into motion with a conviction I had seen a thing which might lead me to a felon.

I dismounted at the castle gatehouse and sought Wilfred the porter. He appeared at the sound of Bruce's great hooves against the cobbles, somewhat surprised at my halt at that place.

"Have you seen a man approach Mill Street from Cow-Leys Corner?" I asked. "He was in haste," I added.

Wilfred scratched his balding pate and peered beyond me into the dusk. "Seen folk about, but none as was in a hurry," he replied.

"Were any of these traveling alone? Did you note where they went?"

Wilfred chewed his lip in thought before he replied. "Two was alone. They went on past the castle. That's the last I seen of 'em. Mill Street can't be seen from the gatehouse once folk near Shill Brook," he explained.

Nor can an observer at the castle gatehouse observe those who might turn away from Mill Street to enter the Weald. I began to think I might guess who it was I had seen at Cow-Leys Corner. The fellow had waited 'til near dark, the better to complete his errand unseen, yet early enough that John the beadle would not yet be about the streets of Bampton to enforce curfew. And if the man entered the Weald John would not see him, for the beadle's duty lay only in Bampton. The vicars of the Church of St Beornwald, as representatives of the Bishop of Exeter, have responsibility for enforcing curfew in the Weald, a thing which neither they nor any other men trouble themselves to do.

I sent Bruce to the marshalsea with the porter's assistant, advised Wilfred that I might return late, and set off for the Weald. Behind me I heard Wilfred cranking down the portcullis.

If it was Edmund Smith I saw scattering entrails about Thomas atte Bridge's grave, I wondered where he might have found a goat. Wealthier tenants of Lord Gilbert and the bishop possess a few sheep, and some own goats. I did not think Emma in such company, and before the smith wed her he owned nothing but a few hens.

I walked in the dark to the end of the path and Arnulf Mannyng's house. A faint gleam through the skins of his windows told that the family had not yet sought their beds. No man wishes to hear pounding upon his door at such a time, but I was impatient to learn the reason for what I had seen at Cow-Leys Corner.

I rapped upon Mannyng's door and shouted my name to ease the fellow's mind about who his late visitor might be. A moment later I heard him raise the bar and lift the latch.

I did not seek Arnulf Mannyng because I thought him the man I had seen at Cow-Leys Corner. Rather, I thought he might know who in the Weald possessed goats.

I apologized for disturbing the peace of his evening, then asked about goats. Mannyng stared at me for a moment, then invited me into his cottage and shut the door behind me.

"Why do you ask of goats?" he said. A cresset upon his table provided enough light that I could see a puzzled expression upon his face.

I did not wish for Arnulf, or any other man, to know yet what I had seen along the road. "Have any in the Weald who own goats seen one go missing?" I asked next.

"Strange you ask," Mannyng replied. "We began shearing the wethers today. I keep six goats with the sheep, but this day I found but five. No sign of the other. Thought it'd run off, or got took by some wild hound."

"It was killed, I think."

"A hound?"

"Nay, a man."

"Who?" Mannyng asked indignantly.

"I am yet uncertain."

"But you have suspicion?"

"Aye."

I bid Arnulf good eve, and walked north in the dark toward Mill Street until I stood in the path before the hut of Edmund and Emma.

I was about to put my knuckles to the door, then reconsidered. I am no coward, but neither am I a fool. No man knew where I had gone this night, or to what purpose. Was Edmund the man I had seen at Cow-Leys Corner, and he took amiss my interest in his business there, he might employ those muscular arms to silence me. Edmund has the heart of a cur in the body of a bull.

I have heard it said that the man who fears God need fear no man. That may be so, but I did wish to live to become a father. I set off silently for Mill Street.

Next morn, after Kate and I broke our fast, I sought Arthur, and with him to help draw explanation from Edmund, walked again to the Weald. Emma answered my knock and told me that Edmund was at work this day at his forge. Arthur and I retraced our steps to Mill Street, crossed Shill Brook, and found Edmund pumping his bellows over new-lit coals.

The day promised warmth, and already sweat stood upon Edmund's brow and lip from his effort at the bellows. He glanced up at our approach, then resumed pumping, as if to say without words that his work was more important than any matter concerning me. Arthur recognized the slight and scowled at the smith's back.

A smith cannot pump air to his coals forever. He must eventually set about his work. Edmund's hammer lay upon a table, aside his anvil. I walked to it and picked it up. He would answer my questions before I returned the hammer to him, else he would accomplish no business this day.

Edmund saw me lift the hammer but continued at his bellows for some time, until the blaze was white with heat and even Arthur and I felt beads of sweat upon our brows. The smith finally ceased his pumping, folded his smoky, sweaty arms across his chest and glared at me. We had disagreed about his conduct in the past, so I did not expect a cheerful welcome, but the scowl now leveled at me bespoke more than a year-old dispute. So I thought.

"What have you done with Arnulf's goat? You needed only the entrails to cast on Thomas atte Bridge's grave."

Edmund blanched. His face went from red with heat and exertion to white in a heartbeat. His words denied my accusation, but his visage said otherwise.

"Goat? Whose?" he protested. "I've no man's goat."

"You discarded the flesh after cutting free the entrails? A terrible waste."

"Don't know what you speak of," he protested, seeming to gather his wits.

"Perhaps we should inspect your house, to see if there be some carcass there upon a spit. Mayhap Emma will remember if you left her last eve for a time, just before curfew."

"You got no bailiwick in the Weald," Edmund spluttered.

"True, but you are a tenant of Lord Gilbert, and I saw you last eve casting the entrails of some beast – a goat, I think – over Thomas atte Bridge's grave, which lies upon Lord Gilbert's land at Cow-Leys Corner. I suspect the vicars of St Beornwald's Church will not take offense if I do their work and find a thief and murderer in the Weald."

My words were not entirely true. I had seen a man at Cow-Leys Corner. This may have been Edmund, or mayhap not. I thought to show the smith confidence that I knew him to be the man and see what was his response.

"I'm no murderer," Edmund protested, and cast his eyes about as if seeking some unremembered place in his forge where he might hide. There was no escape, for Arthur and I blocked the entrance. Arthur does better at obstructing a door than do I, but together the smith would not get past us. And I yet held his hammer.

"No murderer? But a thief. If one, why not the other?"

Edmund's shoulder slumped, and he leaned against his anvil as if likely to topple over without its support.

"He torments me, does Thomas."

"Thomas atte Bridge?" I replied. I was confused. Atte Bridge was two months dead. How could he vex another?

"Aye," the smith mumbled. "Comes in the night, when all others be sleepin', an' wakes me."

"Why? What does he wish? To trouble the man who took his life from him?"

"Nay. I'm no murderer. 'E was plowin' Emma's furrow before 'e died. When I was to wed Emma she told me of it. Thomas was dead an' gone then, and naught but Maud to protest did I seize the land what Thomas took."

"Maud protested?"

"Aye. To me an' Emma. Not to the vicars, 'cause she knew I was right an' the land Thomas was takin' was Emma's."

"Maud and Emma had words about this?"

"Aye, but not after we was wed. Didn't argue with 'er, just took back what was Emma's."

"And now Thomas afflicts you in the night?"

"Aye. Tells me I'll soon join 'im do I not give over them furrows 'e took from Emma."

"You cast the guts of Arnulf Mannyng's goat upon his grave."

"Aye," Edmund reluctantly agreed. "'Eard tell that'll keep spirits in their grave."

"Did it? Last night did Thomas afflict you again?"

The smith brightened. "Nay. Worked well, as folk do say."

"Thomas did not rise from his grave to trouble you because you took his life?"

Edmund blanched again. "Nay. Never murdered no man."

I believed him, and did I not I had no way to prove otherwise. But I would see justice done in the matter of Arnulf Mannyng's goat.

"You will pay Arnulf a shilling for his goat."

"A shilling?" Edmund complained. "Was worth no more than ten pence."

"A thief cannot bid the value of his plunder. A shilling, and you will pay the debt before hallmote or I will have you up on charges. Then you will pay a fine to Lord Gilbert as well."

The smith's shoulders dropped again in submission. I had made no friend here, nor had I discovered a murderer, as I thought I might. Edmund Smith had been no friend before this day, so I was forfeit nothing, and whoso hung Thomas atte Bridge at Cow-Leys Corner was no more unknown to me than when the day began. I had discovered the theft of a goat, so I could boast of some small achievement.

Next day was Sunday. Kate was pleased to see, as we walked to the church past the site of Galen House, that Peter Carpenter had seen to clearing the place of burnt timbers and ash, and Gerard had supplied the first cart-load of elm timbers with which Peter and his crew might begin raising a new house. All that remained at the site was some blackened earth and my new brick chimney.

There was much work for me in the next days. I must see to the shearing of Lord Gilbert's sheep and the sale of the wool, and it was time for the last plowing of Lord Gilbert's fallow fields. Villeins who owed week-work I set to these tasks. This did not please them, as they had their own labors to complete, but such is the way of the world and my work. I must persuade folk to do things they would wish to avoid, whether this be laboring upon their lord's demesne or suffering me to repair their injuries and wounds. Both oft require pain from those to whom I must direct my toil.

At least once each day I made time to observe Peter Carpenter's progress. On Tuesday he brought another load of timbers from Alvescot, and late in the week two carts loaded with bricks came from the kiln at Witney. Two more cart-loads, Peter said, and Warin would have enough to build a second chimney and fill the spaces between the timbers he was raising.

I watched the carpenter wield his mallet and chisel to cut a tenon and rubbed my arm where Sir Simon had pierced me. To think that I had once considered that Peter might have delivered the blow with a chisel. There is no more amicable man in Bampton, I thought.

He spoke fondly of his daughter's child. Jane's babe, he said, was strong. He was placed with the cooper's wife, who had a babe of her own to nurse. Peter seemed not to wish to speak more of the child, which I understood, considering how the infant had come to be. The part of the babe that was Jane would be loved; the part that was Thomas atte Bridge would be despised. It would have been easier, I think, for Peter and his wife to have accepted a lass. I hoped, for the sake of the child, that as he grew he would resemble his mother in character rather than his father.

By St Botolf's Day Peter had erected scaffolds and with his assistants and apprentice was at work raising posts and beams for the upper story of the new Galen House. Beneath the poles and planks of the scaffolding Warin was at work with mortar and trowel, filling in the walls with layers of red-brown bricks. I found myself drawn to Church View Street several times each day, to monitor progress and watch as craftsmen put together a fine house from wood and clay.

Chapter 15

One afternoon I stood in the toft watching Peter and his apprentice hoist a beam from ground to scaffold. This timber was heavy, hewn square, six paces or more long, and thick through as a large man's hand from fingers to wrist. The weight of two men and the beam proved too much for one of the poles supporting the scaffold. It bent under the weight. I saw it begin to bow and shouted to the men to look to their safety. They did so, but not before the pole snapped. Three poles yet supported the scaffold, and Peter and the apprentice seized two of these and so were spared a fall which might have required my services to repair their injuries. They had released the beam when I cried a warning. It thudded to the earth, doing no harm.

Peter clambered down from his perch, thanked me for advising him of danger, scratched his head while he inspected the fractured pole, then set to work raising another so the scaffold might be made whole and he might continue his work.

I watched as Peter selected a solid pole from the stack Gerard had delivered for rafters and set it in place of the splintered shaft. When it was in place he instructed his apprentice, a slender youth whose wiry form was more suited to the work, to mount the scaffold and secure the plank to the new post with a length of hempen cord wrapped thickly about both pole and plank.

Hempen cord. I was not pleased with the thought which then came to me. It had not occurred to me that a carpenter might have use for hempen cord.

My enthusiasm for observing the rebuilding of Galen House withered with this discovery. I left the site and walked slowly to the castle, considering the import, or coincidence, of what I had learned. I was distressed at what it might portend, but could not allow the revelation to pass unexplained.

I kept my own counsel for the next hours, but as dusk darkened the window of our chamber I told Kate what I had seen.

"Many craftsmen may find need of rope in their work," she advised. "You said such cord was common."

"Aye, I did, but a common thing in the hands of a man wronged by another may be put to uncommon purpose."

"You believe the carpenter capable of such cunning, doing murder made to seem suicide?"

"Do you think me capable of such a thing?"

"Nay," Kate replied with some heat. "Why do you ask?"

"I am not a father... not yet," I added, responding to Kate's smile. "But when I think of the injury Thomas atte Bridge did to Peter, and consider what vengeance I might seek should our babe be a lass, and some felon deal with her as Thomas did with Jane, then I am no longer certain of Peter's peaceable nature."

"You could slay a man who did harm to a daughter?"

"If no other penalty seemed in store for the man."

"You believe all men be of such a mind?"

"I do."

"What will you do?"

"I will go to our bed. Mayhap a new day will offer new counsel."

It did not. Sleep was elusive. It came reluctantly and departed eagerly. I arose from our bed in a sour mood, which Kate saw and so busied herself about our chamber wordlessly. A kitchen servant brought a loaf and pot of ale, and when I had broken my fast I felt ready to face my duty. I made ready to depart the castle and Kate finally spoke.

"What will you do?"

"I intend to seek first Father Simon. I have two questions for him which will go some way to resolving this business, I think."

"I pray you succeed," she replied.

"Best pray I do not," I answered wryly.

Father Simon's clerk responded to my knock on the vicarage door and admitted me to the house. The rotund priest soon appeared, puzzled, I think, by my early appearance and black visage.

"Good day, Master Hugh. How may I serve you?"

"Two questions, then I will depart and trouble you with the business of Thomas atte Bridge no more."

"Atte Bridge? I've heard nothing of that matter for many weeks. Thought you'd given up pursuit of a felon an' laid the death to suicide."

"I gave up quest for a murderer several times. But each time I did so some new matter arose to restore my interest. I never thought Thomas did away with himself, nor do I now."

"And you seek me now because some new evidence presents itself?"

"Aye. The hempen cord your clerk purchased to fashion your new belt, whence did it come?"

"Many in the town grow hemp, soak the stems in Shill Brook, and wind the fibers into rope," the priest replied.

"This is so, but not all hempen cord sold in Bampton is missing a length which matches the span of rope used to hang a man."

Father Simon made no reply, hoping, I think, that I would give over my questions and depart. I did not.

"Peter Carpenter," he said finally. "But you should not assume the carpenter guilty of such a felony. Others may have known the unused cord was in my shed and snipped off a length."

"Did Peter know you kept the unused coil in the shed?"

"Don't know. Robert made the purchase of Peter. You

might ask him."

"I may. I have another question for you. Does Peter confess his sins to you, and seek absolution, or does he confess to Father Thomas or Father Ralph?"

"You know I cannot reveal what is said in confession," Father Simon said indignantly.

"I do not ask you to do so. I ask only if Peter confessed to you, or to another."

"I cannot say," the vicar said firmly, and folded his arms across his belly as if punctuating his denial.

"Very well," I replied. "Your answer is helpful."

The priest's brows lifted at this, but I saw no need to enlighten him. He had told me a valuable thing but knew not he had done so.

Had Peter Carpenter confessed to Father Thomas or Father Ralph, Father Simon would, I think, have had no reluctance to tell me he had not heard of the man's sins. Since he refused to answer when I asked, I was sure it was Father Simon who had heard Peter's confession. If this was a confession of murder, the knowledge would explain why he tried to deflect my suspicion from John Kellet and save me a fruitless journey to Exeter.

Or perhaps he feared that I might construe some evidence against Kellet which would see the man punished again, this time for a thing he did not do, and of which Father Simon knew him to be innocent.

I walked north from the vicarage, past the bishop's new tithe barn, and watched as John Prudhomme directed the folding of new-shorn sheep on to demesne lands. He saw me and waved cheerily, but I had no heart for gladsome reply.

All I suspected might be coincidence. I hoped it was so, but I was not satisfied with uncertainty. I wandered the town until dinner, considering and disposing of methods whereby I might find truth, and above all fearing what knowledge of the truth might cost me, the town, and Peter Carpenter.

Kate saw my solemn demeanor at dinner and divined the cause. She did not ask of me what I had learned from Father Simon, but guessed it was unsettling. When we were alone in our chamber she asked of me what news, and I told her.

"The priest speaks true that many folk cultivate hemp and flax for rope and flaxen yarn," she said. "Some have plenty and enough to sell."

"But do they sell a length of cord which matches the rope found about Thomas atte Bridge's neck, when joined together with the cord coiled in Father Simon's shed?"

"Why would Peter seek cord in Father Simon's shed if he had of his own enough to sell?"

"There has been little employment for carpenters since the plague," I reasoned. "Perhaps he needed money and sold unneeded possessions to find it."

"Mayhap," Kate mused, "but he has rope now, you say, to fasten scaffold together."

"And he has fifteen shillings I gave him as early payment, so he might hire laborers and begin the work. Enough cord to build his scaffold would cost little more than a penny."

"How will you discover if Peter hanged Thomas at Cow-Leys Corner," she asked, "and what will you do if it be so?"

"I do not yet know... on both counts."

I could not stay away from Church View Street, no matter who it was who assembled my new home. I left Kate stitching a new kirtle for her enlarging form and set out.

Peter, his apprentice, and two laborers had nearly completed setting posts and beams for the upper story. One worker, a poor cotter whose family was large and whose lands were few, was at work fitting wattles between posts. Warin had nearly completed brickwork upon the ground floor and would soon set to work upon the second chimney.

Peter Carpenter glanced down from his perch above

me on the scaffold, acknowledged my presence with a nod, then returned to his labor. The man had wife, children, and now grandchild to provide for. What poverty would come to them if I found Peter had indeed slain Thomas atte Bridge? But what guilt would I incur against my soul did I learn of a certainty of Peter's guilt and allow the crime to go unpunished? Or was it a crime? Perhaps it was justice, wrongly discharged.

I felt drawn to the hempen cords which bound the scaffold together. Without considering why I did so, I drifted close to the framework and unthinkingly fingered a length of the brown cord, as if touch could tell me whence it came and what it knew.

The hemp remained silent. From the base of the scaffold I raised my eyes again to the place where Peter and his apprentice were driving home a tree nail to fix a beam in place. Peter swung his mallet a last time, wiped sweat from his brow, and glanced down through the lattice of the scaffold to see me examining the hempen cord and studying him.

Some unaccountable recognition flickered between us. I knew then from the look in his eyes what Peter had done, and he saw that I knew. He stared at me, sighed heavily, then turned back to his work.

Peter's oldest child, now Jane was gone, was a lad of twelve or so years. I saw then how Thomas atte Bridge might have met his end.

I suspect Peter was lurking about Thomas's hut, seeking how he might avenge his daughter, when he saw in the moonlight John Kellet enter atte Bridge's toft and harry the hens roosting there. He saw Thomas respond to the troubled hens, watched as Kellet and atte Bridge spoke, and perhaps was close by to hear what was said.

Next eve, when all was dark and quiet in the Weald, Peter and his lad tried the same ruse, disturbing Thomas's hens until the noise once more drew him to his toft. Perhaps atte Bridge expected to find John Kellet there again. But instead Thomas saw a shadow approach and from out of the dark came a blow which laid him insensible in the mud.

Peter then bound atte Bridge's wrists and ankles, and perhaps crammed a wad of fabric in his mouth should he wake from the blow. Then with his lad Peter carried his victim from the Weald toward Cow-Leys Corner. Mayhap Thomas regained his senses while carried thus, and struggled, so that the child lost grip on his ankles and there were then two grooves made in the road; these ruts Kate and I found next morn, and also mud from the road on the back of the doomed man's heels. Perchance Peter delivered another blow to quiet Thomas before continuing to Cow-Leys Corner.

But what of the stool? How would Peter have come by that object? He traveled the Weald to appraise Philip Mannyng's shattered door. Perhaps as he passed he saw Maud sitting at her door, working at some task in the sun, and later made off with the stool she sat upon when she left it. Might he have even then had use in mind for it? Who can know?

Peter, the apprentice, and the laborers continued their work, stretching wattles between posts to make ready for the plaster. I lost interest in the business and departed the toft. As I set foot on Church View Street I saw and heard a large cart approach, drawn by two horses. I stopped to see what this conveyance was about and watched as a man atop its load pulled upon the traces and halted his beasts before Galen House.

"Where's the carpenter?" he asked.

"He is at the rear of the house, framing wattles."

"Peter requires these tiles an' here they are. Not ready yet for 'em, I see," the tiler said with a glance at the empty sky where ridgepole and rafters should soon be placed.

"Need another load anyway. We'll just leave this lot in the toft an' return next week with more. Wat," he called to his apprentice, "lead the 'orses 'round back an' stack the tiles. I'll be there shortly. Good worker," the tiler said to me, with a nod to his apprentice, "but bull-headed."

"So long as he lays a roof which keeps me dry, his disposition is of no concern."

"He'll do that well enough. I'll see to it. Got to return to Witney, so best help the lad."

The tiler touched his cap with a finger and hastened off in the track of his cart. I set off for the castle, where I hoped a few circles of the parapet would clear my mind and set me toward my duty, when I decided where my duty lay.

I had made one circuit of the castle wall and leaned against a merlon, staring at the forest which hid Cow-Leys Corner from view, when I heard Kate call up to me from the castle yard. Her expression indicated peevishness that I had returned and not told her of it. She strode to the gatehouse and a moment later appeared on the parapet.

"What news?" she asked breathlessly. Climbing the circular stairs of the gatehouse was becoming more of a task for her as her belly grew.

"I have no evidence to charge a man before the King's Eyre," I replied.

"But you know the truth of Thomas atte Bridge's death all the same," she asserted, reading my unspoken thoughts.

"Aye, so I believe."

I told Kate then of what I had seen in the hour past. She looked away as I spoke, and together we studied the Ladywell and Lord Gilbert's millpond beyond.

"Will you seek more proofs against the carpenter?"

I could not answer, for I did not know.

"Mayhap he is innocent," Kate brightened, "and you will be spared dealing with him... or if you charge him before the king's judges a jury may discharge him."

"I wish he was guiltless, but of all men he had best cause to slay Thomas atte Bridge, and because he is not a practiced miscreant he could not hide his guilt when I looked him in the eye an hour past."

"The town needs a carpenter," Kate added softly.

"Aye, there is that."

"And Peter is not likely to slay any other. It does not seem to be his nature."

"Nay," I agreed. "He has always been a peaceable sort, since I came to Bampton. But might a man who has succeeded in murdering a foe, and escaping penalty, find it less irksome should the desire again arise to eliminate an adversary?"

Kate made no reply, nor could I answer my own question. We stood thus for some time, until we heard below us Wilfred closing the castle gate and cranking down the portcullis. Kate then took my arm and drew me silently from the parapet to the stairs and our chamber. "Sufficient unto the day is the evil thereof," so says Holy Writ. I had experienced enough evil this day. I would seek my bed and await the evils of another day.

I placed my feet upon the cool flags of our chamber floor next morn before the Angelus Bell ceased ringing from the tower of the Church of St Beornwald. I had resolved in the night to seek the carpenter and confront him with my suspicion against him, so departed the castle before even breaking my fast. The task before me was onerous and I wished it over and done so soon as possible.

Peter's apprentice, the laborers, and Warin were at their work, but Peter was absent. I watched the apprentice busy himself with placing wattles while he occasionally glanced to the street to see was his employer arrived. He soon tired of this, left the workmen to the task, and clambered down from the scaffold.

"Peter seemed unwell when we quit work yesterday," the apprentice said. "I'm off to Rosemary Lane to see is he ill."

I circled the structure to where Warin was placing bricks and his apprentice mixing mortar. From this place a few moments later I saw Peter's apprentice appear at a run from two hundred paces down Church View Street.

The youth skidded to a stop before me and breathlessly gasped a single word: "Gone."

"Who?" I asked stupidly.

"Peter, an' all his household."

"His house is empty?"

"Aye. None there. Goods is gone, tools an' such. Horse an' cart, as well."

Before the lad finished his declaration I set off apace for Rosemary Lane. There I found Peter Carpenter's house and yard as the apprentice said, all abandoned.

I entered the empty house. No chests or pots remained. Tools were absent from Peter's workshop, and the crude shed which had sheltered his horse and cart was vacant. Peter had fled in the night, loading possessions upon his cart and slipping away while the town slept, after the beadle had completed his rounds.

I returned dolefully to Galen House. The apprentice stood where I had left him, open-mouthed.

"Are you competent to complete the work Peter has begun," I asked him plainly, "or must I seek another?"

"Uh, aye," he stammered. "But what has become of Peter?"

"He has fled the town."

"But why so?"

"I am uncertain," I lied. May the Lord Christ absolve me of this sin. "Go this day to Alvescot and tell Gerard the verderer what you need in the way of roof-tree and rafters to complete my house. Then carry on as before. I will pay you what you are due. The tiler promised soon to bring another load of tiles and I wish the rafters ready when he comes."

The apprentice nodded and immediately set off afoot for Alvescot. No matter, he may ride back on Gerard's cart with the timber and rafters.

From Galen House I walked to Father Simon's vicarage and announced my presence with vigorous thumping upon the door. The clerk soon appeared, recognized by my scowl that some grave matter troubled me, and hastened to announce my presence to the vicar.

"Good morn, Master Hugh," Father Simon greeted me pleasantly, although I suspect he guessed that my reappearance at his door brought little good. "How may I serve you?"

"You may send servants and clerks to Cow-Leys Corner to unearth Thomas atte Bridge, then bring his corpse to the churchyard and bury the fellow properly."

"What? I cannot. A suicide..."

"Thomas atte Bridge did not take his own life, as you well know."

The vicar was silent for a moment. "How would I know this?" he finally demanded.

"Because you heard Peter Carpenter confess to the felony."

"But... but..." he stammered, "how can you know this? Did the carpenter confess to you?"

"Aye, in a manner. He has fled the town."

"Fled?"

"Gone in the night. He knew yesterday of my suspicion, and in the night has stolen away. You knew Thomas was no suicide, yet you allowed him to remain in unhallowed ground."

The priest was silent for a moment. "How could I do otherwise?" he said softly. "To say I knew murder was done would be to betray Peter's confession. No matter what course I took, I was in the wrong. And you say you thought him guilty of murder yesterday, but permitted him to escape in the night?"

"I had suspicion only. His flight has provided the proof."

"Will you seek him and carry him to the sheriff at Oxford?"

"Did you set a penance for him?"

"Aye, as for all who sin."

"Was this penance harsh?"

"It was, and is, and will remain so."

"He has not yet fulfilled it?"

"Nay, nor will he for many years."

"Or perhaps never, should I seek and find him and deliver him to Sir Roger."

"Blessed are the merciful," the priest said, "for they shall obtain mercy. He was much provoked."

"Is it for me to grant mercy, or the King's Eyre?"

"Mercy is a duty thrust upon us all," Father Simon replied, "else we would deserve none from the Lord Christ."

"Aye, but for murder?"

"You must answer as you will. You are Lord Gilbert's bailiff, not me."

"Regarding Thomas atte Bridge," I changed the subject. "Send servants and clerks to Cow-Leys Corner and empty the grave. Bring atte Bridge to the churchyard and bury the man as is his due. Tell Maud of this so she may attend. The man was a knave but does not deserve to rest beneath the vines and bracken at Cow-Leys Corner."

I had no authority over the vicars of St Beornwald's Church, but Father Simon did as I required of him. After dinner I stood with Kate on the castle parapet aside the gatehouse and watched five black-garbed men, two with spades and two with a litter between them, as they walked toward Cow-Leys Corner. An hour later they returned, the litter sagging with some lumpen object covered with a black shroud.

Shortly after the procession disappeared across Shill Brook I heard the bell of St Beornwald's Church toll twice. 'Twas many weeks too late for a passing bell, but some formalities must be observed.

"Will you follow the corpse?" Kate asked.

"I did not mourn Thomas atte Bridge dead. I should be false to myself and to all men did I set foot in the churchyard this day."

"Do you mourn Peter Carpenter?"

"Aye. I mourn the living, but not the dead."

"You think he will travel far?"

"Nay. He had a heavy load upon his cart and but one horse to pull it. His wife must carry Jane's babe, and his own small children will not walk far, I think, before they tire. Soon they must seek another nurse for the babe, else it will perish."

"So you will not need to travel far to find him?"

"If I seek him he should be easily found. The cart will have left tracks upon the road. They could not travel many miles before dawn, the nights being short. As they passed through a village they would be observed, come the day."

"Then you have but to find the direction they traveled and soon you will catch them up."

"Aye."

"Will you do so?"

I could not reply for a moment. I was at war with myself and sure to lose.

"Nay," I finally replied.

Kate slipped her arm through mine. "What of justice?" she asked.

"What of mercy? God is just, and merciful, and though His justice is sometimes tardy, it is more sure than any man's. The prophet wrote that men are 'to do justly, and to love mercy,' but he offered no advice when the two seem in conflict."

"What will Lord Gilbert think?"

"He will return from Pembroke in a month, before Lammastide. He will not be pleased for the town to lose a good carpenter, and another tenant will not be readily found. If he is unhappy with the resolution of this business he may replace me."

Kate's face bent to a worried frown. "What then?"

"We will have a fine new house, and I will eke out a living repairing men's bodies when they are incautious."

Galen House was near complete when Lord Gilbert, Lady Petronilla, Master Richard, and the retinue of valets and grooms accompanying them arrived four days before Lammastide.

Lord Gilbert was much angered to learn of Sir Simon's destruction of Galen House, and pleased to learn of its reconstruction. He listened intently while I told him of Peter Carpenter's vengeance against Thomas atte Bridge and my decision to consider the matter closed.

Lord Gilbert was silent for a moment when I had concluded the tale. His lips were drawn tight across his teeth and a frown darkened his features. I feared for my position.

"Peter was a good man," he finally said. "Lady Petronilla is with child. If the babe is a lass and some rogue deals with her the way atte Bridge did with the carpenter's maid, I'll see him hounded to his grave."

Nobles and commons feel much the same about daughters.

"Kate is also to give birth," I announced.

"What? I give you joy, Master Hugh! When?"

"All Saint's Day, or thereabouts."

"The children shall grow to be playmates," he laughed. "Lady Petronilla will be delivered near the same time."

I left Lord Gilbert chuckling in the solar, found Kate, and together we walked to Church View Street where the tiler and his assistant were completing the roof of the new Galen House. While we observed the tilers at work Father Simon appeared from Church Street, saw us, and approached. I greeted the priest and enquired of his day.

"I am well," he answered, "and have this day heard tidings you will wish to hear. John Kellet is to return to St Andrew's Chapel," he said rapidly.

I made no reply, but stood in the street with my jaw sagging in dismay at this announcement. The vicar saw my regret and explained: "The prior at St Nicholas's Priory wished to be rid of him. He was near to bankrupting the place. 'Tis not a wealthy house. Kellet could not be dissuaded from seeking the poor and bringing them for succor to the priory. The almoner's purse is gone, due to Kellet's zeal. The prior appealed to the bishop, and as no curate has yet been found for St Andrew's Chapel, it was decided to return him."

I was prepared to believe John Kellet as Father Simon insisted, a changed man. But I was not prepared to welcome the man to my bailiwick. I spoke a silent prayer as Kate entwined her arm in mine that Kellet was truly transformed, and neither he nor any other would cause me vexation in the future.

The Lord Christ saw fit to honor this request, temporarily. All was peaceful until a fortnight past Martinmas of 1367, when a strange coin was discovered in a strange place.

Afterword

The Bampton Archive has published a booklet, *The Story Behind the Naming of Bampton*. On page 33, under the heading "Cowleaze Corner", is the following information:

> The name comes from the "Cow-Leys" or pastures... But Cowleaze Corner is better known for the ghost stories associated with the location. Crossroads were traditional places where suicides were buried, being forbidden burial in consecrated ground. [A nineteenth-century author] wrote in 1848 that "all memory of the unhallowed corpses which have there mouldered, would long since have perished, if it were not for the troubled spirits... there are persons still living, who assert that they have seen supernatural appearances in the neighbourhood of Cow-Leas Corner."

The Tainted Coin

An extract from the fifth chronicle of
Hugh de Singleton, surgeon

Chapter 1

I would have preferred to lie abed a while longer. The October morn was cool, my bed warm, but Bessie stirred in her cradle and Kate was already up and bringing the coals to life upon our hearth. I arose, clothed myself hurriedly, and bent to lift my daughter from her cradle. She smiled up at me from the woollen layers into which Kate had tucked her the night before. Elizabeth was now nearly a year old, and beginning to sleep through the night, much to Kate's joy, and my own. Children are a blessing from God, but not when they awaken before dawn and demand to be fed.

I had placed the babe upon my shoulder and turned to the stairs when from below I heard an unwelcome pounding upon the door of Galen House. When some man wishes my attention so soon after the morning Angelus Bell has rung it can be to no good purpose. A window was near, so rather than hasten down the stairs I opened it to see who was at my door so early in the morn.

My visitor heard the window open above him and when I peered down I looked into the gaunt, upraised face of John Kellet, curate at St Andrew's Chapel.

"Master Hugh," he shouted, "you must come at once. There is a man wounded and near dead at St Andrew's Chapel. Bring your instruments and make haste."

I did so. Kate had heard Kellet's appeal and awaited me at the foot of the stairs. She took Bessie from me, and over her shoulder I saw my breakfast awaiting upon our table: a loaf and ale. It must wait. I filled a satchel with instruments and herbs from my chest, unbarred the door, and stepped into the foggy dawn.

"Quickly, Master Hugh," the skeletal priest urged, and set off down Church View Street at a trot, his bare, bony feet raising puffs of dust from the dry dirt of the street. I flung my bag over a shoulder and followed. I had questions about this abrupt summons, but Kellet was already too far ahead to allow conversation. I loped after the priest, the satchel bouncing against my back.

Kellet led me to the High Street, thence up Bushey Row to the path to St Andrew's Chapel. 'Tis little more than a quarter of a mile from Bampton to the chapel, and soon the ancient structure appeared through the fog. Kellet plunged through the decrepit lych gate and led me to the porch. There, upon the flags, I saw a man. The priest had placed the fellow upon a pallet so he did not rest upon the hard stones. I bent over the silent form and thought Kellet's trouble unnecessary, for the man before me seemed insensible, if not already dead.

"Found him here at dawn, when I rose to ring the Angelus Bell. I heard a moan, so opened the door an' found the fellow under the porch roof, just where he now lies. Put a pallet 'neath him an' sought you. I could see he was badly off, even in so little light as in the porch."

The curate lived in the chapel tower, in a bare room but four paces on a side. He need not go far from his bed to ring the bell of St Andrew's Chapel, for the bell rope fell through a hole in the center of his chamber to the base of the tower at ground level.

The porch lay in shadow, so the nature of the man's wounds was obscure. I asked Kellet to take one end of the pallet, and I grasped the other. Together we lifted the unconscious stranger to the churchyard, where the rising sun was visible through the thinning fog and his wounds and injuries became apparent.

The man had been beaten senseless. His nose was broken and askew, his scalp lacerated just above an ear, where a blow had found his skull, his lips were purple and swollen, and it seemed sure his jaw was broken and teeth were knocked loose.

"You heard him moan when you rose to ring the Angelus Bell?"

"Aye," Kellet replied.

"Did he say anything when you found him?"

"Nay. He was as you see him now."

Whoever this man was, he had used the last of his strength to reach sanctuary, as I think he assumed the ancient chapel to be. I looked closely at the face, but could not recognize him as any man I knew. I asked the priest if he knew the fellow.

"Nay. 'Course, he's so abused he might be anyone. In his state his own mother'd not know him, I think."

I silently agreed with the priest, then bent to examine the man's injuries more closely, in case there was anything I might do to save his life and speed healing of his wounds.

I am Hugh de Singleton, surgeon, trained at the University of Paris, and also bailiff to Lord Gilbert Talbot at his lands in Bampton. Many would find the work I must do as surgeon disagreeable, repairing men's bodies when they have done themselves harm, but I find my duties as bailiff the more irksome of the two. Now I took my dagger and cut away the wounded man's cotehardie and kirtle, the better to inspect his hurts. As I did so I considered that the supine form presented me with two tasks: I must treat his injuries, and also discover who had dealt with him so.

The man's body presented as many wounds as his head. So many bruises covered his ribs that they might have been one great contusion. I tested one purple blemish and felt the ends of a broken rib move beneath my fingertips.

My examination roused the unconscious fellow. I saw his eyelids flicker, then open. Perhaps he saw my face above him, perhaps not. His eyes seemed not to focus, but drifted about, hesitating only briefly when they turned to me. Did he take me for a friend? Who can know? He surely did not think me one of his assailants, else he would not have spoken as he did.

With pain and effort he opened his swollen lips and said, so faintly I had to ask John Kellet if he heard the same words, "They didn't get me coin."

I had learned two things: whoso attacked the fellow had sought a coin, or perhaps many coins, and more than one had done this evil. I would learn no more from him, for as I began to inspect a bloody laceration between two ribs his chest heaved and was then still.

"Dead?" Kellet asked after a moment.

"Aye. You must think back on finding the fellow. Is there anything you can remember of this morn which might tell who he is and who has done this?"

"I will think on it while I ring the passing bell. I have already offered extreme unction, before I sought you. I could see how ill-used he was, even in the dark of the porch, and feared he might not live 'til I returned."

"While you do so I will fetch the coroner. Hubert Shillside must convene a jury here before we may do any other thing."

I heard Kellet ring the bell of St Andrew's Chapel as I left the churchyard and its tumbled-down wall. I noted several places where someone – Kellet, I presume – had replaced fallen stones so as to halt the decay. My eyes traveled to a section of the wall where, three years past, I had hidden to escape Thomas atte Bridge and the priest, who intended my death. Kellet, for this felony and others, was sent on pilgrimage to Compostela. He returned a transformed man, and was assigned to assist the almoner at the Priory of St Nicholas, in Exeter. There he was so assiduous at seeking the poor that he came near to impoverishing the priory, it not being a wealthy house, and the prior beseeched the bishop to be rid of him. As no curate had been found for St Andrew's Chapel, Kellet was reassigned to the place. He left it three years past a corpulent hedonist, but returned a year ago an emaciated pauper, who wore no shoes at any season and gave to the poor nearly all of the meager living he was awarded as curate. I have never seen a man so reformed, and indeed, when first I learned of the change, doubted it was truly so. May the Lord Christ forgive me for mistrusting the alteration He can work in a repentant man's life. All saints were once sinners, and any sinner may become a saint.

Hubert Shillside was no more pleased than I had been to open his door so early, but accepted his duty as coroner when I told him of the death at St Andrew's Chapel. He set out to assemble a jury while I walked to Church View Street and Galen House.

I told Kate of events at the chapel, hurriedly gobbled the loaf she had set out for me, swallowed a cup of ale, then retraced my steps to the chapel. I arrived with Shillside and his coroner's jury. The haberdasher asked of the priest what he knew of the corpse, and was told what I already heard. Kellet could think of nothing more to explain the dead man's condition.

All who viewed the corpse agreed that the death was murder, not misadventure, and so Shillside did readily declare. No deodand was to be found, so the coroner, no doubt hungry to break his fast, absolved himself and his jurymen of further responsibility in the matter and turned the death over to me.

As the coroner's jury departed the place I told Kellet to once again take in hand an end of the pallet. Together we carried the corpse through the porch, into the chapel, and deposited it on the flags before the altar.

"I'll say a mass, have a grave dug, and bury the man this day," the priest said.

I wished to know where this stranger had been attacked, to see if there might be at the place some evidence of his assailants. It could not have been close to the chapel, for he would have cried out when attacked, and Kellet would have heard him. But the dead man had been so badly injured that he would not have crawled far. I searched the grass of the churchyard for blood, and found traces which led to the lych gate. The curate saw, and followed. Beyond the gate was the path, dry from absence of rain for the past fortnight. In the dust it was easy to follow the track of a crawling man back to the east, for the sun was now well up over the fields and meadow which bordered the narrow road. Nearly two hundred paces to the east the path entered a wood, and a few paces beyond that the marks of a crawling man disappeared into the verge.

I studied the place where the man had crawled from the forest. Why did he struggle to leave the place and crawl to St Andrew's Chapel? In his battered condition this required much effort. Was he familiar with Bampton so that he knew help might be found could he reach the chapel?

John Kellet had followed from the lych gate and with me studied the path where marks in the dust told of the man's entry upon the road.

"Look there," the priest said, and pointed a few paces beyond. Between road and forest was a swathe of dry grass and across this patch of vegetation two parallel tracks of bent-down foliage showed where a cart or similar wheeled conveyance had turned from the road and entered a narrow opening which led into the forest. Marks of the cart wheels, a horse's hooves, and the footprints of men were visible in the dust of the path where the vehicle entered the wood, but although we searched for many paces in both directions from the place, neither Kellet nor I could find any mark where a cart might have left the wood and regained the road. Whatever had entered the forest was yet there.

The priest followed as I traced the path of the cart into the wood. Fallen leaves covered the forest floor, so the track was soon obliterated, but it was possible to guess the way by seeking openings between the trees and bushes large enough to admit passage of a horse and cart.

We had walked perhaps fifty paces from the road when I heard a horse whinny. Another forty paces brought us to a shaded clearing in the wood where before us stood a horse, harnessed to a cart, its reins tied to a small beech. The horse neighed again, no doubt pleased to see men who might offer it water and food.

"Why is this beast here, so distant from the road?" Kellet wondered aloud. "And did it belong to the man now lying dead in St Andrew's Chapel?"

My mind had posed the same questions, and I thought it likely the answer to the second question was "yes." An inspection of the cart might confirm this. It was well made, with two wheels. A waxed cloth had covered the cart, but was drawn aside and hung from the cart to the forest floor. I peered into the cart and saw there several chests, open and upended. Their contents were strewn about. There was a packet of combs, some of wood and cheaply made, but others of fine ivory. Another small chest had held an assortment of buckles, pins, buttons, and a package of needles. These were all tossed about in the cart. A larger chest had held several yards of woolen cloth in a variety of colors. This fabric was flung about, and one bolt lay partly over the side of the cart, dragging upon the leaves. Here was a chapman's cart. The owner made his living selling goods in villages too small to have haberdashers and such like merchants.

I began to form an opinion of what had happened here. The chapman, I thought, had decided to sleep the night under his cart, the weather being yet mild. He led his horse deep into the wood, away from the road and felons who might prowl the countryside, but was followed. Perhaps men saw the track his cart made in the dust of the road, as did the priest and I, or mayhap he was trailed from the last town where he did business.

Here in the forest men surprised the chapman and

demanded his purse. He refused to give it up, so they set upon him with a club, but yet he would not tell them where it was hid. They beat him senseless, near to death, ransacked his cart, then left him in the forest to perish.

Kellet had inspected the contents of the cart from over my shoulder. As I pondered the discovery I saw him reach for a sack and untie the cord which closed it. He examined the contents, then poured some into a wooden bucket which lay in the cart aside the sack. The horse smelled the oats, and neighed in anticipation. The priest took the bucket to the beast, which plunged its muzzle in eagerly. No doubt the animal was thirsty as well.

A fallen branch next caught my eye. It lay at the edge of the clearing, three or four paces from the cart, and seemed freshly broken. One splintered end was white in the dappled sunlight, and the limb lay atop the fallen leaves, not under, as should be had it occupied that place for a day or more.

I lifted the broken limb and saw a thing which caused me to recoil. At a place where a twig had broken from the branch and left a raised and thorn-like barb was the dark stain of blood and what appeared to be a bit of flesh. The priest saw me examining the club, and when the horse had consumed his ration of oats Kellet joined me in studying the cudgel.

"Broke it over his head, I'd say," Kellet said.

The limb was as large around as the calf of my leg, and as long as I am tall. Blows from it would easily break a man's ribs or skull.

I was not optimistic that I could find the felons who had done this murder. Had they taken goods from the chapman's cart I might seek in villages nearby for men who had wares to sell, or whose wives wore new buttons upon their cotehardies or bragged of ivory combs. But if the villains did take goods from the cart, they left much behind. Why so? Unless some men boasted of this attack, I would have no clue which might lead to the assailant.

Even the horse and cart might be carried away to some town and sold. The beast would fetch ten shillings, perhaps twelve, and the cart another eight or ten shillings, for it was well made and sturdy. Whoever murdered the chapman had left here in the woods goods to the value of as much as two pounds. Did the chapman cry out loudly as he was attacked, so as to frighten the felons away? Kellet had heard no such screams, but I could think of no other reason thieves might leave such loot here in the forest.

"Whose goods are these now?" Kellet asked.

"Unless we can discover some heir to the dead man, they become Lord Gilbert's possession, being found upon his land."

"Oh, aye. There is much wealth here. I had thought some might be sold to help the poor through the winter to come."

"Lord Gilbert is not a greedy man ... well, no more so than most of his station. Some of the buttons and buckles of the meaner sort he will give to his grooms and valets, but there may be some he will allow to be sold. I will speak to him about it."

I replaced the waxed cloth atop the cart, then led the horse through the wood to the road. Here I halted to again study the dust of the road to see if it might tell me more of what had happened here. Many men had walked this way since the last rain, and horses also. It was impossible to tell which of the tracks might have been made by men who had slain the chapman.

We walked to St Andrew's Chapel, where Kellet left me to set about his duty to bury the chapman in the hallowed ground of the churchyard. I led the horse and cart through the town and under the Bampton Castle portcullis to the marshalsea, where I told a page to unharness and care for the beast, but to leave the cart where it stood. I then sought John Chamberlain and requested of him an audience with Lord Gilbert. I awaited John's return in the hall, but was not long abandoned. John returned with announcement that Lord Gilbert was at leisure and would see me in the solar.

That chamber, smaller and more easily warmed than the hall, was Lord Gilbert's choice when the weather turned cool and damp. There had been no rain for a fortnight, and the day was mild, but a fire blazed upon the hearth when I was ushered into the solar. A great lord cares little for use of firewood, as he will always have supply. And, in truth, the warmth was pleasing. If I had such resources to hand I would this day have a blaze in all of the hearths in Galen House. Mild it was, but even a mild day in October may be improved with a fire upon the hearth.

"Hugh, what news?" Lord Gilbert said, looking up from a ledger. Lord Gilbert is a bearded, square-faced man, ruddy of cheek and accustomed to squinting into the sun from atop a horse. Unlike most lords he desires to keep abreast of financial dealings within his lands. Each year I prepare an account for his steward, Geoffrey Thirwall, who resides at Pembroke. Thirwall visits Bampton once each year, for hallmote, when he examines my report. Most nobles allow their stewards final say in matters of business, as, in truth, does Lord Gilbert. But, unlike most, Lord Gilbert wishes to keep himself informed of profit and loss first hand, rather than rely only upon the accounts of bailiff and steward. Many great lords have lately been reduced to penury, and must sell lands to pay debts. The plague has taken many tenants, and dead men pay no rents. Lord Gilbert is not in such straitened circumstance. Perhaps his inspection of my accounts and those of his other bailiffs is reason why.

"A dead man was found this morning upon your lands," I said. "Well, he was not dead when found, but died soon after."

"A tenant, or villein?"

"Neither, m'lord. A chapman, I think. We found a place in the wood where the man was attacked, and a horse and cart were there."

"We?"

"Aye. John Kellet found the man moaning and near dead under the porch roof of St Andrew's Chapel. I have brought horse and cart to the castle. Neither I nor Kellet recognize the dead man, nor did Hubert Shillside or any man of his coroner's jury. If no heirs can be discovered the goods in his cart are yours, m'lord."

"Oh, aye... just so. What is there?"

"Two chests of combs, buckles, buttons, pins, and such like, and another of woolen cloth of the middling sort."

"The dead man is a traveling merchant, then," said Lord Gilbert.

"Aye. 'Tis why he is unknown in Bampton. Hubert Shillside sells much the same stuff. The man has probably passed this way before, perhaps traveling from Cote to Alvescot or some such place, and this may be why he sought St Andrew's Chapel when men set upon him."

"If thieves," Lord Gilbert wondered aloud, "why did they not make off with his goods?"

"Before he died he looked at me and said, 'They didn't get my coin.' Poor men might find it impossible to hide possession of ivory combs for their wives. Even selling such things would raise eyebrows. But coins... even a poor cotter will have some wealth. Perhaps whoso attacked the chapman thought disposing of his goods might point to them as thieves, so wished only for his purse."

"Did you find it?"

"Nay. He had no purse fixed to his belt, nor was there one in the cart or the forest, unless it is well hid."

"Then why, I wonder, did he say the fellows had not got his coin?"

"This puzzles me as well. Perhaps the purse was in

his cart, and he was too knocked about to know that the thieves made off with it."

"Aye," Lord Gilbert agreed. "Let us have a look at the cart, and see what is there."

"John Kellet has asked, if the chapman cannot be named, and no heir found, some of the goods found in the cart might be sold and the profit dispensed to the poor, to help them through the winter to come."

Lord Gilbert is not an unjust man, but the thought of surviving a winter, or possibly not, does not enter his mind, nor do any nobles give the season much thought other than to make ready a Christmas feast. That many folk might see winter as a threat to their lives and the survival of their children was an unfamiliar thought to my employer.

"Oh, well, let us see what is there and I will consider the matter."

Most great lords need an extra horse or two, even if the beast be of the meaner sort. Lord Gilbert ordered the chapman's horse placed in an empty stall, and after inspecting the contents of the cart, commanded two grooms to take the goods to John Chamberlain's office, where he might hold them secure while I sought for some heir to the unidentified chapman. The empty cart was placed aside the castle curtain wall, behind the marshalsea, there to await disposition.

My stomach told me 'twas past time for my dinner, and as I departed the castle gatehouse the noon Angelus Bell rang from St Beornwald's Church tower to confirm the time. Kate had prepared a roast of mutton, which I devoured manfully, though such flesh is not my favorite. I have never told this to Kate, as I dislike disappointing her. So I consumed my mutton and awaited another day and a dinner more to my pleasure.

After dinner, of which a sizeable portion remained for my supper, I decided to revisit the clearing in the forest where John Kellet and I found the cart, then travel east to

Aston and Cote. Perhaps the chapman did business in the villages and some there would know of him, or perhaps his murderers lived there and might be found out.

The path to the forest took me past St Andrew's Chapel, and as I approached the lych gate I saw the curate and another man leave the porch, the dead chapman between them upon the pallet. In a far corner of the churchyard was a mound of earth where a grave lay open to receive its unidentified tenant. I turned from the road, passed through the rotting lych gate, and became a mourner at the burial.

Kellet lifted his eyes from his task when I approached and this caused him to stumble as a toe caught some uneven turf. He tried to regain his balance while maintaining a grip on his end of the pallet, but was unable to do either. Kellet's gaunt frame seems hardly robust enough to keep himself upright, much less carry a burden, and the chapman was a well-fed man.

Kellet had provided no shroud for the corpse. The priest gives away so much of his living that he probably had no coin with which to purchase a length of black linen. So when he dropped his end of the pallet the chapman rolled uncovered to the sod, face down.

I hastened to help Kellet to his feet, and together with his assistant we lifted the corpse back upon the pallet. But when the chapman's face was raised from the grass I saw there a thing which arrested my attention and caused his dying words to return to my mind. A small coin lay upon the turf where a moment before the corpse had lain face down.

When the dead man was again upon his pallet I searched in the grass and retrieved the coin. It was worn and corroded, and looked like no coin I had before seen. It was of tarnished silver, smaller than a penny, very near the size of a farthing.

Kellet and his assistant watched as I inspected the

coin. The priest finally spoke. "How did that come to be here in the churchyard?"

"It fell from the dead man's lips when he was turned onto the grass," I replied.

"Is that what he meant when he said the felons had not got his coin? He had hid it in his mouth?"

"Perhaps."

"'Tis an odd thing," Kellet said.

"Aye. Words are inscribed upon it, and the profile of a king, but they are so worn I cannot make them out."

"Why would men do murder for a small silver coin?" the priest asked.

I shrugged and said, "That is the service Lord Gilbert requires of me: to find who would do such a thing on his lands, and why."